# PRAISE FOR RICHARD B. SCHWARTZ

## *Proof of Purchase*

It's like this guy is just channeling Raymond Chandler on every page. . . . The ending . . . would make Mike Hammer proud.
   — Jochem Steen, *Sons of Spade*

In this engaging hard-boiled mystery, one of three in Schwartz's Jack Grant series (Frozen Stare; The Last Voice You Hear), the seasoned California PI looks into the disappearance of an ex-girlfriend at the request of the woman's husband. When her mutilated body turns up in the woods, Grant makes it his mission to track down her murderer. With the assistance of Lt. Diana Craig, an attractive fast-riser in the San Bernardino police department, Grant follows leads that point to his client, as well as to a consortium of underworld bosses who are branching out into a mega-real estate project. The pair find time, between car chases and gun battles, to begin a relationship. . . . Fans of Robert Parker will enjoy encountering Grant . . . .
   — *Publishers Weekly*

## *The Last Voice You Hear*

It's not often that an author's second book is as good as the first, and even less frequent are the instances when an author . . . top[s] it with an extraordinary second . . . deliver[ing] a walloping good tale as well. Richard B. Schwartz has done just that. In *The Last Voice You Hear*, Mr. Schwartz places himself on par with our finest contemporary murder-mystery writers. This is a book you won't want to miss. . . .
   — Alan Paul Curtis in *Who Dunnit*

The author . . . writes vividly, putting the reader right into the scene. Schwartz explores the meaning of right and wrong, crime and justice.
   — Mary Helen Becker in *Mystery News*

The story rockets along . . . a fast-moving, well-told story with a surprising conclusion that blurs the line between crime and justice.
— Joseph Scarpato, Jr. in *Mystery Scene*

Jack Grant, the Vietnam vet and Pasadena-based PI who debuted in Frozen Stare (1989), returns in this engrossing sequel by Schwartz, author of several scholarly studies of Samuel Johnson. Schwartz knows his London, but surprisingly he evokes California with equal ease, mainly with vividly etched strokes. An apparently maniacal killer is on the loose in London, someone strong and very practiced at impalement. So far, so nasty. But when a victim is dispatched in similar fashion in Disneyland, of all places, Jack Grant is called in. He discovers the killer's identity, but there's a problem: there's a method to the killer's madness. Moreover, Grant has an ethical problem of his own: he's plagued by his conscience, since he understands and even sympathizes with the murderer's cause. The cinematic climax takes place high above the floor of the California desert, and Schwartz squeezes every last drop of suspense from his setting. . . . The result is a high-tension thriller awash in sanguinary detail. Paper towels, anyone?
— *Publishers Weekly*

## *Frozen Stare*

I welcome Richard Schwartz to the club. It's been a long time since I've seen two more engaging characters entering the series scene.
— Sandra Scoppettone

Grant and White play nicely off each other and the switch-on-a-switch works well.
— *Kirkus Reviews*

This tale, in the California private eye tradition, has a rousing finish and is an enjoyable read.
— *Publishers Weekly*

A new author devoted to the hard-boiled tradition. . . . Schwartz has the hard-boiled formula down pat. . . . Schwartz does not break any rules in Frozen Stare. . . . He writes crisply. The narrative moves at a slam-bang pace as bodies pile up. . . . As a dedicated student of the hard-boiled school of detective fiction [Schwartz] has learned his lessons well.
— *The Washington Post Book World*

Gives a whole new meaning to the phrase 'cold-blooded murder'. . . . This is a quick read with plenty of action. Schwartz's first novel is a winner!
— *Sarasota, FL Herald Tribune*

This is a delightful tale, full of amusing touches, and the relationship between Grant and his good cop friend, black Frank White, is a joy. I hope that Schwartz can keep this standard up for a long time to come.
— *The Armchair Detective*

## *Nice and Noir: Contemporary American Crime Fiction*

Opinionated but always fascinating, shrewd and smart, but always readable. . . .
— *The Thrilling Detective*

<u>BOOKS BY RICHARD B. SCHWARTZ</u>
## FICTION

### The Jack Grant Novels

*Frozen Stare*
*The Last Voice You Hear*
*Proof of Purchase*

### The Gwen Harrison Novels

*No Exit*
*Red City*
*The Gray Twilight*
*The Last Temptation*
*The Singular Moment*

### The Tom Deaton Novels

*Into the Dark*
*The Survivor's Song*
*Nightmare Man*
*Death Whispers*
*Poison Touch*

### Short Stories

*Townhouse and Other Stories*

## CRITICISM

*Samuel Johnson and the New Science*
*Samuel Johnson and the Problem of Evil*
*Boswell's Johnson: A Preface to the Life*
*Daily Life in Johnson's London*
*After the Death of Literature*
*Nice and Noir: Contemporary American Crime Fiction*
*The Wounds that Heal: Heroism and Human Development*
*(with Judith A. Schwartz)*
ed. *The Plays of Arthur Murphy, 4 vols.*
ed. *Theory and Tradition in Eighteenth-Century Studies*

## MEMOIRS

*The Biggest City in America: A Fifties Boyhood in Ohio*
*Accidental Soldier: A Reserve Officer at West Point in the Vietnam Era*
*Postwar Higher Education in America: Just Yesterday*

## EBOOK

*Is a College Education Still Worth the Price? A Dean's Sobering Perspective*

A GWEN HARRISON NOVEL

# THE SINGULAR MOMENT

RICHARD B. SCHWARTZ

THE SINGULAR MOMENT

Published by Dark Harbor Books
First Edition 2026



ISBN:     979-8-9899271-9-7 Paperback Edition
          979-8-9957210-0-0 Hardcover Edition
          979-8-9957210-1-7 Digital Edition

Library of Congress Control Number: 2026910652

Author services by Pedernales Publishing, LLC
www.pedernalespublishing.com

10 9 8 7 6 5 4 3 2 1

Printed in the United States of America

*For Judith*
*Ever and Always*

*Inter arma enim silent leges.*
*In times of war, the law falls silent.*

**Attributed to Cicero**

EXT. ROOFTOP — DAY

> **MORSE**
>
> How do you do it?

> **THURSDAY**
>
> Leave it at the front door. Cos I have to. Case
> like this'll tear the heart right out of a man. Find
> something worth defending.

> **MORSE**
>
> I thought I had…found something.

> **THURSDAY**
>
> Music? I suppose music is as good as anything.
> Go home, put your best record on…loud as it'll
> play…and with every note, you remember…that's
> something that the darkness couldn't take from you.

**_Endeavour_: "Fugue"**

# ONE

## Five Weeks Ago

La Plata, Maryland is no longer a simple tourist pass-through. According to a local story the area was named by a Colonel named Samuel Chapman who had taken his son to South America in search of a cure for the boy's tuberculosis. He encountered the Rio de la Plata, which flows through Argentina and Uruguay and decided to name a portion of his 6,000 acre Maryland property in its memory. Back in the day before key bridges were built and interstate highways were constructed the snowbirds would take the town's major highway—rte. **301**—to parts south—principally Florida—but La Plata itself was never the cousin of such **I-95** mainstays as Kennebunkport, Boston, New York, Savannah, Coral Gables or West Palm. What you would find there was nothing in the league of the *Fontainebleau*…more like a mom and pop motel in a slasher film, bathed in flickering neon with floor drains revealing visible movement of skittering brown insects and walls and headboards that would often reveal a long history of dark activity when spritzed with a spray or two of luminol.

I was there at the request of the Director, my role being to observe a Bureau operation and report back on any particular lessons learned, the ultimate purpose of which was to enrich the curriculum of a specific unit of Bureau field instruction, an ongoing activity in which I was scheduled to play a leading role.

In this particular situation we were conducting what should have been a simple drug raid. *Tren de Aragua* may be vicious and seemingly omnipresent in contemporary newsprint and websites but it had not made significant headway in this area, where we found ourselves facing our old compadres from MS-13. Maryland had also been the host of Crips, Bloods, the Latin Kings, the TRG (Tiny Rascal Gang), the 18[Th] Street Gang, Black Guerrilla Family and (a Maryland original) the Pagan's Motorcycle Club, which had recently sparred with the MS-13 team over local territory, but this was a straightforward MS-13 operation, the purpose of which was to package the imported crack, heroin and powdered blow for distribution in the streets of D.C., Baltimore and the edgier sections of Prince George's County. The empire had struck back, but while the designation of the group as a transnational criminal organization and the formation of some Bureau/Homeland Security task forces targeting them had brought some positive results, the gang was decentralized into 'cliques' and it was ugly, violent, resilient, determined and uncommonly effective, given its relatively tiny proportion of gang numbers and activities and its miniscule portion of the total take when compared with the stats of the major cartels.

The members of the local chapter were utilizing a large, abandoned metal building which began as an Earl Scheib painting and body work enterprise (the parent company liquidated decades ago but with an in-name-only operation remaining in Baltimore). Earl might have been willing to paint your car in a host of colors for $19.95, but MS-13's offerings were narrower and a good bit more pricey. Earl had gone to his eternal reward in 1992 and the La Plata building had become *Diamond Jack's Gentleman's Club*, which prospered for awhile until the tiny local population became incrementally more gentrified with D.C., Baltimore and Andrews Air Force Base commuters moving in and its fellow strip clubs eased out by both local piety and the free offerings on the internet.

Disputes continued over the source of the title—an echo of the old Brando western or the border brothel/casino on *Twin Peaks* (both called *One-Eyed Jacks*). The one thing that all were able to agree on was the source of the word 'Diamond'—the stage name of the club's principal pole dancer, whose actual name was Carol Green, a local phenom who later attended the College of Southern Maryland, received an associate degree in Criminal Justice and eventually rose through the ranks of the department of Housing and Urban Development, where she enjoyed an estimable reputation as the skilled author of a report on illegal payouts to organized scam artists.

Her professional name was still emblazoned on chipped red paint over the building's principal entrance but the door was now fitted with multiple hardened-steel locks and the interior was lit by bare bulbs suspended from the ceiling over a series of laminate tables that had once been the central features of a large bingo hall adjacent to a local Catholic church called Saints Peter and Paul. The baggers would work under those lights, the few windows of the building now covered by double sheets of industrial plywood.

The problem was: how would our strike team enter the building without drawing attention to itself? Footsteps on the metal roof would be heard immediately and the building's siding was anchored to its concrete platform with thick beams connected by aged, rusted bolts whose removal would result in sounds and motions comparable with those of a 5.5-6.0 earthquake.

# TWO

The answer was: intelligence. The building itself had been under surveillance for months and still-in-service, simple parabolic microphones had been used to detect voices, music and any other evidence of human presence. Not surprisingly, that was infrequent. The drug traffickers did not operate on a 9-5, 5½-day work week schedule. They went into full-scale operation whenever a shipment arrived, often by truck (rarely by water) on the various ingress and egress routes that had replaced rte. **301**.

At that point it was all hands on deck—gnarled hands of elderly women generally, guarded by a cadre of gang members whose principal role was to insure that none of the ladies light-fingered any of their product in an attempt to increase their meagre incomes. There had been two solid visuals over the past month. In each case the women numbered approximately forty and their guardians approximately five, one for each corner of the building, presumably, with a rover keeping a close eye on stockings, pockets, purses and any other possible receptacles for stolen merchandise.

The Bureau team was led by the Baltimore field office, a unit with responsibility for both Maryland and Delaware. Their SAC was a soon-to-retire veteran named Timothy O'Hara, nicknamed 'Ginger' though most of his hair had been gone for as long as Earl Scheib. Tim was a solid citizen but much of his time had been spent pushing paper in the old Hoover Building and deep-diving for evidence of white-collar crime. Whenever he had the opportunity to reassert his bona fides via a guns-and-bullets field operation he was anxious to embrace the task.

"We're ready to make our move, Gwen," he told me. "Units up the chain are monitoring shipment activity. We want to put MS-13 out of business in our backyard but we also want some major confiscation headlines to reassure the public that we're doing our job—taking bad guys off the street and poison out of the community. If we can use this interdiction to take out some of their supervisors as well as their street soldiers, so much the better."

"So you want it all," I said.

"Always," he said. "The old ladies who sort and bag should be doing something more positive; with the right credentialling they'd make more money as Visiting Angels. We wish that there were more traffickers to net but it is what it is. If three or even four survive the firefight we'll try to turn them and find their suppliers on the ground and ultimately in the cartels."

"A highly speculative activity," I said, "particularly given the gang's preference for silence and imprisonment rather than death."

"I think of the whole process as being something akin to dental care," Tim said.

"It's a *journey*, not a solution to a single problem," I responded.

"Right," he said, smiling.

"Take me through the plan," I said.

"OK. First we got the original blueprints for the body-work building, with the front office, storage spaces, painting bays, and so on. When the building was converted to a strip club the owner (a holding company) was obligated to file new plans prior to renovation. That meant a central platform, bar area, disco balls, fixed tables and chairs for the patrons and dressing-and-makeup rooms for the dancers."

"And private rooms for more specialized activities," I added.

"Yes, but unspecified. A course of rooms in a single hallway were listed as 'administrative'."

"But there were no available plans for the building's current purposes."

"No," he said. "The building has an obscure owner masked by a shell company but it's essentially considered to be derelict."

"They haven't announced any plans to change it so they can steer clear of government regulations and nosy inspectors."

"Right. And the removal of the strip club facilities (the sound system, for example, and the lighting) didn't require any planning approval for their relocation."

"And the bingo tables were brought in by vans in the still of the night, the lighting set up by a single electrician with no estimates, subcontracts, paperwork or payments made on the books."

"Bingo," he said, "so to speak."

"I know that the windows have all been sealed. What about a back door?" I asked.

"Required by code, of course, but now covered by a steel plate and welded shut. The door is no longer required since the building is not in formal use. All that's required is a warning sign to any potential interlopers. It's next to the front door, on a tin plate, in small type."

"Probably your only point of entrance, since the sounds on the roof would be noticed immediately and you don't want your people abseiling through skylights down into the open room, exposed to fire."

"Nope."

"But a little well-placed plastic will blow the front door off its steel hinges. A little on each side will widen the hole and get your people in more quickly."

"Yes, and there are no cameras outside that we can't disable."

"So all you need is a diversion," I said.

"Fortunately that's an easy one," he answered.

# THREE

"And that would be…?" I asked.

"Care to guess?"

"I'm thinking there must be a utility room with a fuse or breaker box. That would probably still be in the same place as it was back in Earl Scheib's day because it would be expensive to move it and do all the rerouting that would be entailed. It's also probably in some remote corner of the building, accessible to technicians but not in the middle of the regular activities where it would reduce space and, hence, cash flow."

"Give that lady an A+," Tim said. "In the original plans there was a lunch room for the painters and body work guys. Just beyond it was the utility room, complete with a heavy-duty hot water heater and HVAC system. It's in the rear of the building, on the east side…just…here." He smoothed out the wrinkles in the blueprint and indicated the location with his right index finger.

"You'll create a problem and draw them into that corner."

"Yep."

"And while they've been working inside like little elves you will have had a skilled demolition guy putting some C-4 around the front door and its adjoining area."

"Yes, also with some mattresses to muffle the sound when we blow the door."

"Not enough to create a silent explosion, but if they're otherwise occupied, focused on a different problem, it could give you a few seconds…they might even consider the door blowing sound to be related to the problem that they're trying to solve. Every agent you could put inside during that time would increase your chances of success…success essentially consisting of the gang members instantly surrendering."

"Yes, we don't know how many of our people that will take because we won't know precisely how many they'll have, what weapons are at their disposal, and their degree of determination. If I'm standing there with three or four other people with AR-15's and I'm surrounded by forty people with HK's with 20-round magazines my decision is pretty simple. Unless I want to be swiss-cheesed I'm going to stand down."

"Yes, they may have a lust for money, power and blood but they're unlikely to enter a fight where their chances are nil. But as you say, you won't know exactly what's in their hands and what's on their minds until you go in."

"Right," Tim said, "but we trust our intelligence and we like our odds. We'll have visuals of them entering the building on Thursday (that's the day the shipment is expected to arrive) and we'll be working with far more than blind guesses."

"I'd like to be just inside the door after your team enters," I said. "I'll stay out of the way and also be available for any mop-up in case one of them slips through your line. Technically my job is to observe and report back to the Director on any lessons learned from the op, but another hand available is always a good thing. My only concern would be…"

"Yes?"

"That they've planned for this eventuality and have some devices in place that they could detonate, perhaps something with an incendiary dimension that would destroy evidence. They could even have some claymores aimed at your ingress point—a cheap way to create an effective kill zone."

"We haven't seen any evidence of them, but they're small and portable and could have been brought in without easy detection. They could be part of a drug shipment. We're thinking that all of their boxes contain coke; they're thinking that there's an insurance box or two containing devices with metal balls that could reach 300 feet in a 60-degree arc."

"Not something you'll know until you get inside, but you *can* be sure that they'll be willing to sacrifice all of the women they're using for the sorting, weighing and bagging."

"We'll be wearing vests and we'll move in and away from the door as quickly as we can," he said.

"If I could…"

"Of course, what are you thinking, Gwen?"

"I'd move away from the door as quickly as possible and have part of your team protecting that spot with interlocking fire."

"The roach motel."

"Right. You're keeping them from checking out, so their kill zone is neutralized as much as possible and they realize that they're going to have to stand and fight, not, as the Brits say, scarper off. With overwhelming numbers and significant weaponry on our side one would hope and trust that they'll see the error of their ways and stand down."

"Like my mother would always say, 'we'll see'."

"And outside of course…"

"We were thinking a semicircle of machine guns," Tim said.

"That should speak to their hearts and minds," I said.

# FOUR

Thursday was predicted to be a mini-bust. The traffic on **I-95** was always horrific but it was scheduled to be further hampered by heavy weather. What was expected to be a mid-morning arrival and drop-off was now projected to be a mid-afternoon slog. The Bureau's follow cars had used drones to keep an eye on MS-13's vans, as they weaved through traffic and reassembled in roadside watering holes. The resulting projected ETA's were very reliable. One thing was certain: if the size of their convoy was any indication, this was a worthwhile trip for the protectors of the U.S. of A, with millions of dollars of poison heading toward La Plata.

I had thought of grabbing a quick meal and a good night's sleep the night before, but I wasn't up for the local fare; when *Tripadvisor* includes four chains in their top ten local restaurants it tweaks your skepticism. More to the point I didn't want to be identified by one of the gang members, any one of whom might be prowling the bars or roaming the streets. I didn't know them but they could have known me. I wasn't a household name but my work in the Bureau had drawn enough attention to make me more guarded, even with my cupboard of hats, dark glasses and wigs. Not that the MS-13 crew would be working facial-rec software 24/7 but discretion is always a good move, particularly on the eve of a major operation. It was one of the points I hoped to drive home when I was conducting field training in the weeks ahead.

Though it wasn't a key issue now, a previous Director had pressed me to serve as a DEI poster girl for the Bureau. My Native American background was something he wanted to hype; I had always resisted, saying as politely as I could that I entered the Bureau to take down criminals, not to be photographed for *Benetonn* ads. We both knew that touting my 'diversity' would have secured brownie points for him from his masters and mistresses but I would have been instantly in danger of being compromised, so he had treaded softly but, unfortunately, insistently. With Walt Gradison as Director the problem had disappeared, but I had still been featured in a number of news stories and some of the bad people out there could have long memories.

I decided instead to drive into Old Town Alexandria, where I could stay for the night and get some passable food to tide me over. On a Wednesday night the streets wouldn't be clogged with vehicular and pedestrian traffic but there would be far more distractions, nooks, crannies, shoppes and scrambling bodies than in La Plata.

I thought about my choices for dinner. One local go-to was *Il Portal*, an Italian ristorante that had been there just after George and Martha Washington arrived. It featured a loyal clientele, a wait staff that knew all of the regulars by name, mountainous heaps of carbs, inexpensive wine and a separate party room in which to dine unnoticed.

I went instead for a personal stand-by, *Le Refuge*. While *Il Portal* was near the river and surrounded by heavy tourist traffic, *Le Refuge* was on North Washington, the main drag, with cars, lights, statuary and a succession of possible distractions. It was also cozy (=small), a bit more expensive but, in its way, more obscure within the pedestrian rush. With a colorful silk scarf I would have drawn attention in *Il Portal*; at *Le Refuge* I would fade into the woodwork.

I rallied there with an old friend from my days at Quantico. His name was Ted Henning. Working out of the new Bureau HQ he was working cybercrime. I hoped to enlist his help in my field classes. My go-to computer jock was Mike Liu, but Mike lives in a cottage in Salt Lake with a room that looks like a slightly smaller version of S.P.E.C.T.R.E. headquarters. He spends his waking days there as well as most of his nights and he doesn't like to leave it for the outside world. The room *is* his world, complete with kitchenette, a shower room and a cot with what appeared to be a scratchy wool blanket. I hadn't actually been there but I had received a full tour once when we were Zooming.

Ted was more the gray suit-wearing, buttoned down professional of J. Edgar's dreams. He arrived on time, just as the second hand was crossing the 12. He shook my hand, kissed me on the cheek, said it was great to see me again, reflexively asked me how he could help and…after more pleasantries…pulled back my chair and handed me a menu.

I told him that I didn't have anything for him that was immediately pressing but mentioned my upcoming tour of regional offices, told him that I would be enlisting his help (if I could) and said that I was in the area for that evening and that I thought it would be fun to catch up. He agreed and we settled in behind a dry *Absolut* Martini and a *Knob Creek* Manhattan.

He insisted that I order first and I opted for the baked onion soup with swiss cheese and a filet with a black pepper, cream, brandy sauce. He chose a thingie with crawfish tails and a filet with a Roquefort sauce. He then went all gallant on me and asked the waiter to set aside two slices of their chocolate mousse cake for dessert.

"I know you'll like it," he said, "and I don't want them to run out." Suddenly we were on a semi-date, except for the fact that I happened to know that Ted's long-time partner was named Gerald and their condo was a short stone's throw from Dupont Circle.

I didn't say anything specific about our Thursday op, but I did ask him about the electronic capabilities of gangs in general and MS-13 in particular. He instantly turned into a living encyclopedia and ran down the received wisdom, stressing the fact that while they had access to more hardware and software than the average person might expect, they still tended to rely on old-fashioned ways and means—threats, pain and the severer forms of violence.

We talked awhile about the new Bureau HQ and the fact that the Hoover Building had become unsalvageable. "There are things I miss about it," he said, "but don't ask me to list too many of them."

"Understood," I said. "Change is always difficult, but 50-to-60 years' worth of brutalist architecture is more than enough, particularly when you think about sections of it falling across your head, neck and shoulders."

"Agreed," he said. "And by the way, I'll be happy to help out in any way that I can with your field-training project. I'm always ready to get out of D.C. and see America."

# FIVE

All in all it had been a pleasant evening and while I could have driven back to my apartment in Cathedral Heights I decided instead to stay at the *Residence Inn* on Duke Street and avoid a portion of the morning traffic. It was still dark when I checked out and headed toward the Wilson Bridge, driving against the bulk of the early-bird commuters. The trip to La Plata was 30 miles in duration, but those miles increased in time with the traffic and I wanted no part of a start-and-stop trek.

I met with Tim O'Hara at his La Plata base—a cottage with backyard parking surrounded by trees and overgrown shrubs. There were several members of his team there, the op leader, the demolitions tech, a bilingual woman to communicate in Spanish and an electrician. When I was ushered in by the guard at the back door they were talking to people who were following the mini-convoy en route to La Plata.

"Two hundred and fifty miles out," Tim said. "They're making better time than earlier." When he saw me he put down his cell phone and introduced me to the members of his team: John Haden, Skip Tyler, Louisa Contreras and Bill Jameson.

"How about some coffee?" he asked.

"I'd love some," I said. "Just black."

He poured from the urn into a ceramic mug. "No cardboard or styrofoam around these parts," he said. "Orders from the governor. We may be unfriendly to MS-13 but in these environs (such as they are) we protect the planet. There are also some cinnamon rolls and donuts if you're in need of a blood-sugar spike."

"Always," I said, passing on a jelly-filled and selecting a cake donut with some frosting and coconut on top.

"Gwen is here at the request of the Director," Tim said. "She's going to be working on a program involving in-service learning for regional offices and she's hoping to pick up some insights based on direct field experience. Not that she doesn't have a lot of that already…"

"I appreciate your letting me tag along," I said. "The story may be a standard one—interdicting drug trafficking—but each operation has its own wrinkles."

"I took some coursework at Georgetown once," John Haden said. "There was a priest there who taught in the School of Foreign Service. He was very big on Just War Theory and fixated on the importance of sustaining communication up and down the chain of command. So long as the people on the battlefield could, ultimately, communicate with the commander-in-chief the war would be just, because the POTUS was elected, represented the will of the people and, hence, kept the will of the people (and, more importantly), the good father's personal theory, intact. We the people were acting together, etcetera, etcetera, etcetera. Only one problem…"

"Was it Cicero?" I asked. "'In times of war the law falls silent.' Or there's Mike Tyson's more direct observation about the fate of plans once you've been hit in the mouth."

"My thought exactly," John said. "That's why they call it the fog of war. The moment after the chocolate confections hit the fan the learning begins. What does the Army call the standard expectation and reaction—the 'School Solution'? That's left on the desk the moment something unexpected happens, as it always has a tendency to do."

"A single step off of the grid; that's where we often live," I said.

"We'll do our best to keep things contained," John said.

"Sometimes that's the major lesson beyond the Army's 4 P's (Prior Planning Proper Performance)," I said. "Keep it simple and straightforward. Stick with the tried and true, the best antidotes for chaos and confusion."

"Roger that," John said. "As old General Forrest opined, 'Get there firstest with the mostest.' We'll never forgive him for serving as the first Grand Wizard of the Klan, but General Sherman certainly admired and respected his cavalry tactics."

"No cavalry on this op," Tim said. "It's just us and forty-five of our best friends."

As I finished my donut and refilled my mug I thought about the fact that the military talk was masking the natural anxiety which precedes every operation. Everyone talks a little faster in an attempt to crowd out the doubts and apprehensions and fears. I noticed that the demolitions tech, translator and electrician remained relatively quiet, but I also noticed that they were carrying *Glock* 19M's and were doing so without any awkwardness or unfamiliarity.

After a second donut and a third mug of coffee I listened as Tim went over the plan with John a second and, eventually, a third time. The estimated time of arrival for the traffickers' vans had now been moved to the early afternoon and John would occasionally step away from the kitchen table to check that his people were locked and loaded and up to date on all of the details of his plan. It was just as we had discussed earlier—once they were inside, Skip would install the C-4, Bill would create the diversion, the main cohort would enter through the blown door and side panel, fanning out on either side, with a third of the group able to cover the single egress point with fire. Outside, a smaller group would cover that point with machine gun fire, if necessary. In general they were thought to be more of a deterrent than a strike force. The members of MS-13 were vicious and evil but not suicidal and stupid. They would know that if they tried to escape they would be caught in a pincer movement from which there was no reasonable exit route (that we knew of).

I would go in at the back of the larger unit and search for the optimal (but still safe) observation point. I was free to enter the fray, as needed, but it was clear that the locals did not want any foolhardy theatrics that could result in my becoming a casualty. This was not so much male protectiveness as it was the desire to avoid having to report to the Director concerning my plight. I checked my *Sig* P320c and compulsively counted my five 15-round magazines. I had also brought along a throwing knife, principally for luck, since there was little chance that I would need it or, for that matter, be able to use it effectively, given the nature of the op.

As we approached the magic hour Tim's group became increasingly more quiet but also more earnest, checking in with the follow team at tighter intervals. One interesting development was that one of the traffickers' vans had peeled off and left the remaining four to their own devices. The most likely explanation for that was that they were making a previously-unanticipated drop-off at some intermediate site. This was not our concern, because we were required to focus on the four remaining vans headed in our direction. After weeks of preparation there was no room in our schedule for any side trips.

We had mulled over the numbers from the get-go: why so many vans? A single vehicle filled with drugs of those kind would have a street value of tens of millions of dollars. A ton of coke would yield around 900 keys. Depending on the local market, we'd be talking $100-$200 mil. MS-13 would be paying wholesale; at that volume they'd be spending $25-$30 mil, a serious investment. The best guess was that the drugs were hidden within other materials that occupied a great deal of space, but the size and scope of their operation remained a major ringer in our planning process. Perhaps they were bringing a different group of sorters? Perhaps the nature of the product they were dealing had changed? Weed is still trafficked, regardless of its legal competitors. Perhaps they needed some special equipment for this stage of their operation? We simply didn't know (and probably wouldn't until we entered the building, because we would lose the most effective lines of sight when the vans were backed flush against the door to unload). Time would tell but it remained a significant point of concern. The bottom line was that this 'simple and straightforward' operation still contained a long list of imponderables.

# SIX

As the vans approached the building Tim instructed John to prepare their forces to move into place. The majority of them had been housed in an adjacent building with faded signage. It was fitted out with inconspicuous cameras focused on *Diamond Jack's*.

The vans moved quickly. As the first one backed in, the door opened, revealing for a moment two individuals with face masks and carbines. The rear doors of the van obstructed our vision but we could see the driver and a single passenger (both equipped with sidearms) helping to unload their vehicle. The process took less than ten minutes and as the first van pulled out the second instantly replaced it. These people knew how to drive, stop, reverse, park and move. Unloading the four vans took all of about twenty-five minutes and as the last van shut its doors and pulled away, the front door of the building was closed, locked and fully secured (or so they believed).

A few seconds later Bill Jameson emerged from the side of the building and gingerly climbed an adjoining utility pole; he then deployed a plastic tent with a SMECO (*Southern Maryland Electric Cooperative*) logo and settled in to work.

"Don't worry," Tim said over the team net, "he's out of the line of sight of their CCTV camera. As is Skip." As he said that, Skip Tyler was high-crawling around the other side of the building and squeezing the C-4 around the doorway and the adjoining steel skin. He looked like the world's most dextrous pastry chef. He had the plastic and the detonator in place in less than three minutes. The mattresses were placed against his handiwork by some middle-linebacker types who could crawl, carry serious weight and chew gum at the same time.

"Let's let them marinate for a few minutes," Tim said, "settle into their routine."

"Copy," Bill said. "I'm ready whenever you are."

"Plan on about ten minutes," Tim said to Bill and John. "By now they're digesting their lunches and downing some coffee. The women are sorting; they're watching them, but also taking bathroom breaks, thinking everything's returned to normal."

"OK, Bill. Time to enter the building and rattle the cages," Tim said.

As I learned later, Bill had accessed their electric feed and was futzing with it, turning their lights on and off, shooting for flicker effects. He wasn't alerting them so much as messing with them, the purpose being to draw them to the utility room to check on the building's circuit breaker switches.

"Give them a few more minutes of that, Bill," Tim said. "Are you ready, Skip?"

"Just say the word," he responded.

I could hear a slight slurping sound in Tim's voice; he was holding the mic in one hand and his coffee mug in the other. Cool under fire. Ticked the good-sign box.

"Skip…"

"On the red button," he said.

"Hit that bad boy," Tim said, and a few milliseconds later the door blew and the mattresses were airborne. The wave, blast and flash had come in no particularly discernible order and the results were dramatic. Before anything settled completely to the ground the foot soldiers were entering the building.

Louisa used a camo-painted bullhorn, turned to full volume. She began in Spanish and repeated in English.

*Tírate al suelo!*
*Tírate al suelo!*
**Get down on the floor!**
**Get down on the floor!**

This was directed at the sorters but if the gangbangers wanted to obey as well that would have been fine. Unfortunately, they didn't. Instead they responded with loud but unamplified voices.

*Seguir el plan!*
*Seguir el plan!*


My remaining memories of High School Spanish kicked in. The traffickers were telling the sorters to 'stick to the plan.' We weren't sure what that meant but the early result was some serious scrambling, some rearranging of product, and, eventually, all hands held high in the air. We had wanted them out of any possible lines of fire and their handlers were opting for the exact opposite, figuring that they could use the women as shields while they prepared to position themselves to fire or to attempt to escape.

"How many?" Tim asked John.

Under the sound of rifle fire he responded. "The usual number of sorters, forty or so, and a handful of bad guys, probably no more than five or six."

"Plan B," Tim said, and John's team promptly threw stun grenades over the heads of the sorters, followed by canisters of CS, the new-and-improved variety of tear gas. When several of the sorters continued to stay standing, the team aimed at their faces and released CS from aerosol canisters. That, combined with the physical presence of serious men and women in armored black suits and space-age helmets proved persuasive.

As they fell to the ground the traffickers were revealed, standing approximately five feet apart and assessing their chances. As they cried *"No dispares! No dispares!"* (don't shoot) one man emerged from the area of the utility room and lifted his automatic rifle to spray the room. When his body jerked in multiple directions from the impact of at least ten rounds of ammunition the room went silent. One of the members of our team was down with what looked like a shot to his left bicep but he was animated and emitting standard curses. The operation was effectively over.

As the traffickers were cuffed and hog-tied the sorters were lined up and marched from the building, each one's pockets and purses being checked before they were arrested, loaded onto small buses and taken in for questioning. The initial searches yielded the equivalent of several keys of heroin and coke; that had, apparently, been part of the original plan that they had been instructed to follow.

What happened next proved to be of particular interest.

# SEVEN

"**S**on of a bitch," Tim said. "Sorry," he added.

"We all forgive you," John said. "We were surprised as well."

The source of that surprise came with the after-action search. The vans had included large boxes of cheap gym shoes with open spaces beneath the soles and the inserts. That bulk accounted for the number of vehicles involved. Within the shoes were packages of what purported to be hydrocodone with an awkward **M365** imprint. That would normally indicate a 5% dose of hydrocodone bitartrate combined with 325 mg of acetaminophen. The problem was that the authentic combination pills were white, while these were a light blue. Amateur night. Someone was passing crappy product to the boys of MS-13 but that product was far more deadly than hydro; these tablets were fentanyl.

"Enough here to kill everyone in Maryland, at least," Tim said. "The boys were about to accelerate their operation and drop a new product line. Be sure to check the sorters for anything like this; we don't want any of their kids to think of this as candy."

"Already in process," John said, holding his cell phone to his ear.

"I'll let the Director know," Tim said. "No, why don't you call him, Gwen?"

"You deserve the props, Tim," I said. "I'm just a spear carrier here."

He smiled, hit a button on his phone and lifted it to his ear.

That night I met with the Director in his office. It was 8:15 but he looked rested and refreshed, with a starched white shirt and an Italian silk tie (perhaps a *Batisti*?). Edgar would have thoroughly disapproved but the Director's armored division from back in his two-star days would have considered his flamboyance fully justified. After all, gold scarves had long been the cavalry's stock in trade.

Before we began the debrief he opened the walnut chest behind his desk and removed a bottle of *Michter's* 10 year bourbon and two Edinburgh Crystal glasses. "I think you'll like this," he said, pouring two fingers' worth over a single, large ice cube.

"I'm sure I will," I said. "I can tell you this, Sir; I liked the La Plata operation."

"Tim's a planner and he's got a solid team. So what did you learn, Gwen?"

"No great epiphanies, Sir, but the bottom lines were not unfamiliar. First and foremost, no matter how great the planning there are always some gaps and uncertainties."

"True that," he said.

"Overwhelming force is never a bad thing, so long as your intel on their numbers is rock solid."

"Indeed."

"Sometimes cooler heads prevail but there's always the chance of some rogue actor with neither good sense nor any measure of discretion."

"He wants to die for his country and we're happy to oblige, as Georgie would have said."

"Expect the unexpected," I said next.

"Right. A rogue shooter or a far more lethal cargo than anticipated."

"Be prepared to respond to altered circumstances."

"Right. The flash-bangs and CS always come in handy, especially when the latter can be delivered through multiple systems."

"I think that's about it," I said, "except for the obvious. Have a strong leader who's cool under fire and a team that is suitably specialized and knows their individual roles."

"That may be obvious but it's also essential," he said. "Never tire of repeating the essential."

"We also have some good body-cam footage," I said, "so when I put on my teacher's hat and hit the field offices I can show some interesting film."

"We always liked the movies" he said. "Military education is weird. The first thing they tell you is that the human attention span is somewhere between ten and twenty minutes; then they schedule eight hours of instruction per day. You come to yearn for those movies, except that now everyone's watching clips on their phones and that has resulted in an even-more-reduced attention span. Go figure."

"That's why they used to put the zaftig woman in the maintenance magazine," I said. "What was the woman's name: Connie Rodd? She taught you how to maintain your weapons and other instruments and held your attention with her…what would you say, ample cleavage?"

"How do you know about Connie?" he asked. "She was way before your time."

"My military-trained Quantico classmates must have mentioned her," I said.

He smiled. "How do you like the bourbon?"

"Perfect end to the day, Sir."

"And you haven't eaten?"

"Not yet."

"I took the liberty of ordering some steaks," he said. "Can I tempt you?"

"Tempt away, Sir."

He hit one of the call buttons on his landline and I heard Peggy Chapman's voice. Peggy never left the office until the Director was halfway to his home in McLean. "Ready to dine, Sir?"

"Yes, Peg," he answered.

"With the good wine?"

"Always," he said.

When she opened the door I saw a caterer standing behind her, making last-minute adjustments to the plates. She brought in a bottle of claret that had just been opened; she must have anticipated his order. It was something big and bold from Saint-Estèphe.

We began sipping before the steaks were served. The Director remained silent until the caterer finished her work and closed the door behind her.

"You're probably wondering about the missing van," he said.

"I *was* actually."

"Turned off and headed for a place in PG county," he said. "They had intended to drop off some product and then head home. Small potatoes. We picked up the delivery boys along with the local dealers. All of them lawyered up after we stopped them. The dealers had concealed the stash (we've found nearly all of it) but all of their hands and clothing lit up the sniffer dogs' sense of smell. As it turned out, the driver and passenger also had some GSR on them along with the remains of the controlled substances. We found handguns in the van—unregistered, of course—so that put another dark cloud over their heads."

"Good," I said. "I didn't like the idea of their getting away from the rest of their compadres."

"We had a secondary team in reserve, just in case."

I smiled and sipped my wine.

"We should talk about your upcoming tour," he said, "but after dessert."

# EIGHT

That would be something with chocolate. The Director's sweet tooth was single-minded and predictable. After it was served the caterer described it in her best continental accent. I didn't catch the full title but I heard two words clearly: *royale* and *decadent*. After two cups of strong black coffee and some cognac we got back to business.

"One thing I need to tell you…" the Director said. "Part of the purpose of this little tour is to broaden your horizons. Most of your work has entailed direct assignments from me and, needless to say, that work has been exceptional. It's also kept you out of the mainstream. In the unlikely event of my being hit by a bus or the more likely event of a new administration putting me out to pasture I want to be sure that you're positioned for a job commensurate with your talents. Bottom line: you're highly respected within the Bureau but you're principally associated with special tasks from the old man. The tour will help extend the awareness of your presence and skills. There's also the potential for a subsidiary benefit…"

"I may learn some things in the process."

He smiled and took a sip of his cognac. "Always a possibility," he said. "Of course, everyone's always anxious to hear from the higher echelons. They think we'll feed their curiosity and possibly share something truly serious. They also realize the degree to which the world has changed. It's just so complicated these days. Take the last operation, for example. Drugs are not our long suit or principal responsibility, but we often (as in this case) get involved because of our cybersecurity specialty. We work relatively independently of the DEA, but the DEA deals with money laundering and bulk currency smuggling. That's something we're interested in, particularly with regard to asset forfeiture. If the drug money is also underwriting terrorism…well…preventing terrorist attacks is our top priority. When it comes to drugs, however, we could find ourselves working with the DEA, Homeland Security, the ATF, the Marshals, Customs and Border Protection, even the Postal Inspection Service and the Coast Guard. We all have our orbits and roles but the world is now (what would you say) a seamless mess?"

"Totally agree, Sir. I had actually planned to begin my sessions with mug shots of Edgar's targets—Karpis, Dillinger, Baby Face Nelson, Machine Gun Kelly, et al. I would probably put up a contemporary 'Most Wanted Fugitives' image to reinforce our continuities with the past, but then put up some pictures, graphs, outlines of chains of command and organizational charts to make the central point that times have changed and that we're now one of a number of large teams that overlap, intersect, and interact, while trying to play to our strengths but not step on each other's toes, feet and ankles. I'd illustrate that with some Venn diagrams and some explosion-in-a-spaghetti-factory charts with lines going in any and all directions."

"Perfect," he responded. "Then you get down to cases that focus on our major activities but illustrate the fact that we don't do these things alone."

"Exactly, but walking the tightrope between teamwork and turf wars."

"Always an issue," he said.

"Ted Henning has volunteered to help me with cybercrime and cybersecurity issues. That overlaps with white-collar crime actions and economic espionage. Since we have specially-trained cyber squads in each field office this will be a bit of a challenge for me. I don't want them sharpshooting me in a Q&A, but I don't want to appear to be showy or pompous in an area where my experience is clearly limited."

"You prefer firefights and breaking down doors," the Director said.

"Guilty as charged," I responded. "I'll need Ted's help and I'll give him full credit for his contributions. I'll also have Mike Liu in reserve to help me with anecdotes and images."

"Both solid citizens," the Director said. "The one is more gray and buttoned down and the other pyjama-clad in mom's basement, but we need both types. There's another issue; the more technical the lesson the greater the risk of boring your audience. I'd start the case studies with something easy, not necessarily easy in execution but easy in concept."

"You're reading my mind again, Sir," I said.

"My secret power."

"I was thinking about the Georgetown Reservoir."

"As a terrorist target?"

"Yes. They've all probably seen it and they've all probably consumed its product at one time or another. It always seems like a possible (and relatively easy) target. Who guards it? When you come up from Canal Road or drive along MacArthur Boulevard you never see anyone there."

"True."

"As you know, it's not formally guarded by anyone. It's overseen by the Army Corps of Engineers, patrolled by the police department, DC Water and occasionally by the Park Police. The security is 'layered'; whether that instills confidence or not I'll leave up to the audience. The point is that we're all in these things together these days; that's the problem, the challenge, the reality."

"And as every simple Google search will tell you, terrorism is our top priority and managing the cyber threat is one of our long suits. So we're ultimately involved in just about…everything. You don't think of 'counterintelligence' as a contemporary watchword but we're still heavily immersed in it. Also WMD's and domestic terrorism. Everyone worries about pulse bombs and dirty bombs but a poisoned water supply in Northwest D.C. could do a significant amount of damage, both to bodies and to hearts and minds."

I nodded in agreement and took a sip of the Director's cognac.

"So where would you prefer to start?" he asked.

"At first I thought, somewhere in the boonies—Anchorage, Billings, El Paso, Little Rock—but while I wanted to warm up there before trying to pitch in New York, Chicago or L.A. I wouldn't want them to think they're on the periphery, so I thought maybe Charlotte or Kansas City, some place like that. I know I'm not the only one involved in the program; what do you think, Sir?"

"I wouldn't inflict all 56 on one person. I've got one AD on the team and several SAC's. I appreciate your thoughts on all this. We'll work up a chart; plan on doing seven or eight visits. This could be an annual activity, depending on the feedback and changing circumstances. My thought was to rotate the trainers each time around so that eventually each would cover all 56 field offices. I'll try to organize the trips in such a way that they'll be of help to you and largely be inscrutable to the locals."

"Sounds great," I said.

"Work on your lesson plans; check back with me when you've got some ideas to share with the whole team. Plan on two weeks to prep, a week to chat and finalize and then we'll take the show on the road."

"Will do, Sir. Thanks for dinner. Always a pleasure."

"And for me," he said.


I drove to my apartment, unloaded my car, showered and got in bed. I felt good. That was because I had no knowledge of what awaited me.

# NINE

I was particularly grateful for the opportunity to get off the road, break out the pencils and yellow tablets and search the Bureau's private corners of the web. It was like writing term papers. Most of my classmates hated them; I loved the opportunity to sit in a dark corner, read books and wordsmith.

I decided to turn the initial stage of my teaching assignment into a mini-vacation. By now my base salary had hit six figures, even if I never had the time and opportunity to spend it on anything beyond essentials. My 450-square foot apartment was appallingly expensive, but those of us who work out of the District draw locality pay that closes the gap between the normal and the surreal.

My destination of choice was Middleburg, in the Virginia version of the 'hunt country' but most of the spas and resorts exacted piratical payments, so I settled for the *Red Fox Inn*, whose rack rate was a little south of astronomical. A little quick talking and flashing of credentials persuaded them to lower the tariff to something like double the government per diem. They also included breakfast, a not inconsiderable perk, given the quality of their restaurant and my ability to balance my dietary timing for maximum effect.

As I settled in with a tall cup of black coffee and my new *MacBook* Air it quickly dawned on me that nearly every segment of my instruction would be computer-driven. All of life is, of course, but protecting against terrorism (both international and domestic), developing counterintelligence (now chiefly the protection of computer networks from data theft), protecting against economic espionage, imposing costs on cyber adversaries and exposing public corruption are all important tasks that are handled with keyboards and hard drives more than Tommy Guns.

I needed particular help from Ted and Mike on the NCIJTF (the National Cyber Investigative Joint Task Force), in which the Bureau takes the lead, with the involvement of more than thirty other agencies from law enforcement and the intelligence community.

Fortunately there were a few areas in which I had some experience (though often minimal) which were not so tech-driven—asset forfeiture, e.g., drug interdiction and the protection of access to 'women's health' clinics.

The bottom line was that I would be caught in the classic position of the instructional neophyte—staying a day or two ahead of my students. My advantage, however, was the fact that so many of my 'students' joined the Bureau to break down doors and take down bad hombres. Riding a slightly-padded chair and operating a desktop was part of the job, indeed an important part of the job, but it often drew as much love as the completion of reports and the undergoing of mandated instruction from the office of Human Resources (actually the Human Resources Division or HRD, which operates out of the District as well as places like Clarksburg, West Virginia). I don't remember whether or not that was one of Senator Byrd's pork delivery enterprises, like the CJIS (Criminal Justice Information Services Division), the computerized fingerprint records office, which scrapes by on its modest campus of 986 acres, approximately the footprint of my beloved alma mater, Kenyon College.

That would not be the subject of extended discourse in the classroom though it could be an interesting topic during coffee or lunch breaks. These reflections did remind me of the fact that the alphabet soup of government acronyms was never fully listed. The DOJ offered a partial list, but it was woefully brief and didn't, e.g., include the aforementioned HRD or even the CJIS. Perhaps this was all part of a larger cultural vision in which government types (preeminently the military) prided themselves on their ability to talk in acronym-speak, a kind of code for the cognoscenti. Food for thought.

The results of these musings were ultimately positive. I had already broken down my larger subject into discrete sections and had some marginal comments on possible illustrative examples or case studies. The musings gave me some themes or leitmotifs that would serve as overarching links in my presentations. Facts can be listed on a pamphlet but inculcating a change or shift in overall attitude is trickier and potentially more important, even as it risks being commonplace and mundane. No one wants to be told the obvious. There was one thing of which I was becoming certain: this was a good exercise for me, something to broaden my horizons, as the Director had suggested.

I stayed in for dinner but changed into something a bit more smart. Opting for their three-course special I went for the parsnip soup, the sea bass and the chocolate pistachio torte. I passed on the wine pairing and did some house chardonnay. I figured I'd splurge the first night and then do their pub food later. I was disappointed to note the absence of their mainstay peanut soup, but into every life a little rain must fall and I took solace in the fact that the wine was great value and chilled perfectly.

# TEN

I slept well, the change in venue apparently working to my advantage. Road warriors often long to sleep in their own beds but in my case the maxim didn't always hold, particularly after a bout of armed field work. There's something about fresh sheets and soft comforters that exceed the effects of the usually tried and true.

For the next six days I worked intently, with the single exception of one afternoon break—a short road trip to Front Royal to soak up some Civil War history and some wine from the local vineyards. Other than that I was on my laptop for 9-10 hours a day, with breaks for breakfast, dinner and multiple cups of black coffee. I was surprised by the fare at the local Middleburg restaurants. Tourists might expect large helpings of game and grog but these days the special of the day was just as likely to be Pad Thai, some concoction with raw fish or a heaping side of Tabbouleh. Some novice restaurateurs came to the area with the thought of reproducing authentic Revolutionary War fare, until they learned what our forefathers and foremothers actually ate (and how they preserved it from spoilage). Calf's head and pigeon pie might have tempted the palates of people in powdered wigs, but today's diners wanted waiters and waitresses in period dress delivering the type of food that could always be found in close proximity to the offices of K Street lobbyists.

With some final polishing of my lesson plans I was ready to Zoom with my fellow instructors. Three were individual SAC's I knew in passing; one (a major score for the Director) the Deputy AG in the DOJ and, a great choice in my judgment, Ralph 'Dex' Dexter, the NYC AD who had been acting in the job and was now permanent. Dex was an Army vet with prosthetic feet and calves and a prosthetic right hand. I knew him from a previous case, an unassuming and jovial warrior who let his actions and personal history speak for themselves.

We were all surprised at the degree of overlap that we had achieved, though we were studiously independent in our preparations. The Director was pleased, since his plan for the program was to tick both the unity and variety boxes. He didn't want anyone wandering off on unexpected tangents; at the same time he didn't want us to be working in straitjackets, parroting some boring party line to a drowsy audience. Since the ultimate plan was for us to continue the program with each of us shifting venues in the succeeding iterations our audiences would be exposed to our individual quirks and insights while each of us (in general) reinforced specific points.

After we all talked and produced a broad outline of the general direction of our presentations they were approved by the Director, with the proviso that we were free to make some final tweaks and, yes, appropriate anything that we particularly liked from our colleagues' documents. After 48 hours of last-minute shuffling we were given our individual schedules. I drew Columbia, SC, Buffalo, Birmingham, Billings, Albany, Denver, San Diego, New Orleans and my old stomping ground, St. Louis. We were given the choice of the order. I began with San Diego, the most distant locale from D.C., with St. Louis on deck.

The presentation in San Diego went well. The SAC was pleased and rewarded me with a 2½ hour dinner in Little Italy. "I especially liked the example of the Georgetown Reservoir," he said. "'Layered' supervision. It was all I could do to keep from laughing out loud. All sweetness and light and friendly cooperation until an event occurs and the circular firing squad is formed. You'll forgive me, Gwen, but I believe that someone has to be in charge. Absolutely in charge. That person can 'coordinate' with a friendly face but when you talk to the SAC's and AD's you'll often find that they have a Harry Truman sign on their desks."

"Indicating where the buck stops," I said.

"Exactly. Anyway, I liked the way you handled that. A little bit of (what would you say) countercultural advice?"

"What do they say at MI5?" I asked, "London rules or Moscow rules?"

"Precisely. In Moscow if you screw up you get a radioactive cocktail or a bullet in the brain; in London you look around and point fingers at everyone else in the Service."

We clinked wine glasses.

A lovely *Riserva*.

I was starting to enjoy this assignment.

My next stop was St. Louis. The new SAC had been a special agent the last time I was there and we were happy to renew our acquaintance. The audience was slightly more buttoned-down and less effusive in its responses to my presentations, but they asked serious questions and took notes. They were particularly interested in the discussion of the complex nature of drug interdiction because that was a significant part of their sphere of responsibility. Their problem was geography. Routes **44**, **55**, **64** and **70** facilitated the distribution of product from the southwest border and there was an ongoing local problem with the manufacture and distribution of meth. They liked the anecdotes from the La Plata operation and added some of their own stories. I connected with them by jotting some down and saying that I would steal them and use them in later talks.

The SAC, Dave Jenkins, brought along two of his female special agents to dinner, indicating that they couldn't have too many mentors and asking me if I would enlist myself in the task. How could I refuse, particularly looking over a $58 steak and the best potato I'd ever eaten, outside of Boise or Presque Isle, Maine. Actually, I didn't think they needed much mentoring. One was an Olympic-level markswoman (25m pistol) and the other a graduate of Yale law. They wore their sidearms comfortably and asked some of the best questions I had yet received.

They shared a medium-rare tomahawk steak and had each begun the dinner with *Corner Creek* bourbon, neat.

The following morning I was scheduled for a flight to *Louis Armstrong New Orleans International*; I loved the sound of that but sadly it was not to be.

The Director called me personally on my cell phone.

# ELEVEN

"I hate to interrupt your tour," he said, "but this is important. At least to me it is and I think it will be to you."

"Yes, Sir…"

"One of our former special agents has gone missing, a man named Richard Ingle. I gather that the two of you were classmates and friends."

"We were," I said, but I didn't add the fact that we had been more than friends, at least for a brief time.

"You may or may not know that he left the Bureau a few years ago…"

"I did know that, Sir. He had served five years of active duty in the Army and done night law school before joining the Bureau. He was assigned to a number of places after Quantico. I think he was anxious to settle down, establish roots, start a family…"

"Right. Normally this kind of disappearance would be handled by local law enforcement, but Richard's wife reached out to the SAC in Buffalo as well as to the locals. Though technically a civilian I still consider him a member of the family. I want all of us to live long and prosper and I abhor anything that might be life-threatening, particularly when that threat involves our own people."

"Fully agree, Sir."

You haven't met the Buffalo SAC yet, have you?"

"No, Sir."

"Good man. I know you were scheduled to speak there later, but we've been, as they say, overtaken by events."

"Understood, Sir."

"If you haven't checked him out yet, his name is Scott Leven. He started out in the boonies of the northern plains, did a great job there and was moved to western New York. As you know, most of our missing persons cases involve criminals, witnesses, people of interest, not family men in quiet neighborhoods.

"His wife actually began with the satellite office in Monroe County, but that's primarily a tip line and a service office for the local communities. When she said that he had been in the Bureau they bucked the call to Scott, Scott talked to her, and then called me."

"What do we know, Sir?"

"Precious little, I'm afraid. Richard works for a Swedish tech company. The Rochester area is very popular for such operations because of the volume of skilled workers ultimately associated with the heydays of *Eastman Kodak*. The job required very little travel, but when Richard did travel he was away for several days. There was also a level of security with his work because the company is a defense contractor as well as a manufacturer of consumer goods. Basically, radios. What I'm getting at is the fact that his wife was used to seeing him come and go and sometimes deal in confidential areas. She waited several days before contacting the police and the Bureau."

"And you want me to see if I can find him, Sir."

"It's what you do best, Gwen. It's probably nothing. He may have been in some kind of car accident that rendered him incommunicado. We simply don't know. If it's something else, something more serious… well, I don't like to think of one of our own in need of help and unable to receive it. Strong and resourceful men generally don't simply disappear."

"I understand, Sir."

"We'll start positive," he said. "You're postponing your Cajun jambalaya and preparing to sit down with an old friend over a plate of chicken wings. If, God willing, he's gone for good we'll pray for him and toast his memory. However, if he's walked into something ugly I want someone on the case who…won't hold anything back."

"I remember him fondly, Sir."

"I thought that might be the case."

"And I won't hold back."

"You never do," he said. "I just wanted to add that I'm sorry about this development and I'm hoping for the best. The bottom line is that a missing friend and colleague trumps a classroom stint in New Orleans."

"I suspect that the route from Lambert to western New York will involve a single-stop on a toy airplane," I said. "I'll plan to leave first thing in the morning if there's space available."

"Already arranged," he said. "You're out at 10:19, flying via Detroit. I figured you'd want to talk to his wife first rather than Scott. Richard lives in the Rochester suburbs; Scott's about an hour and a half away, possibly less, depending on the traffic and weather. We'll have an unmarked Bureau car for you at the Rochester airport. Your contact will be a man named Tony Giraldi."

"May I say something, Sir?" I asked.

"Of course, Gwen."

"I appreciate your speaking of Richard in the present tense."

"I have every confidence because I knew that you'd be on the case," he answered.


That night I slept fitfully. I was struck by the degree to which Richard and I had lost touch. I didn't know where he was living and I didn't know that he was married. All that I did know was that he had left the Bureau and gone to work in the private sector. I was embarrassed by the fact that my own work had been so all-consuming that I had let my private life fall into abeyance. It was a common occurrence but in this case my feelings had run deeper than I had thought at the time.

# TWELVE

**M**y flight from Lambert Field had been on time but Detroit Metro/ Wayne County was a different story entirely. The place is huge, nearly O'Hare-level huge and the powers that control it kept changing our departure gate. This resulted in a series of heel-and-toe races that tested both the patience and the physical stamina of the customers, particularly those in wheelchairs or navigating with canes and walkers. Eventually I caught up with the flight crew, who were seething, and told them I would avoid the public address system's voice of Big Brother and simply follow them. The final departure gate was surrounded by out-of-breath angry individuals who were cursing the airline, the airport, the city and the travel gods.

I settled into my seat and both texted and emailed Richard's wife (her name was Kathleen), introduced myself, asked her to keep my impending visit private and inquired as to her availability that afternoon.

She thanked me immediately, gave me her address (which I already had in the electronic briefing packet furnished by the Director's assistant, Peggy Chapman) and told me she was looking forward to seeing me.

The luggage carousels at the grandly-titled *Frederick Douglass Greater Rochester International Airport* were in a corner close to the parking facilities. As I entered the area a short, swarthy man with jet black hair and dark brown eyes approached me. "I'm Tony," he said. "I've got your car."

"Thanks, I'm Gwen," I said.

"We use the nondescript unmarkeds so you don't look like a tourist in a rental or a storm trooper in a black-and-white," he said.

"Got it; that's good," I said.

"It's right outside."

The broad pickup lanes were just outside the door, presided over by a uniformed officer who looked like he could have been a power forward in the NBA. The traffic was light enough that he was using hand gestures rather than a whistle.

"It's kind of a small town thing," Tony said. "If the traffic is light they'll let you sit awhile and wait for the person who's just deplaned. Your car's just…there." He pointed to the right at a metallic gray Rav4. "Here's your fob," he said, handing it to me along with a map.

"I figured you might like to have a paper map. They say you can get anywhere in this town in twenty minutes, but the arterial highways can get a little complicated. I like to get the big picture on the paper map so that I can use the navigation system with greater confidence. Maybe I'm weird and maybe I have trust issues, but, I don't know, I like the feel of the paper."

"So do I," I said. "Thanks."

"Anyway, the navigation system is already set up to take you to Richard's house in Honeoye Falls." (He pronounced it *honey-oi.*) "You're looking at a little under twenty miles but you should make it there in less than thirty minutes. Nice little town. What you'd call *quaint.* Maybe *picturesque.*"

"I appreciate your help, Tony."

"We appreciate your being here. We're all hoping for the best and whenever you need us we're ready to help."


En route to Honeoye Falls I passed through a suburb called Henrietta. It was the place in which Richard worked. As I hit the outskirts of town I was struck by the fact that I had moved so quickly from a congested area of hotels, chain restaurants and big box stores into farm country. I didn't think of western New York as corn country and I thought even less of it as being peach country, but I saw several hand-painted signs at roadside stands advertising their present and future availability.

Richard's home was in a subdivision of new homes surrounded by some sprawling farms that could have been airlifted from Iowa or downstate Illinois. When I rang the bell the door opened immediately.

"I'm so glad you're here," Richard's wife said. "I'm Kathleen. Come in. Come in." She hugged me and asked if it would be all right if she called me Gwen.

"Of course," I said.

She was relatively tall, probably 5'8" or 5'9", with chestnut brown hair, green eyes and a pleasant but now troubled face. The worry lines had reduced her smile, but she embraced me a second time and invited me to sit on their couch. "What can I get you to drink?" she asked.

"Whatever you're having," I said.

"I'm having black coffee," she said. "I spend most of my time trying to stay alert, waiting for news."

"That would be perfect," I said.

She went into the kitchen and returned with large mugs with wisps of steam hovering at the surface. By then it had fully sunk in that she was 7-8 months pregnant. She hadn't mentioned it; it was a simple fact of life to her, though I (for whatever reason) was struck by it.

"It began about five days ago. Richard left for work at his usual time but he didn't return home that evening. I called the police and they said that it was best to give him 48 hours or so before applying what they called the full-court press. I called the local hospitals and urgent care centers (we have a lot of those here) but no one had seen him. I gave them all full descriptions of him but they reiterated that no one there had seen him. When I called the police back they asked me a host of questions; many of them I thought were…well…intrusive, but I answered them honestly."

"And then you called the Bureau."

"The local satellite office first, but then the main field office in Buffalo."

"And they were responsive."

"Very," she said. "They contacted the Director's office and his assistant…"

"Peggy Chapman."

"Yes. Wonderful woman. She said she'd get back to me as soon as she could. A few hours later Mrs. Chapman said that General Gradison was sending you to help. She said that you handled special assignments and that you reported directly to him."

"A lot of people still use the Director's military title."

"So I gathered," she said, her eyes welling up. "I'm so glad you're here."

"Richard and I were at Quantico together, soon after he had completed law school and joined the Bureau."

"I understand," she said. "He mentioned you often. He was fond of you."

"And I of him. We helped each other get through our training."

I left it at that, not knowing whether or not his wife was aware of our closer connection.

"He said you were aces," she said. "I had never heard that expression before. I grew up in Indiana."

"If I might ask, how did the two of you meet?"

"It wasn't online and it wasn't in church," she said, managing a smile. I was working in one of the medical offices near his company's building complex and we had seen each other at lunch at some of the same local restaurants. One day he asked if he could join me and we had a nice conversation. He later told me that he noticed that I wasn't wearing a ring and that emboldened him to approach me. I thought that was sweet. He's really a lovely man."

"He certainly is," I said. "The best. That's why I'm here to find him."

# THIRTEEN

After a few minutes of small talk she asked if I would like to stay for dinner. "I would really like that," she said. "Talking to you somehow makes me more aware of his presence."

Dinner was simple pasta in a *Rao* vodka sauce. Kathleen made us small salads with Italian dressing and cut us slices of bread which she put on side plates. She offered me wine. "I can't have any," she said, "but you might like some."

"Only if it's already opened," I said.

"Since I've been pregnant Richard's been buying it in those individual cups or tiny bottles. There are always several of them in the fridge. He always says that it tastes much better than it looks."

As she poured it and placed it beside my glass of ice water I noticed the framed display of Richard's medals that hung on the wall above the sideboard.

"Very impressive," I said. "I didn't know that Richard had received a silver star as well as a bronze star with a **V** device."

"They were both from fighting ISIS in Iraq and Syria," she said. "Let me see if I can get this straight—'Operation Inherent Resolve'."

"That's it," I said.

"The silver star involved a six-hour firefight. Some of the men in his Company were wounded and became separated from the main force. Richard was able to reach them and protect them until another unit from their battalion was able to secure the area. The bronze star was a little less dramatic. Richard's unit was assigned the task of securing an area for the locals and refitting some community buildings. They came under sniper fire and Richard was able to protect the civilians by neutralizing the threat. He was nicked in the shoulder in the process. That's where he got the purple heart…"

"I saw that…"

"Richard always jokes that if it hadn't been for the snipers he'd have gotten a simple medal, not one with a device indicating Valor. Then he tells the story about a man in another unit who was hiding under a table during an artillery attack. The man bolted, bumped his head and rubbed the spot until there was a trickle of blood. The man then received the same medals as Richard. I think he was downplaying his own accomplishments. He's very modest and unassuming; it's something that makes him attractive to people."

"But truly skilled and brave," I said, while wondering to myself why he had never mentioned his combat experiences.

"He *is* brave," Kathleen said. "I pray that if he's found himself in some kind of serious trouble that he'll have the inner resources to survive."

I hadn't expected her to say something that serious but she was right. Absent some medical emergency there is no reason for anyone to simply disappear, unless, of course, that is something that they want to do and have planned on doing. That wasn't Richard, particularly not with a child on the way. I shifted the conversation.

"Was he enjoying his work?" I asked.

"Very much so," Kathleen responded. "You'll be talking to the people there. They make radios for both defense work and civilian hobbyists. Richard was hired to help with R&D. His engineering studies at West Point combined with his combat experience made him the perfect person to help with the design and refinement of their products. He loved the field testing, particularly in the mountains that surround us here."

"And he hadn't said anything about any problems at work or with any of the people there…"

"Not at all," she said. "They've been wonderful. The CEO called me directly. He told me not to worry. He said that Richard's salary would continue and that I should call whenever I had any concerns. Richard's wellbeing was their highest priority."

"That must have been very reassuring," I said.

"Yes. They're good people. You may know that it's actually a Swedish company but the vast majority of the people who work there are local. This has always been a town with a great number of people with technical expertise. That's why companies locate here; that's why Richard came here. *Kodak* missed the digital revolution but they've gone into other areas…coating, printing, fabrics…."

"There's always a need for people with technical skills," I said. "Our competitors and adversaries are always ahead of us in their educational programs. They don't have the luxury of studying the liberal arts. I'm a Bureau special agent but I went to a college that was known for the study of literature and languages. I studied geography because I was fascinated with it, not because the government forced me to do so. In fairness, I was exposed to a lot of other things as well."

"But you've also got a family heritage," she said. "Native blood…it counts for a lot. Richard told me about all of your skills."

That was interesting, I thought to myself. Richard had the self-confidence (and the confidence in his marriage) to talk to his wife about a former acquaintance.

"I'm not sure how much of that is myth and how much of it is genetically transmitted," I said.

"I think a lot of it is in the blood," Kathleen said. "I'm not a scientist but I think that things like instinct and intuition are a lot more complex than we know."

"They're the sum of all of our experience," I said, "not some tool that's held in reserve or sparked by a single event."

"Precisely," she answered, "and at the right time and in the right moment you count on that…totality."

"I think so," I said. I was beginning to really like this woman.

# FOURTEEN

"How about dessert?" she asked. "I've got some ice cream."

"How about some more black coffee," I asked.

"I'll make fresh," she said.

After two cups of coffee and another hour of reminiscing, Kathleen (now Kathy) asked me if I would like to stay with her during my investigation. After thanking her several times, I declined politely. "That's very sweet of you, but I should be closer to the Bureau satellite office and to Richard's work place," I said. "I have to check my phone but I believe that Peggy's arranged a place for me in town."

Actually, Peggy had arranged a place for me in an upscale neighborhood called Pittsford. The rather honorific title was the *Del Monte Lodge Renaissance Rochester Hotel & Spa*, not the *Marriott, Pittsford*. "The places in Henrietta are a little more exposed," she said. "The *Del Monte* has several entry/exit points and what appears to be a vast parking lot. There's an adjoining spa as well as some nearby commercial enterprises. I want you to have some room to come and go and maneuver…just in case there's someone there watching you or hoping to obstruct your investigation."

Before I left I gave Kathy a phone to use whenever she wanted to talk to me. I didn't have to explain to her that if someone had actually abducted Richard, or worse, they would have the means to listen in on conversations from her landline and possibly her cell phone. She thanked me and put it next to her purse.

Before I drove to the *Del Monte* I decided to drive by Richard's office building. As I noted earlier, Henrietta had residential areas at its periphery but it chiefly consisted of chain restaurants, big box stores and a host of small businesses. This was the place you drove to if you wanted to shop in familiar surroundings, buy a car, a burger and fries or a carton of discount liquor. The hotel chains were there, but as Peggy had figured they had small parking lots that were easily surveilled. Many catered to families and a single woman could quickly draw unwanted attention from someone wondering about her presence there (or, perhaps, wishing to do her harm).

Amid the household-name commercial enterprises were a large number of medical facilities—outposts for specialist groups, test labs, and urgent care operations—most subdued and formal, but some with gawdy signs, including *The Foot Doctor's* office on Jefferson Road.

Richard's company adjoined a cardiology group's office on Calkins Road, a major east/west artery south of Jefferson. It sat in a parallel industrial park on the south side of Calkins, with the heart docs just to the east. The signage at the entrance to the park consisted of raised, sleek, aluminum lettering in a faux art-deco font: *Kommunicom*. Peggy's read was that this was a forced marriage between the Swedish word for communication and .com. It sounded to me like a branch of the Stasi or KGB.

There were five buildings. The central building was small but tasteful, probably the administrative HQ. At the end of a series of walkway/ tentacles were four larger buildings, probably the sites of company divisions. There were lights on in various floors of each, but only security lights in the entryway and corners of the administrative facility. The good news was that there was no security checkpoint through which I would be forced to pass if I wanted to drive up for a closer look. Unfortunately, there would probably be a succession of CCTV cameras that would have recorded my presence and raised suspicions as to why I might be casing the place after dark.

My problem was that I couldn't investigate without disclosing my identity. If and when I entered the building I would be asked to present some form of credential. A six-year old could have googled my name and come up with thousands of hits and if the credential was forged anyone with basic facial rec software could have unmasked me in a matter of moments. I had to play it straight. The principal goal was to reduce any qualms concerning the level of our doubts and suspicions and make the investigation appear to be serious but, ultimately, routine.

That is why we held off on making appointments and securing search warrants. The satellite office had made brief inquiries and the Buffalo field office had kept their distance and maintained what *Kommunicom* would have been happy to call radio silence.

The fact remained that they were the principal organization of interest. The only other alternatives were that Richard was being nursed back to health by a farmer without a cell phone or computer or that he had become involved in activities that were sufficiently off-the-legal-grid to risk his kidnapping, imprisonment or murder. Given Richard's personality, temperament, skill set, patriotism and personal faith, that was even more unlikely than the existence of a Good Samaritan who had rescued Richard from an accident and then refused to contact anyone in the outside world concerning his plight.

Besides, the company that employed Richard had too many suspicious aspects. They dealt in defense contracts. They probably had global purchasers, some with bad intentions. And they had a Director named Rudolf Bethe; I didn't like that name any more than I liked the name of the company. I would know more after I interviewed him the following morning (assuming that I could see him then) but the name immediately conjured up memories of Bond villains and cold war apparatchiks with monocles and facial scars.

I made some mental notes and drove to the *Del Monte*, where I checked in to my room and then visited the bar. I used my phone to create a checklist for my interview with the company director. I offset the remains of my coffee buzz with a glass (to be honest, two) of brandy and finally retired for the night.

# FIFTEEN

I slept reasonably well, rose early and had a full breakfast of pancakes, bacon and eggs. The company opened at 8:00 (Rudolf's work ethic presumably trumping most local practice). I waited until 9:15 to call; I didn't want to appear to be too anxious.

His assistant identified herself as Karla. Given her vaguely European accent, I assumed it was Karla with a K rather than a C.

"Good morning," I said. "I'm calling to see if I can visit with the Director sometime today."

"May I tell him your name and the purpose of the visit?" she asked.

"Yes. My name is Gwendolyn Harrison. I'm working through the Buffalo field office of the Federal Bureau of Investigation. Your employee, a Mr. Richard Ingle, has been reported missing. Mr. Ingle is a former Bureau special agent and I'm calling to offer any help that the Bureau might be able to provide in finding him."

"That's very kind," she said. "Let me check for a second." A few moments later she came back on the phone. "Would you be able to come in at 11:15?"

"That would be good for me," I said. "Please thank the Director for seeing me on such short notice."

"He always attempts to be as accommodating as possible and I'm sure that he will appreciate your help. He has always valued Mr. Ingle's contributions and is anxious to find him and have him return to work at *Kommunicom*."

"I'll see you at 11:15," I said, thinking that her response seemed just a bit robotic.

I arrived at the *Kommunicom* administrative facility at 11:05. There were five Visitor parking spaces, one next to the reserved spot for the Director, the specially color-coded space outlining the angular reality of a top-of-the-line current model *Range Rover*. The color was 'Santorini Black', a curious designation because most people who think of Santorini think of blue roofs and blue sea. Nice wheels for those with 6 figures to spend and no special need for reliability.

The interior of the building was spare and efficient, with touches of aluminum eye makeup and long panels of indirect lighting. This all changed when I entered the Director's wing and suite, where everything was walnut and Carrara marble. I was greeted by a male assistant and wondered where the woman with the robotic voice was entrenched. Perhaps he was like Della Street's Gertie, the woman who did the receptionist's tasks while Della enjoyed the privilege of sitting in on Perry Mason's private meetings.

When I finally met the Director he was a vision of sartorial indulgence. He had blown past *Hugo Boss* and *Armani* on his way to *Brioni's* private showroom. I couldn't identify the difference between Merino wool and Cashmere at a glance, but I could feel the presence of dollar signs and sliding decimal points. The starch on his collar and French cuffs was impeccable, and the cuffs' links were golden chunks of eye candy that cried out for attention.

The tie was either *Turnbull & Asser* or *Hermès*. Again, I was constrained by my limited experience, but I could recognize conspicuous consumption when I saw it and this outfit qualified. There was no wedding band but there was a tidy little *Patek Philippe* bauble on his wrist that would make a *Rolex* look like a *Timex*. It may well have cost him as much as his *Range Rover*.

He greeted me warmly and asked me if I would like to join him for coffee or tea. I opted for coffee and he asked Gertie-man to bring him tea. "*Yorkshire Gold*," he said. "I became addicted when we had an office in Berkshire." The coffee and tea were served in antique bone china; it was all I could do to keep from slurping mine down and checking the manufacturer's mark on the bottom.

He savored his tea, added a drop or two more of actual cream and then nodded appreciatively. "Thank you, Wilson," he said, and Wilson disappeared. I wondered whether that was his given name or surname.

"First," he said, taking the imaginary podium, "let me say how much we appreciate your offer to help us find Richard. He is a superb young man and a treasured member of our staff. His field experience has been of great value to our Research and Development division. He is also about to become a father; did you know that?"

"I did," I answered. "I met briefly with his wife after I arrived yesterday afternoon."

"But, unfortunately, she was unable to be of help in your search."

"No, she said that he left for work that morning and then inexplicably disappeared."

"Yes," he said. "It's all very sad. I don't understand it. The road in is a straightforward affair and it's busy enough each morning that if there were an accident of some sort it could not have gone unnoticed. Of course, there is always the possibility that he might have made another stop along the way, but those who know him well have assured me that he is a disciplined individual who follows a strict routine and simply could not have been involved in anything untoward. If you drive in from Honeoye Falls…oh, excuse me, you've done that…"

"Yes, it's a straight shot. One little rural roundabout but other than that the country road is an extension of a major city street."

"Clover," he responded.

It was a test. I wanted reassurance that he actually had communed from time to time with mere mortals.

I changed the subject. "I hope it will be all right if I talk to other people within your organization. I'm not hopeful that anyone will have a solution to the problem. If they did they would have already come forward. However…"

"It's simple due diligence," he said. "Of course you may, and if we can provide any assistance just let us know. We can make a room available for interviews, e.g., provide tech support…whatever you need."

"That's very kind. I appreciate it," I said.

"Talk to anyone," he said. "I'll let the division heads know that you're helping us and I'll ask them to make themselves available and anyone else on their staffs who you might want to talk with. I consider this very important, not just from the point of view of our company's needs but from the simple fact of loyalty and concern for our colleague."

I liked the 'colleague' instead of 'employee'. The man may have been a clothes horse but I didn't automatically dislike him. If he were trying to be Jesus he'd probably lose the tunic and sandals and dress more like the Infant of Prague, but there were elements of sincerity and actual concern beneath the Cashmere and gold veneer.

"When would you like to start?" he asked. "We can be ready whenever you need us to be."

"This afternoon?"

"Done. Who do you want to see first?"

"The head of R&D?"

"That would be Patricia Cline." He hit an intercom button and asked Patricia if she was available to see me that afternoon. She responded affirmatively. "2:00?" he asked. "Yes, of course," she said.

He turned to me and said, "Building three. This will give you time to have some lunch and organize your questions."

"Much appreciated."

"I'll also offer you a recommendation. *Steve's Original Diner.* It sounds a little down-to-earth, but it's the most reliable place in the neighborhood."

"Thanks," I said. Somehow I had trouble imagining *him* pulling up in any parking lot that housed an actual diner.

# SIXTEEN

*Steve's* was one of the anchor operations in a nearby strip mall. Its menu was practically as long as the road from Henrietta to Honeoye Falls. The waitress warned me about the pancakes.

"One of those will fill a dinner plate, Honey, so don't order two unless you're starving."

"Thanks for the headsup," I said, "but I think I'll do the turkey club with cottage cheese on the side."

"Good choice. How about for your drink?"

"Iced tea," I said, "unsweetened."

"Not to worry, Honey. We don't put you in sugar shock unless you request it."

The sandwich was good. As I went over my questions I noticed a man in overalls at an adjoining table; he was an all-day breakfast type, with a double order of bacon and two of Steve's so-called love cakes. The waitress was right; one of them was as big and thick as a competition-level frisbee. I imagined a large wolf leaping in the air and catching it in his teeth.

When I returned to *Kommunicom* Patricia Cline was waiting for me. We went through the usual pleasantries, agreed to use first names (in her case, Pat) and sat around a large coffee table in the front of her office.

"I hired Richard," she said. "Exceptional person. A gift, really. The workforce in Rochester is good, but it's not often that you get a seasoned soldier and engineer who can field-test your products. As you probably know, we make radios for the civilian market as well as military-grade instruments. Richard would take the commercial products home on the weekends and give me reports on them. No charge. He just enjoyed playing with them. With the more serious stuff…well, he was our go-to guy. This involved some travel. We would test them for distance in open spaces and for penetration in more mountainous regions. There aren't always cell towers in combat zones. A lot of people weren't interested in that part of the job; they didn't want to travel and they didn't want to get their hands dirty doing field simulations. They wanted routine, 9-5 schedules. Richard was up for anything."

"Maybe because he had seen much worse," I said.

"Right," Pat said. "There were no snipers or ambushers or IED makers in the Allegheny Plateau or Adirondacks, at least to our knowledge. He loved the outdoors, especially the quiet outdoors. When I interviewed him for the job and told him that we would want him to do some field testing as well as some office administration he told me that when he was doing his infantry officer basic course at Ft. Benning he used the little down time that they had to go camping. Of course he wasn't married then and he was never the type to go to the officers' club and spend his time drinking."

I didn't mention the fact that we were at Quantico together. All that I said was that our paths had crossed several years ago.

"Tell me about your own background, if you don't mind," I said. "I'm trying to get a feel for the company culture."

"Not that much to tell," she said. "I was a double-E major at Carnegie Mellon when my husband was doing his graduate work across the street at Pitt. In Philosophy. They're known for that. He got a job at the U of R and quickly received tenure. At first I was the trailing spouse but I got a job at *Kommunicom* and worked my way up. The pay's better than at a university and I've enjoyed the work. It's not enough for me to live like the peacock, but it's good."

"The peacock?"

"Rudolf," she said. "That's his nickname. We don't say it to his face but he knows that he's called that behind the scenes."

"Big money to sustain that lifestyle," I said. "That's why the most frequently-heard expression in D.C. is the 'private sector.' It's usually uttered with damp cheeks under the eyes."

She laughed. "I love it," she said. "I'm sure he does well at *Kommunicom* but the cars and suits come from old family money."

"*Volvo?*" I asked.

"No," she laughed, "*IKEA*."

"So he's not really from a high-tech background…"

"He studied Accounting and Financial Management at Uppsala University. He's a businessman, a managerial type, not a scientist. A good manager, in my opinion, but his previous position with *Kommunicom* was in marketing. That's when he was in England and got into the habit of shopping in Savile Row and Jermyn Street."

Interesting, I thought to myself.

"So Pat, what's your best guess on Richard's whereabouts?" I asked.

"No idea," she said. "None of it makes any sense. He's not the sort to simply disappear, and while this is an area with a population of around a million across six counties it still can feel like a small town. When a person with his background and personality disappears, people notice. He wasn't a joiner but he was active in his church and community, doing volunteer work and serving on the occasional committee…salt of the earth-type. People knew him and liked him. They're all nonplussed, as are we."

"And I gather that there are multiple medical facilities here. If he had been in some sort of accident he would have been cared for promptly."

"Precisely," she said. "I've thought and thought about this but I keep coming up against brick walls. I hate to say it, but I doubt that any of my colleagues are going to know any more than I do. We've talked about it. We've had meetings about it. We've Zoomed and face-timed and texted and we always end up shaking our heads. It's frustrating, Gwen. We really liked him. We're really worried about him and, somehow, we can't seem to be able to do a damned thing for him."

"Who do you think I should talk to next?" I asked.

"Tom Fuse, I suppose. He's our security guy. We haven't had the chance to talk about Richard today. Maybe he has some thoughts."

"Point me in the right direction," I said, "and thanks for your time… and your concern for Richard."

"Tom's in the building to our right. I'll call him and see if he's available."

She did and he was.

# SEVENTEEN

"Tom Fuse," he said, offering his hand. "And please don't make fun of my name" (smiling as he said it).

"Thinking you were a double-E major?"

"Yes. I wasn't actually. I majored in History at City University and picked up the security stuff later when I went to work for the NYPD. Mom was from Buffalo, Dad from Long Island. After he passed she moved back to western New York and I followed, primarily to take care of her but often it's the other way around. The original family name was F-u-s-s, German for foot. Sometimes you see it as Foos. When my ancestors came to Ellis Island the people there suggested that we change the name to Fuse. It's an American word, they said, whereas the Fuss word connoted something different, something that would lead to teasing or ridicule. So we suddenly became the Fuse family."

I could see that he liked to talk. Maybe being head of security was a lonely job.

"No one can actually pronounce my ancestors' name," I said.

"Oh, right," he answered. "Someone mentioned that you were a Native American. You don't…"

"Look like one?" I said.

"No offense meant," he said.

"None taken," I said. "Call me Gwen."

"You're helping us find Richard."

"Trying to," I said, "but not getting very far."

"Let me bounce something off of the wall on you; I'm trying to look at it from a darker point of view. You know…someone kidnapped him and is trying to get information about the company and its products."

"I suppose that's always been a possibility," I said, "but, as everyone has acknowledged, there's no evidence of it. Unfortunately, there's no evidence of anything. Let's back up a second. Tell me about your part of the operation."

"Actually, I wear two hats. I'm responsible for both internal and external security. I work with our IT people to keep our company communication systems secure and do some of the workaday jobs like checking our CCTV system, the codes for our locks, the i.d. cards for staff…that kind of thing.

"On the outside I secure areas when we're testing military products, insure that anyone involved in confidential operations are appropriately credentialled, make sure that each of the items we're testing is accounted for…nothing very romantic, but it's all still necessary. We're in a competitive business and we worry as much about industrial espionage from other manufacturers as we do about intellectual property theft from adversary nations. However, when you get right down to it we're not dealing with things of strategic importance like guidance systems or nuclear technology. If you google us you'll see that what we're doing is pretty basic and straightforward."

"I'd like to hear it from you," I said.

"Sure. We make tactical radios—secure, digital jobbies that use technologies that include frequency-hopping and encryption. These help prevent interception and jamming and are particularly useful in zones with high levels of interference. We deal in satellite communications, secure digital networks, mesh networks that enable devices to communicate directly with one another without the need for a central infrastructure, integrated systems that synch voice, video and tactical data across different branches and platforms, including air, land and sea. Richard was especially interested in SDR's (Software-Defined Radios). These instruments are very flexible and they can be reconfigured in the field using different types of software. Basically he was interested in the 'if only' military applications."

"As in…?"

"As in, 'if only we had had this when I was in combat…"

"Got it," I said.

"For example: emerging technology like quantum communication…using quantum mechanics to create virtually unbreakable encryption keys."

"Making the Nazis' Enigma machines look like Tinkertoys," I said.

"That's the idea," he said. "His training as an engineer combined with his field experience as an Infantry Company Commander were indispensable to our business. But you already knew that, I'm sure."

"I did, but, again, it's always helpful to hear it directly from someone who knew him."

"You probably knew this also," he added, "that we feel his loss at a personal level but also at *Kommunicom's* bottom line. No one is irreplaceable but Richard comes pretty close to it."

"And as to your earlier point, his knowledge and experience could be of use to a military adversary or a commercial competitor."

He nodded in agreement and there was a tinge of sympathy and regret in his eyes.

"Unfortunately," he said, "that may provide a possible motive for his abduction, assuming that he was abducted, but we have no evidence of that, no clues, no lines of inquiry, no suspicious occurrences. He left for work…"

"And he didn't show up," I said.

Again he nodded silently.

"I appreciate your time," I said. "I also appreciate your affection for Richard. And for referring to him in the present tense."

"I suppose you should talk to Gabe," he said. "I'm not sure that he can add anything that you haven't already heard from Pat and me but he lives between the company and Honeoye Falls, along Richard's migration route."

I checked my notes. "Gabe Ruffino," the head of manufacturing."

"Technically *Gabriele*," he said, "an Italian name of course, but with Jewish origins."

"This is like the U.N. here," I said.

"Hopefully we get more done," he answered. "Maybe with your help we can even find Richard."

# EIGHTEEN

The manufacturing division was in a larger building. It was loud (not deafening but loud to the point of annoying) and the people there were dressed to work rather than to talk.

"Come in here," Gabe said, pointing to a glass-enclosed office that provided a 180-degree view of the shop floor. When he closed the door behind us the sound was muted but still noticeable.

"I'm Gabe," he said. "Thanks for being here and thanks for helping us."

"Gwen," I answered. "Thanks for seeing me."

He was wearing black cotton pants and a tattersall shirt. He was shorter than Tom Fuse, but with dark hair and eyes, unlike Tom's more blond/blue Nordic features. Where Tom had worn a light beige poplin jacket Gabe had been wearing a leather apron and a leather baseball cap that was reversed on his head, with the strap encircling his forehead. He removed them and offered me coffee.

"I can never seem to get too much of it," I said.

"Guess what," he said.

"You've got an espresso machine to go with your Italian given name and surname."

"You just grabbed the gold ring," he said. He opened a door at the rear of his office. His bathroom had been cannibalized to accommodate a tiny kitchenette with the coffee apparatus and a mini-fridge. He returned after a few minutes and set a large, half-filled cup on the edge of the desk where I was sitting in his client chair.

"That's actually a triple," he said. "The machine cost a fortune but my priest told me that I owed it to myself."

"My kind of priest," I said.

"Now if only I was also related to the *Ruffino* wine family…"

"You'd be in a Tuscan villa, sitting in the sun," I said, "testing the family's products."

"You know, I've never been to Italy. How is that possible?"

"Your ancestors came here to work on the Canal?"

"Right. And we never left. The positive thing is that there are a lot of us here and the town is filled with great restaurants and almost-authentic Italian grocery stores."

"No stuffed wild boar outside their doorways and hams hanging from the ceiling."

"Nope, but easier parking."

"Richard likes Italian food. We were at Quantico together. Whenever the members of our class took a break and drove into the city for dinner he would vote for Italian."

"We get better here," Gabe said. "True family restaurants with regional dishes. Peasant food often, like tripe, but it's worth trying. Me? I'm more a steak and pasta type, but not the Florentine steak, where you can still hear the Mooo and detect movement in the extremities."

"Not so much medium rare as medium-still-alive," I said.

"Right. Anyway…we should talk about Richard. I don't know anything of substance but I can fill in some of the cultural blanks for you."

"I'd like that," I said. "Tom Fuse said that you were on the same migration route with Richard."

"Yes, more or less. My wife and I are in the Autumn Woods development, just off of Mendon Center Road. You can take Mendon Center and eventually intersect with the road to Honeoye Falls, but Richard wouldn't have normally come in that way. He would have come straight in on 65, which becomes Clover. Actually he might sometimes come the other way if one of our cars was down and my wife needed the other. He'd give me a lift into work but that was…what…once or twice a year? Henrietta is more or less due south of downtown Rochester and he and I are more or less south/southeast of Henrietta, but apart from work we didn't see each other on a regular basis. My wife and I and Richard and Kathleen had dinner at one of the Honeoye Falls pubs about six or eight months ago, but we didn't go out like that on a regular basis. Honeoye Falls is a sweet little town but it's more of (what do they call them) part of the *exurbs*? If you want to get away you go to Buffalo and the real Falls or the finger lakes to take a wine tour. My wife likes to go to Canandaigua; that's like the entry point to the finger lakes, maybe 30 miles or so from Rochester."

"So the day that Richard disappeared was an ordinary one, with each of you coming in on parallel routes, more or less."

"Yes, exactly. And our paths didn't cross every day. A lot of his time was spent in Pat's building, pushing paper, taking phone calls, and so on. I didn't know that he had failed to arrive until late morning, when someone asked me if I had seen him."

"Do you remember who that was?"

"I think it was Tom. Marianne Phillips was looking for him also. She had a question about one of the people in Pat's shop."

"She's H.R."

"Right. You haven't talked to her yet?"

"I think she's the last division head on my itinerary."

"Nice woman," he said. "They can be a real pain in the backside. Rules and forms. Forms and rules."

"I know what you mean. I work for the government," I said, smiling.

"I'm not sure that she can add anything to your search," he said, "but she has all of the records and if anyone suspicious turns up along the way she can give you the background data on him. Or her."

"Just one other thing," I said, "was there anything happening in the company that was in any way out of the ordinary; new products coming on line, new major contracts, anything that could make the day he disappeared special?"

"Nothing that I can think of," he said. "I'm sure you've already perceived that we're a niche company. We make good things; we do important things; we have a strong bottom line and we do both our government and the Swedish government proud, but we're not *Lockheed Martin, Boeing* or *General Dynamics*. We're not building the iron dome or the golden dome or the platinum dome; we're just trying to facilitate communications. Every day is pretty much like the day before."

"Communications are very important," I said.

"Of course, but you know what I mean. The masters of the universe, the Merciless Ming, people like that...they don't lose sleep over what we're doing here, next to the cardiology clinic and down the street from *Marketplace Liquor* and *Steve's Original Diner*."

"I get it," I said, "but if we assume that a West Point engineer in the defense industry, who once worked as a special agent for the Federal Bureau of Investigation was abducted..."

"We may be more important than we think. Or he was," Gabe said.

"Yes."

"Maybe Marianne can be of help. I wish I could be, but in all honesty I don't think I can."

# NINETEEN

It was late in the afternoon when I got to the H.R. Director's office, but she looked fresh and well-rested and told me that she would be happy to help me in any way that she could.

"People tend to avoid this office," she said, "but I'm really here to support, not obstruct. This is not a Dickensian counting house; I work for *Kommunicom* and see myself as a buffer between our company and the people who spend their every waking hour trying to throw molasses into our gearwork. Of course, I have to follow the rules, but I try to absorb a lot of the onerous paperwork and let the people who develop products, manufacture products and sell products do their thing."

"Any interest in coming to work in Washington?" I asked.

She smiled. "I'll take the Fifth on that," she said.

"So tell me about Richard, from your perspective," I said.

"Actually…" she said, handing me a file folder. "This is Richard's personnel file. You already have his vitals—name, address, marital status…probably his fingerprints, right?"

"Yes. The military collects those, as does the Bureau."

"Height and weight, age. His salary is there and his social, his landline and cell numbers. There's some material there on his initial interview. Mr. Bethe interviewed him, along with Pat Cline. There's a note on his previous work experience…when he left the Army and did night law school he worked for a few defense consulting firms in the Washington area…"

"Beltway bandits," I said.

"Right. Nothing special. Mostly what we would consider clerical work. It's a two-way street bargain. You work for a company, receive health benefits, have the time to attend night law school; they get a solid work product at bargain basement prices and in return let you come and go to complete your schooling. As you probably know, the night law school grads are even more prized than the day students."

"Because they've demonstrated that they can work double shifts, effectively. That's what they're going to be doing for their first law firm job or jobs, before they make partner…if they make partner."

"Exactly," she said. "There are notes to that effect on Pat and Mr. Bethe's interview form. We have an in-house counsel but Richard's legal training was a subsidiary benefit for us. We could call on him for legal advice from time to time. The in-house lawyer mostly handles lawsuits, contracts, the daily work flow. Richard could be used more like a…"

"A consigliere?"

"Yes, sort of. And that also had a nice monetary dimension."

"You didn't have to pay him twice."

She smiled for a second and then continued. "Richard preferred it that way, I think. He liked a varied schedule, especially when he was working in the field, testing products. He didn't want to be chained to a desk. You know what they sometimes say about education—it's not so much what you study as the fact that you can show up, apply yourself, complete tasks, and so on. I would also add the need for communication skills. If you can write…well, that always helps. And if you can do public speaking, so much the better. Pat and Mr. Bethe were particularly impressed by his abilities in those areas. Plus he had the right education also; the fit with our company was perfect. And very rare. Specialized knowledge combined with basic skills: priceless."

"At West Point they get a lot of that dual training via math class. It's foundational for engineering, of course, but they use it for other purposes. The cadets are required to make formal presentations and submit proofs to their classmates. They march up to the board, write their numbers and symbols and prepare themselves for challenges and criticism. Educators would call the math experience there a key part of their core curriculum."

"That's interesting; I didn't know that," she said. "In my work you're expected to have specific training in human resources. Organization and management are helpful also, but I minored in Psychology and often feel that that's proven to be the most important preparation for the job. You have to know the laws and forms and economics, particularly with payroll taxes, workman's comp and healthcare contracts, but fundamentally you're working with people and people, well, they have their quirks."

"Did Richard?"

"No. He was a treasure. Sorry, he *is* a treasure. He was always on time with his materials and never a complainer. We just finished a round of annual evaluations (his is there, in your folder); Pat gave him the equivalent of five stars, finishing with her usual comment to the effect that she wished she could have given him six. That's why he's at the top of the pay scale in his division."

"Let me ask you something," I said.

"Shoot."

"Who does your marketing?"

"Pat and Mr. Bethe. Pat knows the ins and outs of our products and speaks from a technical point of view. Mr. Bethe knows the business side and the major international players. They do a kind of tag team operation."

"And how about IT? I was surprised when I didn't see a mini-empire for that within your organization."

"Gabe and Tom split that. Tom does the security aspects and Gabe does the hardware and software setups. We actually run very lean."

"Doesn't hurt the bottom line," I said.

"Part of the secret of our success," she said. "This is where the Psych stuff comes in. Whenever you build bureaucracies the people who run them try to gain brownie points by creating new programs that require new staff."

"They proliferate."

"Like minks. And the additional staff also need computers, printers, office space and heat and light and H.R. support and on and on and on. Whereas, if you take existing personnel and assign them additional duties they compartmentalize and prioritize rather than breed. Of course they have to be good people to begin with."

"If you want something done, give the task to a busy, highly competent individual."

"Yes, so it's a basic principle after all. The bureaucratization… that's for people who like to drink coffee, eat sweet rolls and convene endless meetings."

"Coffee as comfort, not fuel."

"Maybe even a dramatic prop. When you're sipping you don't have to be thinking and saying wise things. You let others do that for you: 'what are your thoughts on that, Mary Jane?' 'Bill?' 'Larry?'"

The more she spoke the more I liked her.

"Let me just ask one more thing," I said.

"Of course."

"You said that you just went through a round of annual evaluations."

"Yes?"

"Anything else happen lately that would represent a break in the usual schedule?"

"Just the retreat."

"An administrative retreat?"

"Yes. We do it annually. It's a chance to think about knotty problems, to dream dreams, team build…the usual stuff."

"Who would attend that?"

"The division heads and key players in their organizations. Twenty people or so."

"Including Richard?"

"Especially multi-faceted people like Richard, backbone types, the key links between upper management and success on the ground."

"When was this?"

"Less than a month ago. Two and a half weeks? I can check…." She turned to her computer and made a few keystrokes. "We returned… sixteen days ago."

"Did you go some place in the finger lakes?"

"No, we usually try to make it a real road trip. Last year we went to a place just outside of Lake Placid. This year we went to a place in rural Maine."

# TWENTY

"Who arranges those retreats?"

"The place is selected by Mr. Bethe's office and then the specific logistics are handled by me. It doesn't really amount to much. Once we've nailed down our facility I tell the people in charge there how many people we'll bring, the catering that we'll require, the IT facilities to support talks and discussions…all basic stuff. Business school 101."

"M1A1, Richard would have said."

"Yes, probably."

Before I left I called Rudolf Bethe's office to thank him for his help. He was unavailable but I spoke briefly with his assistant (Karla/Della, not Wilson/Gertie) and she told me that I should feel free to check back with them if they could help in any way. She took down my cell number and said that she would call me if anything occurred that could possibly be of interest.

I then called Scott Leven's office in Buffalo to brief him on what I had learned. There wasn't much.

"Richard's company seems completely legit," I said. "It's well-managed, successful, and leads in its particular niche market. The Director is a Swedish national. Business type, not an engineer. He dresses to the nines, thanks to the fact that he's connected with the *IKEA* fortune. He's the company front man and handles marketing for their major-league clients. As you know, they do both defense industry stuff and commercial, hobbyist stuff. The rest of the team are local, with a security branch, H.R. branch, manufacturing branch and R&D branch. The R&D person does the low-end, commercial marketing. Everyone was as helpful as they could have been, but no one really knew anything."

"Richard left for work one morning and never arrived there," Scott said. "A straight shot of about ten miles. A heavily-used, common commutation route; many of the people who work in Rochester live in the hinterlands to avoid the taxes."

"Exactly. And I've been over his route. Actually, the usual route and a secondary one. Rural, but, as you said, heavily-traveled in both cases. Any significant traffic accident would have been seen and reported promptly. The area is filled with hospitals and urgent care centers and there were no reports of his presence at any of them."

"Unless he was making an unusual stop (in the wee hours of the morning) he must have been abducted in some way."

"Or persuaded to alter his route and then abducted."

"But almost surely not by anyone at his company."

"None that I could see," I said.

"And, of course, no ransom demands or bodies found."

"Nothing. I spoke with his wife. Very nice woman. She couldn't add anything beyond her profound concern. She's also pregnant; I didn't ask for dates but I'd say she's due in a month or two. Did you know that?"

"We did. It adds to the urgency, as well as to our concern and frustration."

"I asked the H.R. director if there was anything in the recent past that someone might consider to be out of the ordinary. She shook her head, checked and re-checked her calendar and told me that they had just been through their annual evaluations and that Richard had been given the highest ranking possible. By the way, she also gave me his personnel file. I'll copy it and send it to you through an encrypted channel."

"I appreciate that, Gwen. Thanks."

"Unfortunately there's nothing there that is likely to prove of help. Much of it is public information and the confidential stuff like his salary and evaluations all reflect well on him but don't include anything that would be of interest to a potential adversary."

"Still, I appreciate it. Anything else?"

"The only other thing was that the upper echelon of the company has just held its administrative retreat. Previously scheduled, an annual event, nothing out of the ordinary."

"The site of your next stop?"

"I don't have anything else," I said. "If something of note had happened there someone would have mentioned it, so it's almost surely a waste of time, but like I said…"

"You don't have anything else."

"Right."

"Where was it held?"

"A place in Maine. The venue is a bit of a jaunt from Henrietta, but not completely out of the ordinary. They tend to avoid the obvious places nearby. Last year they went to Lake Placid."

"Wish there was some support for you in that state. There are resident agencies in Portland and Augusta but nothing serious beyond the Boston field office. You're heading to the boonies."

"Indeed. Washington County. A town called Milbridge."

"That's where you might stop off for a bathroom break if you're going to Campobello Island. Otherwise…zilch."

"I know," I said, "but then…"

"You don't have anything else."

# TWENTY-ONE

After a quick 6:30 breakfast I pulled out of the parking lot at the *Del Monte* and checked my sat nav. I had a hefty drive of just under 700 miles between my comfortable 4-star hotel room and rocky shores, pine trees, stoop-workers in search of clams and roadside shacks that featured mediocre hot dogs and hamburgers and excellent lobster rolls. I figured I'd stop to eat in either Worcester or Lowell and then push on into the deep northeast. If you google the top hotels in Milbridge, Maine the ones that pop up are generally around 50 miles away, in or near Bar Harbor. I put myself in Peggy Chapman's hands after filing my tentative report to the Director. She found me a rental cottage named *Gull's Way* about three miles from Milbridge proper.

"You're heading to the blueberry capital of the world," she said. "I think there may be a nice *Shop 'n Save* nearby, along with a bustling population of around 1,400 people. That's the boonies, honey."

"That's what Scott Leven said," I answered. "I hope the trip turns out to be more than a fool's errand."

"You're no fool, Gwen," Peggy said, "and from what I can see you don't have any other options, at least not at this point."

"The one thing we can all agree on," I said.


Three hours outside of Pittsford I stopped for coffee and called Kathy on the secure phone I had given her.

"How are you Gwen?" she asked. "I was hoping you'd call." There was neither hopefulness nor despair in her voice.

"I'm fine; I'm just checking in," I said. "I met with Richard's colleagues at *Kommunicom*. They all love him there and miss him. Unfortunately, none of them had any information that contributed significantly to my search."

"That's what I expected," she said.

"There was one little thing…" I said.

"Yes?"

"I asked if there was anything that had occurred recently that was in any way out of the ordinary. Two things happened, but neither was unscheduled or unexpected. They did the annual evaluations of all of the people at the company. Richard received the highest marks possible. The other thing was that they had recently completed their annual administrative retreat…"

"Yes, that was a few weeks ago. They went to this island in Maine."

"Did Richard have anything to say about it?"

"Not really. He said it was an interesting place, basically a medium-sized center that doubled as a meeting place and a hotel. Richard commented on the fact that there was no water on the island and that the owners of the facility had installed a desalination plant to service the operation. He thought it was interesting from an engineering point of view. Major plants cost millions and even billions, of course, but smaller ones are doable depending on other economic factors. In this case, for example, the island came at a tiny fraction of the usual cost. On the other hand there was the problem of pollution. The plant releases brine which has a number of chemicals which, added together, can cause harm to the local ecosystem…"

"But a resort or meeting center could also bring a lot of dollars to a community sorely in need of them."

"Precisely," Kathy said. "The prospective owners had to wend their way among the pros and cons and do a lot of serious public relations work. In the end there were some compromises and investments and good faith efforts and the project was approved. Richard thought that it might be used as a model for other sorts of enterprises."

"But it was mostly of interest as an engineering project…"

"Right. Other than that the facilities were, well, like a basic *Marriott*, but with great views, peace and quiet…space to think and talk."

"Interesting," I said. "I'll check it out when I get there. Well, actually, it may be pretty dark by the time I get there."

"So you're driving there now."

"Yes."

"I appreciate your telling me. I wish I had something to reciprocate with, but everything here is quiet. Disturbingly quiet."

"I understand," I said.

I actually pushed past Worcester and Lowell and had a late lunch in Portsmouth, New Hampshire at a trattoria called *Il Bellagio*. It had an authentic Neapolitan pizza oven; I had a basic Margherita pizza with a side salad and a single glass of wine, followed by a double espresso. "Do you want another for the road?" the waitress asked.

"I'd love one," I said. "A double that is."

That kept my eyes open and my reflexes sharp for hours. When I finally pulled into Milbridge I followed Peggy's instructions and went to the local *Sunoco* station (still open, but barely) where I asked for Marty. An elderly man lifted himself from a stool with a thick rubber pad and asked if I was the woman who had rented *Gull's Way*.

"I am," I said, showing him my driver's license.

"Mr. Wyatt's gone home for the day," he said, pointing to a two-story building some fifty or sixty yards to the south. He does real estate, law, and some other things here. He left me your key. *Gull's Way* is a mile and a half north. It's actually the smaller of two cottages. The larger is called *Eagle's Way*, the one to its south is called *Gull's Way*. There's no one in *Eagle's Way* right now. I think somebody's coming up from Boston for the weekend. In your cottage…"

"Yes?"

"There's a cord that hangs beside the sink. Don't pull it."

"I won't. Why?"

"It rings a bell in *Eagle's Way*. Nobody there to hear it."

"So this was the jungle tom-tom between the buildings that rented to large families."

"Right. *Gull's Way* was for the kids."

"OK, thanks."

"But don't worry," Marty said.

"Why's that?"

"*Gull's Way* is nicer. The flush works better."

"I appreciate that," I said, and took the small brown envelope containing the key from the top of the counter.

# TWENTY-TWO

When I entered the cottage there was the smell of mold. At first that concerned me but as I did a brief tour of the space I could tell that the scent was coming from the basket of wood that sat on the edge of the fireplace. Places like this would have a rack or an outbuilding that held a cord or more of firewood. In this case they were all local pine. If I had been there in February rather than late June I would have been grateful.

The sitting room adjoined the kitchenette. One corner was a cutout with a bay window, ocean view, comfortable armchair and a large bookcase that contained some 50-100 year-old classics that also carried the scent of mold. On top, at either end, there were homemade tchotchkes: three round 6" poles secured by wire bands to resemble wharf pillars. Each had a ceramic seagull attached at the edge of the top by metal prongs. I wondered if the other cottage had eagles atop theirs.

The 'flush' was serviceable, the water pressure good, the spare supply of toilet paper ample. The bedroom had a set of bunkbeds and a single, separate bed with fresh, crisp linen and a cupboard that included an additional pillow, thermal blankets and a comforter. All were encased in plastic.

I unpacked, checked my phone for messages and was asleep in less than ten minutes. When I woke up the next morning the area was covered in fog. That's why the cottage was available for rental. It must have contributed to the privacy (and, I thought, the isolation) of the setting for *Kommunicom's* executive retreat.

At 9:00 I met with the manager.

"Ed Wyatt," he said, "welcome to Milbridge. How's the cabin?"

"It's very nice, just what I needed," I said.

"And how was breakfast this morning at Lou's?"

"Whoa," I said. "I knew this was a small town but not that small."

"It's not so much that we're nosy," he said. "We're just bored. Everything here is pretty cyclic. The trees grow; the tides come and go, as do the ice and snow. The kids move out for school and seldom return, except for an occasional visit. The lobstermen and the clammers make their rounds. The local grocers restock their shelves. The gas station attendants play video games on their phones. Those of us who service the tourist trade are slaves to the weather. That fog this morning…"

"Yes, I couldn't help notice it."

"It'll pretty much be gone by the beginning of July, but people who come here to look out over the ocean don't want their vision obstructed. That's why the rentals are nearly all available now. The size of the town doubles in the summer. That's our Christmas. That's when the money flows. Now? Not so much. The fact that you had breakfast at Lou's will help their bottom line. There's always some regulars there, but the margins are thin. Some say that the depression came to Maine and never left."

"Well, I have to say that Lou has good coffee and that's one of my few absolute requirements."

"But you came here to meet me," he said, "so I'm thinking there's something else that you might need."

"Just some information," I said. "There was an administrative conference out on the island about a month ago. Around a week ago one of the participants disappeared. I had some time off from my government job and I decided to see if I could be of any help to local law enforcement. The man who disappeared is an old friend."

"And you're with the Bureau."

"Yes, actually."

"Somebody from Washington made your reservation; she sounded like she knew what she was doing. Plus, I'm cheating…"

"Cheating?"

"Yes, there was a story that was picked up by the *Bangor Daily News* a couple of days ago. The company that met here was from a place in western New York and it said that the man who had disappeared was a former Army officer and a former FBI special agent. The woman who made your reservation sounded like a hardened D.C. veteran, not like some young E-4 whose major job was to pin pieces of paper to bulletin boards."

I just smiled. "Mr. Wyatt, you could be in law enforcement rather than in real estate," I said.

"My mother taught me to pay attention," he said. "So how can I help you?"

"Tell me a little about the facility where they met," I said.

"Well, it's owned by a couple and the property's listed on the masthead of a small hotel chain, but the owners actually developed the property and they carry all of the risk. Fortunately, they're experienced hoteliers—George and Ann Carlson. They're from Massachusetts. Woburn."

"Boston suburb," I said.

"Right. They had a mom and pop place there, a B&B kind of thing with a colonial theme. They were eased out by the *Hilton* hydra."

"The hydra? You mean their list of brands."

"Right. You've got your basic *Hilton*, your *Garden Inn Hilton*, your *Hampton Inn*, your *Homewood Suites*, your *Embassy Suites*, *Home2 Suites*, your *Conrad*, your *DoubleTree*…it seems like it never ends. Anyway, as their market share shrank they found out about the availability of Mary's Island and they bought it, developed it and turned it into a successful operation. I'm not sure about their Woburn property; I think they sold it to a medical group, possibly a group of psychologists? Anyway, the little chain that they're linked with is useful for referrals, registration software and general branding. The facility is great for Milbridge because they've developed good links with the town. They buy as much of their food here as they can; they contribute to the tax base; they're good neighbors and solid citizens. Smart, too. People who go to islands…they want to be set apart but they don't want to be completely isolated. You take something as simple as parking. A lot of island properties don't have adequate parking or transportation systems, so they make people park on the mainland and come and go on little boats with oily smells and slippery seats. People don't like that. They worry about their cars and they worry about getting in and out of dinghies and tenders, especially the elderly and the comfort seekers with deep pockets."

"So you can park on this island."

"Yes. George and Ann have a little ferry boat. It'll hold a couple of cars along with a number of passengers. It makes several trips a day for the people who want to stretch their legs on the mainland, but you can also rent it. I'm not sure about the cost but it's somewhere in the neighborhood of what you'd pay for lunch in Boston. A lot of people come to Washington County, saying they want to stay clear of the tourist throngs but after a day or two they want to go to Bar Harbor, grab some blueberry pie, do some shopping, hike up Cadillac Mountain…it's a serious hub with multiple features. There are also the outlet stores in the strip malls on the road from Ellsworth, craft sellers on Blue Hill Bay, antique dealers working out of refurbished barns…any number of things that you can't find here on the island. This is for solitude, pure and simple, and the more people think that that's what they want, the more they feel like getting away from it for a day or two."

"You said it was called 'Mary's Island'."

"Yes. Mary Cabot. Good old local name. True Boston Brahmin stock. Her married name is Taylor. Tom Taylor. Banker-type, from Connecticut, I think. Before that—back when she was a Cabot—her branch of the family had a factory in Lowell. They came up here for August. They actually still own *Eagle's Way* and *Gull's Way*. Mary and Tom live in Concord; I serve as their rental agent and also do some legal work for them, as necessary. When Mary turned 18 her parents bought her the island that bears her name. Without water the property was more or less worthless. It was the sort of place you'd go to for a picnic on the shore or a walk among the rocks and trees. Beautiful, but without the water it was just another dot along the coast."

"Very interesting," I said. "That's why I came to see you."

"For the local lore? I'm full of it," he said, smiling.

# TWENTY-THREE

George Carlson was a tall, thin man with sandy blond hair and bright gray eyes. Statistically rare, they were his best feature. He was dressed for the kind of work that kept him from a desk but also from any activity that might require him to wear gloves or an apron—a plaid flannel shirt, tan chinos and upscale deck shoes—Mr. L.L. Bean himself.

We introduced ourselves. He told me that Ed Wyatt had given him a heads-up call. "He's a sort of unofficial mayor of Milbridge," Carlson said.

"Lawyer, Realtor, Executive Director of the Chamber of Commerce, Rotary President..." I said.

"That's him," Carlson said.

"He told me a little about your operation," I said, "the mini-ferry, the on-site parking...he didn't mention the desalination plant, which surprised me."

"It's not that big of a deal. The up-front costs were challenging, but we were blessed with some family money on Ann's side. We have to maintain the system but we use it sparingly. We put bottled water in all of the mini-fridges and we try to persuade the guests to drink beer or wine. Our clients? That would be their normal preference anyway. At dinner we sell *Pellegrino* and *Acqua Panna*, so they can have either sparkling or still. You know—the European way, where you pay for everything on the table except the ice cubes and cutlery."

"So the desalinated water is for showers and baths and wash-ups."

"Right. It's a cost for us but we have the benefit of being in an area of relatively high unemployment so we can hire staff at modest rates. A great tradeoff. Most of them are high school kids or students at the University of Maine branch in Machias. Let me show you something…"

We walked from the entry hall to a room that I thought was going to be for meetings or greetings; it turned out to be a library. A stunning library.

The casework was in dark cherry and the materials were legit, not stained pine or oak. I did a quick guesstimate of the shelf space and came up with enough running feet to accommodate something in the neighborhood of 5,000 volumes. The books were organized by genre and the authors were well-known. This wasn't the sort of thing that you'd find on a corner shelf in *Gull's Way*; this was the kind of material you'd see in the *University Club* library in New York. Interspersed among the shelves and side tables were armchairs in leather or rich Clan tartans. This was modeled after an English gentleman's club but one that didn't discriminate against the ladies.

George said, "Look here," and lifted the panels on one portion of the cabinetry. "The *Armagnacs* are popular after dinner; the *Macallans* are great before. For the bourbon drinkers we have a range of *Pappy's*. We have a selection of age statements so we can sell flights, do vertical tastings, and so on. That's for the companies that want to give their senior staffs a treat. Most of the guests just buy by the glass and when you're talking about something like a 25 year-old *Macallan* you're talking $200 a glass, if you're lucky. That 'old sherry oak' there (pointing) retails for about $2500 a bottle."

"And having a captive audience doesn't hurt," I said.

"Exactly," he answered. "And as you can well expect, most of our guests can afford it and most have been ripped off regularly in Boston and New York so they don't blanch at the price."

"And they can't read and hang out for hours in a city bar, the way that they can here."

"The more you read the longer you stay in your comfortable chair and the more thirsty you become."

"It illustrates the oldest lesson in fine dining," I said.

"You make all the money on the alcohol."

"Bingo," I said.

"Interesting that you say that," George said. "My brother went to Princeton and whenever he had a great day he would go to dinner at the *Nassau Inn*..."

"The place that has the Norman Rockwell Yankee Doodle painting behind the bar."

"So you've been there," he said.

"Once. All I had was black coffee."

"Well back in the day they were on the *Wine Spectator's* all star list. I always thought it was odd. You'd go in there for a hamburger and then decide whether or not you'd want to spring for a $2,000 bottle of wine. They're not on the list anymore and they sell workaday pinot grigio by the glass. But still..."

"They make money on the alcohol," I said.

"It's always about the math. You do much better selling oceans of plonk than a single bottle of good stuff at a slightly inflated price. And with the good stuff it's all about the provenance and the timing. Before they blew up the twin towers you could get top wines at bargain prices at *Windows on the World* because they had filled their cellar years earlier. That's how we got our desalination plant."

"Tell me," I said.

"Ann's grandfather was a bigwig in the Hartford insurance industry. He loved wine and he only bought the best stuff. His son, Ann's dad, was a Trump guy. Trump didn't drink and neither did he. Grandfather's collection was properly stored, properly cooled and properly managed. When he passed on, my father-in-law (and his favorite daughter) reaped the benefits. For example, 1961 was a great year in Bordeaux; there was some spottiness but it was still memorable. A Margaux from '61 now goes for 2-3K a bottle, depending on provenance, storage, etc. Do you know what it sold for upon release?"

"One hell of a lot less," I said.

"Something like $20-25 bucks a bottle. The '61 Palmer, which I prefer, sold for 7 francs. Grandpa's cellar sold for a gazillion dollars; Ann received enough to pay for the desalination plant, and then some."

"Sweet," I said.

"I know you didn't come to talk about our business model, but I thought you might find the history interesting."

"Very," I said.

"You also want to talk about your friend who was here with his company a month ago."

"I do," I said.

"Unfortunately, I don't have anything for you. That company was the best-behaved we've had in years, but they weren't drinkers. The Director had some brandy one night after dinner, possibly two snifters' worth, but that was it."

"Anything happen while they were here that you would consider out of the ordinary?"

"They stayed on the island the whole time…no road trips to Acadia. That's unusual."

"Anything else?"

"We have movies if anyone wants to take a night off from their corporate meetings. Most don't take advantage, but they did."

"What did they see?"

"Let me check," he said, looking at his iPhone. "They saw 'Year of the Comet'."

"Wine movie, William Goldman script."

"Yes, a sleeper. Unfortunately it didn't make them buy anything as expensive as the bottle in the movie."

"Pity," I said. "Anything else happen while they were here?"

"Not that I'm aware of. Let me check with Ann…"

# TWENTY-FOUR

He told me to make myself comfortable in the library while he went in search of his wife. They returned in about ten minutes. She looked very New England—close cropped hair, thin lips, light makeup and a carbon copy of downeast couture, Mrs. L.L. Bean.

"I was checking some inventory in one of the outbuildings," she said, extending her hand, "Ann Carlson."

"I'm Gwen," I said.

"You're checking on the missing man from *Kommunicom*."

"Yes, trying to, but not making much headway."

"You're FBI," she said.

Before I could answer, she said, "Not trying to pry. I read that the man had been in both the military and the FBI. You look more like an agent than an Army officer."

"I'll take that as a compliment," I said, smiling.

"I just figured that if you were military you'd be running through a prescribed spiel, standing stiffly and presenting me with credentials of some kind."

"Probably true," I said. "Actually I'm doing this on my own time as a favor to the Buffalo field office. The missing man was in my class at Quantico and we knew each other briefly. Technically he's a civilian now, but he was once one of our's and the Bureau likes to remember past service and be of help in any way that we can."

"I understand," she said. "I find that comforting in its way. Somebody still cares about you."

I just nodded and offered a warm smile.

"I assume you've ruled out anything obvious like a car accident."

"Actually, we haven't ruled out anything. We just haven't found any evidence that could help us in our search."

"The company is in the Rochester suburbs. This was their annual administrative retreat. Maybe about twenty people came…"

"Right."

"I spoke to somebody in the Human Resources office there and worked with her on arrangements…rooms, catering, IT needs, etc. As I recall they were a particularly nice group of people. No rowdiness. No misbehavior. Good tips."

"It's interesting that you remember that they were good tippers," I said.

"Actually, it's part of an old joke. My much-younger sister Ellen teaches English at Smith College. Back in the day, maybe 40, 50 years ago the *New York Times* reported on the *Modern Language Association* annual meetings; they listed the convention seminar subjects and made fun of the titles. They did this every year. In one of the stories they asked the manager of one of the convention hotels (I think it was the *Sheraton* that they used to call the *Americana*) about the nature of the MLA clientele. He said that his staff had never seen so much booze, so few girls and such small tips."

"Girls as in hookers."

"Right," she said. "Not the professors, but it could have applied to them as well. Now the departments are nearly all girls."

"Great story," I said.

"My sister claims to be an expert on postcolonial gender studies, or something like that. At Thanksgiving we just smile and pass the stuffing and gravy. When I was at Yale we read people like Milton and Chaucer, Alexander Pope and Emily Dickinson. That was in the dark ages."

I smiled. I liked this woman.

"Anyway," she said, "I'm afraid I can't add much to whatever George has told you, but let me check something."

We followed her back into the reception room. She walked behind the receptionist's desk, smiled at the young girl there (her nametag read SARAH) and borrowed her laptop. Ann clicked her way through several screens and stopped, then scrolled.

"This really wasn't terribly odd," she said, "but it was a little bit out of the ordinary. The first ferry to the mainland goes in at 9:00. When the *Kommunicom* people were here some of them chartered a trip in at 7:00. That happens sometimes but it's not particularly common. Our breakfasts are pretty good, certainly better than what you'd get in Milbridge. Besides, they were included with the package deal that *Kommunicom* had purchased."

"Any record of who chartered it and who was aboard?"

"No, sorry. The $85 was just added to the general bill."

"Was the $85 itemized on the bill?"

"No, it would be under *miscellaneous* unless it was a sizeable amount. Just a sec…(she changed screens and scrolled). OK, the miscellaneous charge was less than $200. For a group that large and for that long… budget dust."

"Who operates the ferry?" I asked.

"A man named Bill Lowell. Retired lobsterman. We have an apartment fitted out for him above one of the garages. He gets his meals *gratis*; that and his room are basically his form of compensation. You could talk to him. He might remember something. He's pushing 80 and his hips and knees aren't what they once were, but he's got a good memory and he's as reliable as the tides."

I looked at my watch. It was 9:35.

Ann read my mind. "He'll wait to pick up any passengers or cargo in Milbridge and dock here in about twenty-five minutes. How about some coffee?"

"Perfect," I said.

"Black?"

"So you could float a horseshoe in it."

"You got it."

# TWENTY-FIVE

When I met Bill in his apartment he was wearing a set of rubber overalls and a long brim hat with no logo. There was some dried salt spray across the front of his overalls and a damp spot on the right elbow of his red flannel shirt. Before we spoke he got me a refill on my coffee and filled his mug with what I figured was probably his third or fourth of the day.

"Bill Lowell," he said.

"Gwen Harrison," I answered.

"Ann said you wanted to talk to me about the early morning run I made for that radio company, about a month ago."

"Right," I said. "There were about twenty of them here for their annual administrative retreat and on the morning of the 5th they chartered a run at 7:00."

"It's not all that rare," he said. "Some people have a plane to catch. It's a three-hour drive to Portland and an hour and a half to Bangor, give or take. By the time you drop off your rental and get to the check-in you can be in for a fairly long trip. I've had people who wanted to go out at 5:00, one—last year—at 4:30. Not much fun on your departure day, but if you're trying to stretch out your time here, well, it's the price you pay. Me? I like to get to an airport two hours in advance. I don't trust them. There's always a problem, always a delay, always an upcharge. Now, my grandson, Michael, he says he hates them too, so he doesn't want to be there until the last minute. He says he wants to be the guy who's one ahead of the person in line who gets the 'late arrival' tag put on his luggage."

"I'm like you, Bill," I said.

"Anyway, I remember those radio company people. They came here in a mini-coach. I met them at the dock. All leather seats, very nice. I thought to myself that this was one very smart company. The luxury mini-coach would set you back less than two grand for a day's trip, but if you had everyone driving their own cars and getting the government reimbursement rate it would cost you five times that amount. With the rental you'd spare the passengers the need to drive. They could sit back and enjoy the trip."

"And they might even talk business along the way, so the company might get more work out of them," I said.

"And have plenty of money left over for a gourmet lunch," he added.

"Well, Bill," I said, "there's one thing I've learned here…"

"What's that, Hon?"

"Your mother didn't raise any stupid children."

"Why, thank you."

"So if you took the radio company people into shore they wouldn't have had any means of transportation waiting for them there."

"No," he said. "Unless they made prior arrangements. They'd be standing at the dock with their hands in their pockets, wondering what to do next."

"I wonder what they all did."

"I should have been clearer on that," he said. "I didn't take all of them in."

"You didn't?"

"No, just two. Both women. One tall, the other short. Mutt and Jeff."

"What else do you remember about them, Bill?"

"One was older, the shorter one. They were dressed about the same, ready for a walk in the woods or a trip to the tourist traps. Not sure when their day was actually going to start that morning. Allowing for breakfast…probably around 9:00 or so. Not sure why they didn't have breakfast here at the Center; they probably already paid for it and it would have been better than what they would have gotten at Lou's place."

"Ann said that as well."

"Obvious point. If I was going off for a day trip I'd have had breakfast here first and then gone in on the scheduled ferry run. Cheaper and better all the way around."

"Do you remember returning them to the island?"

"I wish I could. The morning return trip is usually crowded. People come out for the day, walk around the shore or in the woods. The Carlsons will do picnic lunches for you, if you're interested. I may have brought back the shorter one, but I can't be sure. That was a month ago and I've ferried a lot of people since then. How are you doing with that coffee?"

"I could drink another cup if you're making some."

"No problem. I've got one of those Keurig cup thingies and the water is always hot and ready to go."

"You know how I like it," I said.


When he went into the galley kitchen I looked at some of the plaques and pictures that lined his walls. When he returned I asked him about them. "You got a bronze star with a **V** device in Vietnam."

"Near Pleiku. Central Highlands. I was a medic. Our unit came under mortar fire and it took a long time to get in some air support."

"You saved people who were under fire."

"I tried to. Got most of them."

"And back here…you were the mayor of a town."

"Tiny place down the coast. It was more ceremonial than anything else. Part-time position, provided more of a stipend than a salary."

"And then you became a lobsterman."

"Actually I ran the VFW Post in Bangor for a few years. Then I did some security work for a bank and some other businesses there. I don't know why I spent so much of my life behind a desk; I always preferred to be outside."

"Fascinating," I said.

"You know what I find?" he asked.

"What's that, Bill?"

"The longer you're around the more you discover that you're surrounded by people with interesting stories. If you live long enough and you're willing to get off your porch and get out in the world there's all kinds of things that you can accomplish. The thing is…no one ever asks you about it. They think of you as an old man or old woman who was never involved in anything before they met you. Those older people have personal stories. Some of them are serious and impressive. Sometimes we're actually surrounded by heroes and heroines, teachers, business people, nurses, even some artists sometimes. Painters and glass blowers, carvers, potters…I liked those programs they used to have where they took schoolkids into nursing homes and asked people to tell their stories. Me? Not so much. I like the quiet, the solitude. The people who knew my story…well…I mostly just carry them in my heart."

"And you were married; you mentioned your grandson."

"Married for forty-seven years," he said. "Mary's gone now but I have two great kids and wonderful grandkids. Bill Jr. is a heart doctor in Boston and my daughter Claire is a lawyer in Portland. They come visit often and we talk about their mom and the old days. They've built their own lives and families now and the Carlsons let me take the clan out on the boat whenever they're here. They love it, especially when the seals are sprawling on the rocks, sunning themselves. June to October is the best time to see the whales, especially the humpbacks. Sometimes the grandkids call me *Grandpa Captain*. I get a kick out of that. All in all it's a good life."

"My people are close to the land, not the water," I said. "Northern plains."

"All part of the same world," he said. "I think the different places all speak to different parts of our experience. They're like scenes from the movies that make up our lives. Some may be more important than others but we carry all of those things with us, both the good and the bad."

"They're at our beck and call," I said. "In the tight moments, the moments when we can't think things through and make lists of pros and cons…they tell us what to do, how to act, sometimes how to survive. As a soldier you'd know that."

"I expect you do as well," he said. "I wonder about your friend, the man who disappeared, the one you're looking for…what did he do in that moment? Why is he gone? Where is he now?"

"I wish I knew," I said.

"I wish I could help," he said.

"Maybe you already have," I answered.

# TWENTY-SIX

The next morning I got up early and drove into town for breakfast at *Lou's Diner*. Before that I took a slow drive along the coast. The closest house to the dock for Mary's Island was a substantial cottage that consisted of multiple additions that were covered by cedar shake siding in various shades of silver and gray. I jotted down the address and the name on the mailbox in the Notes app on my iPhone. When I got to Lou's I parked to the side of the rest of the cars and trucks there and did some research on the address in my notes. The home was owned by a man named Robert Sharp. He had purchased it decades ago for a pittance. From the look of the structure and the age of the additions I figured that he had been responsible for most of the improvements. I googled his name but nothing came up except for a white pages notation of his likely age (65-) and a reference to a ten year-old human interest piece concerning his lobster business in a local paper.

The morning rush was on in Lou's. When I entered I could smell a mixture of good things—fresh coffee, grilled sausage and bacon, bread popping from toasters. I stood a few feet from the checkout counter where I was approached by a middle-aged woman with one hand full of cutlery wrapped in paper napkins and the other juggling a sheaf of plastic menus. "Sit anywhere you want, Honey," she said. When she walked toward an open table I followed her there.

"Here you go," she said, putting a wrapped place setting and menu in front of me. "I'll give you a couple of minutes; there's a lot to choose from."

I slipped off my jacket as she put an empty mug in front of me. "Coffee?" she asked.

"High test, black," I said.

When she returned three or four minutes later I ordered some buttermilk pancakes with sausage patties.

"Any eggs or toast with that?" she asked.

"No thanks, but how about some crisp bacon?"

"Always my choice," she said. "When you can't decide on bacon or sausage you have both."

We continued to socialize as she refilled my coffee. "Can I ask you something?" I said.

"Sure," she said, looking around and seeing that the booths were coming open and the seats at the breakfast bar were empty except for an elderly man at the end, reading a newspaper. "He'll be here most of the morning," she said.

"I just wanted to ask you about one of the people here in town. I'm not a reporter or anything. I wanted to talk to him but I didn't want to appear at his door and spook him. Some people are invalids, some with failing memories…you know what I mean. I'm fascinated by the town and I saw his lobster traps by his boat and, well, I figured he might be a good person to talk to about life in a small town in Washington County."

"Bob Sharp?" she said, except she pronounced it like *Bahb Shahp*.

"Yes, I think that was the name I saw on his mailbox."

"I'm glad you asked me first," she said.

"Why's that?"

"Well, Bob's a little odd. Some might say…abnormal."

"In what way?"

"Oh, he's not angry or bat-shit crazy or anything. He just sticks to himself and, well, he kind of lives in his own world."

"Don't we all?" I asked.

"Yes, in a way, but, well, he really does. Maybe I'd put it that he lives in a different time. He doesn't care for, well, the way we do things now. I mean…it sure as hell isn't perfect, but most of us, well, we get used to it.

We deal with it. Bob doesn't. He rarely leaves his cottage, except to check his traps or dig some clams out on the beach there. He's safe though. You don't have to worry about that. I'm just thinking that if you want to talk to somebody about the town you'd probably get a better account from someone like Ed Wyatt (if he isn't busy) or maybe Marty Adams down at the *Sunoco* station."

"Already met both," I said. "Enjoyed talking to them. I just thought that somebody right there on the water, somebody who can hear the ocean, well, they might be a little more vivid when it comes to describing what it's like to be living in this part of the world."

"I don't know about *vivid*," she said, "but I doubt that he would be dull. Now how about some more black coffee. I just made fresh."

"You don't have to twist my arm," I said.

"Lorraine," she said. "You were wondering about my name."

"You're a very intuitive person, Lorraine," I said, "not that I'm a big believer in what they call intuition."

"It's more *experience*," she said. "*Intuition* is what the women have in the Hollywood movies and the shows on the streaming services. Those companies that produce that kind of thing…they don't make movies about the people who work in Washington County."

When I knocked on Bob Sharp's door it took him awhile to get there. He was carrying an oblong magnifying glass. He looked at me expressionless, waiting for me to speak.

"Mr. Sharp?"

"It's on the box," he said.

"My name's Gwen Harrison. I was wondering if I could talk to you for a few minutes."

"About what?" he asked.

"Life, times, the ways in which we try to get by now."

"Come on in," he said.

He told me that I should sit on his couch. "I don't have any tea or anything," he said. "I've got some coffee on."

"Coffee would be great," I said.

He returned with mugs that had business logos on them. "I have cups and saucers," he said, "but they don't hold anything. I hope the mug's OK."

"You don't know the half of it," I said.

"Yeah? How's that?"

"In my line of work we call it plasma. One of my coworkers once said that they should put an IV in his arm and run the coffee straight from the kitchenette to his desk."

He smiled slightly. "What's your line of work?" he asked.

"I'm a kind of tracker," I said.

"What does that mean?"

"Well, you asked…"

"Yes?"

"I'm a fibbie," I said.

"You work for the FBI?"

"On my own time right now. We had an agent a few years ago. He left the Bureau and went into the private sector. Now he's disappeared. No body found. No accident recorded. He just fell off the earth. He and I went through Quantico together. When I heard he was missing I asked the powers that be if I could use some of my leave time to check around. Nothing heavy. Nothing official. Just trying to be of help. He was here about a month ago, at a business conference, out there on Mary's Island…"

"Can't say I'm fond of the place," he said. "They bring in a lot of money but they leave these briny chemicals in the water. I think the town did a deal with the devil, but I can see their point of view on it. This is a literal backwater with constant money problems. I've never had any extended dealings with the people who run the retreat. They're called the Carlsons. Our paths cross from time to time and they seem decent enough. They have a lot of traffic; I'll give them that. I didn't think the operation would survive more than a season or two, but they've made a serious go of it. How's the coffee?"

"Perfect," I said. "You've got a nice place here." That was an exaggeration because the living room was small—a couple of chairs and a couch by the fireplace, some tools and a rack of pine firewood with that telltale scent of mold. I was struck by the fact that the wall behind his chair contained some black and white framed photos. The frames were simple and unobtrusive but obviously pricey. Both were local scenes and they were exquisite. Ansel Adams-level.

"I see that the pictures have drawn your eye," he said.

"They're lovely," I said. "Museum quality."

"Not El Capitan," he said, "but I'm not ashamed of them."

"You took them."

"Yes. Trying to hold their place in time, before somebody brings in an *A&W* root beer stand."

"Edward Hopper could do both—put in the old site and the contemporary business operation."

"He could indeed," Bob said, "but he was always going for isolation and loneliness; I'm going for natural beauty. Well, actually, that's not entirely honest. I would include some of the works of man on the list of natural beauties, but I'd see them in their original form, before they were commercialized or what some people consider modernized."

"I understand," I said.

"Bring your coffee," he said. "I want to show you something."

# TWENTY-SEVEN

He took me into a huge adjoining room, at least three times the size of the living room. The walls were covered with framed photographs. They weren't displayed individually; they abutted one another and formed a display that was more like splendid wallpaper. Most were in black and white.

"Look here," he said, pointing to a picture of a lighthouse.

"That's the Nubble, isn't it?" I asked. "In York."

He looked at me with an expression that hinted of connectedness, possibly even of some degree of affection. "How would you know that?"

"I did some homework before I came up here," I said. "It's a historic structure; it's special."

"I used to operate it," he said, "back in the day before it was automated. Now there's a gift shop there."

"Sacrilegious," I said.

"That was the word I used," he responded. "It's an abomination; it's appalling."

"What kind of camera did you use?" I asked, trying to reduce the temperature and keep him talking.

"*Hasselblad* 500C/M. *Zeiss* lens."

"That's an old camera, a legendary camera."

"Cost me a lot less then than it would now," he said. "They used *Hasselblads* on the moon," he said. "The astronauts left the camera bodies there to keep the weight down, make more room for the samples of rocks and whatever other stuff they wanted to collect for their return trip."

"Setting priorities can be a bitch," I said.

"Amen," he answered.

For the next fifteen minutes I looked at the pictures. Most of them were large; the medium format cameras will enable you to do that without any loss of resolution. "And you still do this," I said.

"Oh yes," he answered. "Some people believe that you can't buy film anymore, that everything's digital. That's ridiculous. A good drug store will develop your 35 mm in a couple days. If you go 24x24 as I usually do it can take some weeks. And it's not cheap."

"But look at the result," I said. "How do you put a price on that?"

"You can't, but you have to pull in a lot of chickens to afford it."

"Chicken lobsters."

"Yes, the tasty ones. About a pound to a pound and a quarter. They take seven years to grow to that size. The small ones you have to throw back."

I was looking at a picture that he had taken of a group of clammers. "I like this," I said. "You were going for something like that painting by Millet, with the women stooping over and collecting things from the ground. What is it, the 'Harvesters' or 'Gleaners,' or something?"

"You've got quite an eye, young lady."

"I also love the old clam baskets."

"They're usually called hods," he said. "You can rock them back and forth and clean the clams in the ocean water. You need to fine-tune the cleaning process before you make your chowder but they're a nice rough-and-ready implement. Now they often just use metal baskets…"

"But the old ways are often the best."

"I'd say the most *authentic*, but not necessarily the most efficient. Authentic is important to me."

"Tell me, Mr. Sharp…"

"Yes?"

"Do you ever take pictures of Mary's Island?"

"Back in the corner," he said, leading me to a place next to a window with a full view of the beach. The picture hung about five feet from the ground, museum-style.

"That's it there, before the conference center was built. It looks larger, doesn't it?"

"It does," I said. "Lovely composition, with the rocky shoreline, the evergreens and the cloud formations."

"Did you see the human figure in the left corner?"

"Oh yes," I said. "The little girl with her back to the camera. Is that Mary Cabot?"

"It is."

"It's interesting," I said. "It's as if the natural setting is looming over her…as if, well, we shouldn't actually *own* such a thing. Is that what you were going for?"

He just nodded. "If you look down the row of images they each reveal seasonal changes. I put the one at the bottom there because it's ugly and I was trying to make a point, something that in retrospect I think should have been more subtle."

The picture just above the quarter-round baseboard molding showed the conference center under construction. The framing had just been completed and it looked like a skeletal form that was taking over the island. "Sacrilege again," I said.

"Yes, but too heavy-handed, I think. A cheap shot. The camera has to be more…accepting. This is more like a 2x4 across the bridge of the viewer's nose. Nobody likes preachy. At least I don't."

"Sometimes we can't help ourselves," I said. "It's a cry to be heard, maybe a cry for something like justice."

"Your line of work, but I don't think it should be mine," he said.

"Did the Cabot woman visit it often, over the years?" I asked, trying to change the subject.

"Not really. I think she's happier with her husband in the Boston suburbs. Concord, I think. Historic. Been there several times. I like it."

"How about more recent shots?"

"Of the island?"

"Yes."

"Sure. I take pictures of it all the time. It's at the center of my view; I can't look away and forget that it's there. At the top there…"

The image was of a party on the lawn between the conference center and the shoreline. There were well-dressed people in conversation, holding Martini and Manhattan glasses.

"The temptation was to go all Gatsby and smarmy decadence," he said, "but I was in a forgiving mood and wanted to show the people dressed up in a natural setting, as if they respected it and drew warmth or inspiration from it."

"That comes through very nicely," I said. "I can't help but ask…"

"Don't be shy," he said.

"Any images of the people at the radio company conference last month?"

"I think they just arrived from the processor," he said. "I didn't open the box yet to check. I took two that I thought were interesting enough to have developed."

He walked over to the editing table in the center of the room and picked up an unopened box. "These just arrived yesterday," he said.

The photos were each 24x24, shipped flat between sheets of heavy-duty cardboard, with corner protectors and several layers of bubble wrap. The box itself was reinforced to prevent crushing or bending and sealed in heavy plastic to protect it from the weather.

"Your developer is very careful," I said.

"Yes. Here are the negatives. He puts them in plastic cases, the kind that the grading companies use for rare baseball cards. After all, they're the pictures' souls. If I find one that I like, one that could be profitable, it goes in a safe, not in a drawer."

He picked up the top photograph. "I was going for pleasant solitude, not the Hopper loneliness," he said. The image was of a man sitting in an Adirondack chair at the side of the conference center, facing an inlet from the sea and a stand of trees beyond. He was completely absorbed, clutching the book as if he was trying to squeeze the essence from it.

"I felt a little guilty," Bob said. "I moored my skiff on the other side of the island and positioned myself just within the tree line. Any jury would find me guilty of invading the man's privacy, but, well, to me he was a part of the picture, a man with a book, sitting in the sun, absorbed. I wasn't trying to reveal any secrets or steal something from him. I was, well, trying to turn him into a modest form of art."

"I'm glad you did," I said.

"You like it then," he answered.

"More than that," I said. "That's my friend, the person I've been looking for."

# TWENTY-EIGHT

"What's his name?" Bob asked.

"Richard. What did you imagine it might be?"

"Man with a book."

I had to work hard to suppress a smile. "And there's a second picture there."

"Yes, completely different," he said.

"May I see it?"

"Of course."

He unwrapped the picture and put it on the editing table.

"Could you turn on the overhead light?" I asked.

"Sure."

The picture *was* completely different.

"This was taken from a totally different angle," he said. "I was in my skiff, near the island but close to the mainland shore. I had to use a *Zeiss* Superachromat T* Telephoto lens. I found it on *eBay*; cost me a fortune."

"But worth every penny."

"Of course."

"Did anyone see you take the picture?"

"No, I don't believe so. There was a light rain and I was wearing a poncho. I had a line in the water, fishing. When the image appeared I slipped the camera out from under the poncho and got the shot."

"You weren't trespassing or anything."

"No, but some people think you're stealing their souls and it doesn't make them happy."

"Or catching them in the act of being themselves, perhaps doing something they prefer to keep secret."

"Yes, I suppose that could be possible."

The picture contained an image of two figures. The first was little more than a wisp of motion, recognizable as human, because forest animals don't wear scarves. It appeared to be a woman, almost like a ghost or spirit, disappearing into the woods which were enveloped in fog. Behind her (assuming it was a her) was a clear figure of a youngish woman, standing on the edge of the woods but with her face fully exposed, her head turned in the direction of the island. It was as if she was looking to see whether or not she was being followed. There was concern in her face, not something approaching fear, but something involving apprehension or uneasiness.

She was plainly dressed, but in decent clothes suitable for travel. The wind was moving her dark-colored hair and the fog lay at her feet, almost as if she was floating above it, escaping into the woods, but guardedly.

"I wish I knew her name," I said.

"Downeast wood spirit," Bob said. "Seeking protection."

"Would you mind if I took pictures of each of them?" I asked.

"No, go ahead," he answered. "I can get you originals. I'd rather not give up the negatives."

"Just keep them safe for now," I said. "And can I offer you some advice?"

"Of course."

"Don't let anyone else see them until you hear from me."

"You think someone might make me disappear too?"

"We have to consider all of the possibilities," I said.

"You mean the fact that the man you're looking for might have been murdered."

I looked into his eyes.

"I understand," he said.

"One other request," I said.

"Sure…"

"I'd like you to take me to the precise spot on the shoreline where the woman disappeared into the woods."

"I can do that," he said. "You're wanting to see if there's any remaining physical evidence."

I nodded yes.

"Then we can have a fresh mug of coffee."

"Maybe after I make a phone call or two, depending on what I find, if anything."

"I won't get in your way," he said.

"I appreciate that, and everything else you've done," I said.


The entry point into the woods above the mainland shoreline was no more than fifty yards from the back of Bob's cottage.

"It was right there," he said. "I was over there (pointing), floating close to the dock. The woman (or two women) got off the ferry from the conference center, turned right, walked up the beach and went into the woods, just by that set of rocks."

Bob left to replenish our supply of coffee as I walked into the woods. There was an actual path between the trees but no gravel or asphalt walkway. Dried pine needles covered the ground but there were exposed roots every few steps so that I had to walk carefully and avoid tripping or falling ass over teakettle.

My hope was to find physical evidence—torn threads, for example, that might later be linked to specific items of clothing, but the width of the walkway was frustrating my attempts. I did, however, find a single cigarette butt. This one was damp and degraded but I noticed immediately that it had a tube filter. These exist in America (with *Parliaments*, I think) but they are far more common in Europe. Who, in America, would go to the trouble of purchasing European cigarettes? They are apparently 'safer' than their American cousins, but smoking itself is now rare, the going number somewhere in the vicinity of 11% of American adults. That number might be higher among fishermen, lobstermen and clammers but I doubt that *they* would be so fastidious as to order their coffin nails from Europe or, for that matter, smoke *Parliaments*. I slipped the butt into an evidence bag, realizing that this was a long shot. If there *was* a suspicious European in our midst it would be highly unlikely that we could match any DNA extracted from the cigarette to something in any of *our* public records. Interpol was a long shot. Its DNA data base has less than 300,000 records and many of the criminals on file would be dead, incarcerated or still operating in a foreign country. The majority of them were unlikely to look like the attractive woman in the picture.

A few yards farther on I found something much more interesting. The pathway ended on an unpaved road with a cutaway area with parking spaces for three or four vehicles, depending on their size. It had been there awhile. The rough-cut logs that outlined the space were filled with rot and insect ingress/egress points. This space would have been known by the locals seeking access to the beach in an isolated area devoid of traffic, people or parking meters. It would also have been a convenient way to drop off or pick up one or more individuals who did not want their presence in the neighborhood known to anyone there, particularly members of law enforcement.

I walked the pathway four times, twice in each direction, but failed to find anything other than the chi-chi cigarette butt. When I returned to Bob's cottage I could smell the scent of fresh-brewed coffee.

"Do you want a sandwich to go with that?" he asked.

"That would be very nice," I said.

"Cheese or meat?"

"Cheese."

"Swiss or cheddar?"

"Swiss."

"Rye or white bread?"

"Rye."

"Mustard, I presume?"

"Have to have mustard," I said, smiling.

"Simple yellow or heavy-duty Deli?"

"Deli, but not too much of it."

"As you ordered," he said, putting the paper plate with the sandwich and some olives on the coffee table. "Any luck?" he asked.

"Unfortunately, no," I said, "but I did see the parking area at the end of the trail. Does that get a lot of use?"

"Not too much," he said, "but when the tourists are thick on the ground it's a nice alternative for the locals. It's not advertised up on the main road. You're thinking maybe that the woman entering the woods was picked up there?"

"It's possible," I said, "but it would be unlikely that any guest coming from the island would know about it, unless, of course, the woman was a local."

"I didn't recognize her," he said, "and I've lived here for thirty-seven years."

I didn't tell him what I had been considering but he saw the possibility immediately. "What if the island was a stepping stone?" he asked.

"In what sense?" I responded.

"She may have been dropped off there by someone who wanted to retain his (and his boat's) anonymity. If this was something hush-hush the captain (or drug dealer) would have wanted to avoid pulling up on a public beach, particularly one that's now frequently used. An easy alternative would have been to drop off the passenger on the east side of the island and let her slip in with the other members of the group that were coming ashore on the early run, but as I remember this was much earlier in the morning."

"The man who pilots the ferry…"

"Billy Lowell."

"Yes. He lives in an apartment over one of the island outbuildings."

"You met him."

"Yes. Anyway, he seems like the kind of person who would value his privacy. He wouldn't mix and mingle with the paying guests. He might even feel awkward doing so and he wouldn't want to have to change his clothes to fit in. He's basically a loner."

"So someone could board the ferry who was unrecognizable to him, whether they were going in early, on time, or later. And 'unrecognizable' wouldn't mean much to him because he was more focused on the clock and the workings of his vessel than the identities of his passengers."

"Yes, particularly if that person was being shepherded by one of the more prominent, well-known guests."

"The person with the scarf."

"Right," I said.

"This is getting interesting," he said, "but like you suggested earlier…"

"Maybe a little scary as well. My advice to you still stands, Mr. Sharp. Don't say anything about this. To anyone."

"How's the sandwich?"

"Excellent. Where do you get these olives?"

"They're Castelvetranoes; I get them at a Deli in Machias."

"Worth the trip," I said.

"Your body language is talking," he said.

"How so?"

"You want to thank me, say good-bye, get on your cell phone and get back to work."

"Is it that obvious?"

"No, I was just guessing," he said, smiling. "I hope I've been of help."

"I don't yet know how or why, but I'd bet serious money on it," I said.

"I'm always here if you need me," he said, handing me a blue post-it note with his phone number and email address."

"Let's use this if we need it," I said, handing him a secure cell phone.

# TWENTY-NINE

The first person I called was Peggy Chapman.

"You're probably going to drive straight to western New York rather than stopping and resting like a sane person," Peggy said.

"I don't know if Richard's still alive, but I don't want to waste any time looking for him."

"I'll get you a late-arrival reservation for the place in Pittsford."

"Thanks. Could you also contact Scott Leven, in Buffalo?"

"Sure. What do you need?"

"As soon as I stop somewhere to unload some of this coffee I'll send him a picture. There's an image of a woman on it, with her face toward the camera. I'd like somebody to photoshop the background out of the picture and just home in on her face. The background can be white or black; it doesn't matter. If someone could overnight it to my hotel I'd very much appreciate it. I want to use it like a mug shot and ask Richard's wife and some of the people at Richard's company if they recognize her."

"We can do that," Peggy said. "Anything else?"

"No. Before we put out a call to the cavalry I want to make sure I'm not wasting a lot of peoples' valuable time. The person in the picture could be well-known and the whole process to date a wild goose chase."

"But you doubt it. Your gut's telling you that this could represent a break in the case."

"It's not so much my gut," I said. "It's the expression on her face and the general circumstances of the event being recorded."

"Stay in touch, Babe," Peggy said. "I'll let the General know where things stand. Do you want to send us a copy of the full picture?"

"Maybe I should," I said. "I don't want to waste any one's time, but if, somehow, I was taken off the board, I'd want others to pick up the thread."

"Let's not go there just yet," Peggy said.

"I'll send the picture," I said.

I stopped at one of the new rest stops on the NY Thruway for a sit-down dinner. I didn't see how these new facilities were great improvements over their predecessors. They seemed smaller and there were fewer bathroom stalls. I checked the secure website on my phone and found that Peggy had secured my room and Scott had put my doctored mug shot in the mail. Then I settled in over my meal: chicken nuggets, honey-mustard dipping sauce, some very salty fries and a large, caffeinated cola. I figured I had already had enough coffee to keep Juan Valdez in business for the better part of a year.

When I arrived at the *Del Monte* the desk clerk had red circles under her young eyes. The hotel was deserted except for the sound of an electric sweeper vacuuming the common areas. I saw the man with an industrial-strength, 30"-wide model as he passed by; there wasn't any spring in his step.

I rested for several hours, had an early breakfast and called Kathy. I told her that I just had a question or two; I tried to allay her concerns by telling her that I didn't have any significant information on Richard, positive or otherwise. When I reached her home she looked tired. I asked her how she was doing and she said that their baby was restless. "It's fascinating," she said. "You know all about it and you expect it, but when you see your belly moved by the motion of the baby's foot everything becomes more real, even more real than the image from the ultrasound."

"Magic," I said, "but not necessarily conducive to sleep."

"No. There was a lot of activity last night, almost as if the baby was worrying about its dad."

I didn't know how to respond to that beyond placing my hand on Kathy's shoulder and doing my best to communicate a sense of warmth and sympathy.

She smiled and asked me about the questions that I had.

"Well, really only one, unless it occasions a follow-up."

I took out the mug shot of the lady in the woods and asked her if she recognized the face.

"I've never seen her," she said. "Are you telling me that Richard might have known her…in some capacity?"

"No. You shouldn't worry about anything like that. I did see a picture of Richard at the conference center in Maine. It was taken about the same time as this picture. The two figures were separated by a considerable distance and Richard was sitting in a chair, reading. There was no perceivable connection between them."

I could still see some concern in her expression. "Again," she said, "I've never seen this woman. Do you know who she is?"

"Not yet," I said. "All I can say is that there was no particular indication that she was a part of the company group. She was simply seen in the general area there and I'm wondering if someone might have been trying to conceal her presence."

"And you think Richard might have seen something that he shouldn't have."

"It's possible," I said. "It would provide a motive for his disappearance."

"But that happened weeks later."

"Yes, I know," I said. "Again, this is all in its early stages and I'm feeling my way through some literal and figurative fog. The fact that you didn't recognize her helps, though I don't yet understand how or why."

"Maybe someone else at the company might recognize her."

"My next stop," I said.

"Let me tell you again how much I appreciate your help, Gwen."

I smiled and put my hand on her's. "I understand that time is of the essence," I said.

"You look like you drove all night," she said.

"Well, now that you mention it…"

"Let me get you some coffee," she said.

We tried to make small talk. I asked her about the sex of her baby.

"A little girl," she said. "At first we weren't sure that we wanted to know, but the technician doing the ultrasound blurted it out."

"My cousin says that little girls are easier to raise," I said.

"Until they become teenagers," Kathy answered.

"I wouldn't worry about that," I said. "She comes from a good gene pool."

"Sweet of you to say," she responded. "Right now my half is pretty nervous. I could do with some meds or some cocktails—any of the things that I'm not supposed to have."

"There'll be time for that later," I said.

# THIRTY

Rather than appear unannounced at *Kommunicom* I called first and asked Pat, Gabe, Tom and Marianne if they were available for a brief chat at *Steve's Original Diner.* I staggered the times and asked them to keep the meetings private. I was still concerned about the figure with the scarf who appeared to be leading the mystery woman through the woods. From the proportions visible in the photograph neither Pat nor Marianne would have qualified as potential candidates.

I thought about talking to Rudolf but I didn't have the same level of trust with him that I did with the others and I figured that the division heads and the H.R. Director would be more likely to know a person that was far enough down the corporate food chain to escape the attention of Kathy Ingle.

I began with Gabe. "Sorry," he said. "Never seen her. Where was the picture taken?"

"I'd rather not go into any detail at this time because it's such a long shot and I don't want to invade anyone's privacy."

"I understand" he said. "It looks like she's concerned that someone's following her."

"I had that impression too," I said, giving him just enough feedback to sustain our trust.

Tom didn't recognize her either. "Nice photograph," he said. "Lots of drama in her face. Reminds me of that Meryl Streep picture from, what was it, 'The French Lieutenant's Woman'?"

"You're right," I said. "Very observant. I think her face was in a reverse profile…in the movie still."

"Yes," he said, "but the eyes and the expression are similar."


Pat said, "Nope. Never seen her. Do you have any idea who she is?"

"I was hoping you'd be able to help," I said.

"Sorry. She doesn't look like a techie to me, more like a drama queen. Fortunately I don't have to deal with too many of those."


Marianne looked at the picture intently. "It's not the kind of shot I'd usually see. People who send pictures with their resumés usually pick the ones from their scrapbook that make them appear all bright-eyed and bushy-tailed. Their pictures say 'Hire Me!' This one's saying something different, something like, 'Did You Hear Something?' 'Is someone following us?'"

"Interesting that you pluralized it," I said, "you know…you added another person to the scene."

"Right, I did," she said. "I'm not sure why. I guess I saw some motion in her expression, as if she's walking somewhere and heard something that the other person might not have heard. Has the picture been cropped in some way?"

"I'm not really sure," I lied. "The picture turned up on a CCTV system and this was all that the tech could salvage from it."

"Got it," she said. "Anyway, I'm sorry I couldn't be of any more help."


As she stood up to leave I thanked her again for her assistance. The waitress approached me and said, "You look like you could use some more coffee."

"Is it that obvious?" I asked.

"Coffee can't cure everything, but it helps people focus."

"I agree," I said, and picked up my phone. It was time to call in a big gun.

# THIRTY-ONE

I texted Peggy, brought her up to date on my progress, such as it was, and called Mike Liu on a secure line. Mike was the master computer jock in the Salt Lake City field office. We had done business before.

"So," he said, "you're calling to put the band back together."

"Peggy already mentioned it to you."

"She gave me a headsup," he said. "She also cleared it with my SAC, Sandy. Officially I'm to give you as much of my time as you need. A lot of that will probably be front-loaded."

"Your SAC was acting in the job. Santiago Martinez."

"Just made permanent," Mike said. "His family nickname is Santi, but he said that might be a bridge too far for the Anglos in our office."

"How about the Chinese?" I asked.

"My name is very uncommon," Mike said. "How did you possibly deduce that I was Chinese?"

"Call it a lucky guess," I said. "How many Lius are there in mainland China?"

"Only about seventy million," Mike said. "The family name was originally Lipschitz; at Ellis Island they suggested we use something more common and recognizable."

"I've missed you," I said.

"What have you got for me, Ms. Gwen?"

"Have you heard about Richard Ingle?"

"Just what Peggy said. Former special agent. Went civilian to have a normal life. Working in the commercial (slash) defense industry making high end radios in western New York. Suddenly he disappeared."

"We went through Quantico together," I said. "The Bureau sees loyalty as a two-way street. I've been asked to try to find him."

"What do you need from me?"

"A couple weeks before he disappeared, the members of his company were holding their annual administrative retreat. This was in Washington County, Maine."

"What's that, a couple days' drive from the Arctic Circle?"

"Depending on the vehicle," I said.

"Talk about wanting to get away from it all…"

"Interesting place—a facility on a waterless island, now with a desalination plant."

"Pay me now or pay me later," Mike said. "An island without water is not going to set off any bidding wars."

"Exactly. Anyway, I visited the island and met a local photographer (slash) lobsterman (slash) clammer (slash) former lighthouse operator. He showed me two examples of his handiwork. One was a picture of Richard, sitting in the sun, reading a book. The other was of a figure and a half…"

"A half? Top or bottom?"

"The edges of a scarf with the full body hidden by a stand of pine trees. Actually, white spruce. I figure it's a she because the scarf has a design that would be more likely to be worn by a woman."

"Ornate."

"Not over-the-top Bette Midler, but not something you'd expect to see on a downeast logger. Plus, from the distance between the scarf and the ground the wearer would appear to be just over five feet tall."

"So it's as if she just walked into the woods and all you can see is the end of her scarf blowing in the breeze or resting on her shoulder."

"Yes, and did I happen to mention the fog?"

"Early June in northern Maine? You could wake up and see nothing *but* fog."

"It's hovering just above ground level."

"How about the other figure?"

"Full size."

"You mean zaftig?"

"No, the whole body is visible. Tallish. Well-proportioned. Maybe 5'10". She's looking over her left shoulder, as if she heard something behind her or was worried that someone might be following her."

"And Shorty is leading her through the woods?"

"Entirely possible," I said. "There could be others, fore and aft, but the photographer focused on the one woman and said that if there were others there they were well out of the picture frame."

"I take it he wasn't using his *iPhone* to take the picture."

"No, a medium-format classic *Hasselblad*."

"Nice," Mike said, "the high-priced spread. My facial rec software will be pleased."

"The guy's a stickler for the best and the most authentic."

"But no one knows who this woman is or you wouldn't be calling me."

"I talked to Richard's wife and I talked to the division heads at Richard's company; no one recognized her."

"Including the H.R. person, presumably."

"Yes."

"Unless we're talking a large company…"

"We're not. Less than a hundred people, probably little more than fifty or sixty, assuming that some of the manufacturing is outsourced."

"If anyone would know, the H.R. woman would."

"I didn't say it was a woman."

"H.R. is a feelings-driven organization," Mike said, laughing.

"Except when they're cooperating with the feds or local courts to garnish your wages."

"There is that," he said, again laughing.

"I'll send the picture to our standard drop site," I said. "You might be interested in what one of the company directors said about the woman's facial expression…"

"What's that?"

"He said that she looked like Meryl Streep in that famous marquee still from 'The French Lieutenant's Woman.' Meryl's facial profile is different from that of the woman in the picture, but the expression is very similar."

"Concern…terror…surprise…uncertainty?"

"All of the above," I said.

"She's standing on the Cobb, I think, the stone breakwater in Lyme Regis," he said.

"You truly are the cosmopolitan one," I said.

"All I do is look at pictures all day," he responded. "Tell me that the woman isn't wearing a hoodie, like Meryl."

"No, you've got her full face to work with."

"Deo gratias. Why was she walking into the woods?"

"That's my next question. Possibly the major question, but as you know, she could simply be a good-looking tourist from Ashtabula, Ohio who saw an osprey that was a little too close for comfort."

"Or someone who was herself being kidnapped."

"Could be," I said.

"How soon can you get me the picture?"

"Five minutes? Maybe four?"

"I'll get right on it. With me you always have most-favored-nation status."

"And you know how much I appreciate that."

"Always," Mike said.

# THIRTY-TWO

I texted Peggy and thanked her for clearing the way with Mike, treated myself to a 45-minute power nap, and checked the drop site through which Mike and I communicated. There was nothing there but a winking smiley face emoji indicating that he had received the picture.

I slept a few hours more and made it to the hotel restaurant in time for a late dinner. I had some French onion soup, meatloaf and whipped potatoes and a glass of house cabernet, passing on the black coffee since I wanted some uninterrupted sleep, as many hours of it as I could manage.

There was still no message from Mike when I woke up the next morning. This time I did have coffee with my meal, three cups of it. I returned to my room and waited for my phone or laptop to send me some sign-of-life signal from Salt Lake City.

Three hours later it came in.

"Your young lady is quite elusive," Mike said. "I found a solid match with my facial rec software, but it took hours to cycle through the possibilities. You'll be surprised to learn that she's now a long way away from the Maine woods."

"How far?" I asked.

"I'm not so sure about the route that the crow flies," Mike said, "but as the car drives let's say about 3,300 miles."

"She's in California."

"She *was* in California. Last week."

"What was she doing there?"

"Trying to find a good book," he said.

"I guess she hasn't heard about *Amazon*," I said.

"This is an all-purpose experience," he said. "*Vroman's* in Pasadena. Ever heard of it?"

"Sure. It's where Hollywood shops, along with all of the rest of us little people. Right on the Rose parade route."

"Colorado Boulevard," Mike said. "Readings, talks, signings… the entire enchilada, along with all kinds of interesting tchotchkes and geegaws. You want some Harry Potter action figures? Some Winnie-the-Pooh dolls or bookends? Maybe some *Pride and Prejudice* statuettes? One of my most treasured possessions from that store is a plastic figure of a gentleman by the name of Bibendum."

"Bib. The *Michelin* man."

"The very same."

"So you were shopping for something other than books. What was *she* doing there?"

"Hard to say, exactly. I picked her up on a public camera out on the sidewalk and then started checking the CCTV systems of the adjacent businesses. There was only one good screen grab—in the bookstore. She was simply standing against a blank wall, 'looking on' as we say."

"And you'll send me the date and time along with the image."

"It's in the mail," he said.

"And she hasn't surfaced anywhere else?"

"Not as yet," he said. "Enjoy your trip to the city of the angels."

"Actually I'll start in the city of the old Protestant money nestled in the San Gabriel Valley."

"Don't get all frustrated and jump off the Arroyo Seco Bridge; I couldn't function without your business."

"I'll keep it coming," I said. "I have to say…she gets around…and suspiciously enough to suggest that it's worth following up the lead."

"First she's downeast, looking over her shoulder in the fog, then she's shopping among the beautiful people. For me…I'm hearing a lot of bells ringing and whistles whistling."

"Thanks again, Mike."

"I live to serve," he said.

I caught the delayed, late-afternoon *United* flight through Chicago and landed at LAX at sunset. Peggy had found me a room at the *Westin* on Los Robles, a 15-minute leisurely walk from *Vroman's*. I had grabbed a sandwich in O'Hare, so I skipped dinner, tapped into my stash of snacks and turned in for the night. There had been no news from Mike and a simple note from Peggy, wishing me well. The bookstore didn't open until 10:00, so I had time for a hot shower, a decent breakfast and a tour-de-Pasadena walk.

# THIRTY-THREE

I found the store manager at *Vroman's*, a woman named Anne Gilson, explained in general terms my position in the Bureau and the fact that I was conducting a routine investigation. I asked her if the woman in Mike's picture looked familiar.

"I'm not usually on the floor the way my clerks are," she said. "You should probably talk to them. We have a lot of foot traffic along with the established customers. People come into Pasadena to shop or eat or go to the movies and check in with us the way you'd walk into a favorite store at the mall. I don't recognize the person in your picture as a regular."

"And I'm sure you've been working here for awhile."

"Eleven years. She appears to be nicely dressed, but not as a Midwest tourist or a day-tripper in a full, over-the-top Palm Springs, Palm Desert or Rancho Mirage beads-and-buckles outfit. I'm thinking almost European. Of course we've got lots of those in SoCal."

How about the positioning within the store?" I asked, "the place where the picture was taken."

"I'll show you," she said, walking me to an open space towards the front of the store. "When we have readings or signings we set up tables or podiums here. The day she was here…"

I reminded her of the time and date.

"We had a signing by an author named Karen Dennett. She's written a first novel with great word-of-mouth. I remember being surprised at the size of the crowd that she drew. The person in your picture was here in mid-afternoon and the signing was at 7:00, so we wouldn't have set up the table yet. This would have been a nice opportunity for the Dennett woman but not a big deal for us, not like a Michael Connelly or James Ellroy signing, where we would have to set up cattle chutes and have hundreds of books on hand."

Hard to imagine a person standing around for four hours waiting for a signing, I thought to myself, particularly not to buy a book about the troubled upbringing of a woman from Arkansas with a crippled boyfriend named Hap and an aging dog called Shep.

Anne introduced me to the clerks who were rearranging shelves and running credit cards through readers. She respected my wish that we could do this in a low-key manner. I found it amusing that the clerks were all suddenly speaking in whispers. Unfortunately, none of them recognized the woman, though one did say that she reminded her of a younger Meryl Streep. "She *does* live in Pasadena now…well, and in New York and Connecticut too…but she comes here every now and then. I saw her once. She was wearing a coat that cost as much as my first car. I think she lives down by the Huntington…"

"I didn't know that," I said.

"The woman in your picture is probably fifty years younger, but there *is* a resemblance."

"I agree," I said.


Having exhausted my search I returned to the *Westin*, lay down on the bed and stared at the ceiling, hoping for messages or images to appear there. None did. I could have investigated Meryl Streep's house and satisfied my curiosity but instead I went to the *Huntington Gardens and Library*, which now operates a café and coffee shop, neither of which require you to pay the admission charge for the general grounds (a cool $29-34 depending on the day of the week). I went to the coffee shop and secured a tall black coffee and an almond croissant.

Rule #1 in FBI work: as soon as you kick back and get comfortable you'll receive a message that interrupts your break. This one was from Mike.

"I have good news and bad news," he said.

"What's the good news?"

"Actually there's good news, bad news and bad news."

"I'm sitting down," I said.

"There's been another sighting. In a *Hilton Garden Inn*."

"What's the bad news?"

"I still haven't identified her. No name, no nationality, no background, no personal history."

"What's the other bad news?"

"The *Hilton Garden Inn* is in Cincinnati."

"Where, in Cincinnati?"

"Norwood, sort of. Evanston, sort of. Not far from Hyde Park. On Dana Avenue—not too far from Xavier University. Semi-historic part of town. The old Coca-Cola bottling plant there is an art deco masterpiece."

"She was seen in a bottling plant?"

"No, it's the alumni center for Xavier these days, but it would be worth a side trip."

"OK, I appreciate the travel advice."

"I haven't checked local CCTV systems, but there's no question that she was in that hotel."

"When was she there?"

"A week and a half ago."

"Keep checking on the local systems. I'm heading to LAX."

# THIRTY-FOUR

There was space available on the *Delta* red eye, which saved me the trouble of an intermediate stop at BWI or Chicago/Midway. The Cincinnati airport is actually in northern Kentucky, as experienced Midwest travelers all know. Peggy had booked me into the *Hilton Garden Inn* and provided me with a Bureau car. The trip in was just under twenty miles, but I was fortified with a small ocean of coffee and after a brief delay in our takeoff time I had been able to sleep for most of the four-hour flight.

Fortunately the hotel had not been fully booked the evening before and I was able to get into a room long before check-in time. The breakfast service was still available and I made myself a waffle with those pre-measured batter cups and the device which you load and then flip 180 degrees. Or is it 360? Too early in the morning for higher math.

I was finishing a side order of bacon when I got a text from Mike, directing me to a fresh drop site. I filled a large cardboard cup with coffee and returned to my room.

"Surprise," his message read. "I was cruising the neighborhood and found a bookstore something like *Vroman's*. It's called *Joseph-Beth Booksellers* and it's in a place called the *Rookwood Pavilion*. Rookwood is the name of a famous Cincinnati pottery factory. *Joseph-Beth* is a huge place and it also sells geegaws and all kinds of point-of-purchase items."

"So she's making a tour of bookstores?"

"I don't know," Mike said.

"Clarify, please."

"If she was in the bookstore I couldn't find her on their CCTV system. However, the so-called *Rookwood Pavilion* is an upscale shopping district with all kinds of things on offer. I found her on the CCTV system of a restaurant near the bookstore, a place called the *Redlands Grill*. It's a steak/pasta/salad-y kind of place. The image of her is interesting."

"How so?"

"Well, the image in the hotel is what you'd call normal. She's walking through the lobby, checking her cell phone. At the restaurant she's posing."

"Your picture just came through," I said. "She's standing at the end of a long table, but there's no one else there with her."

"Right. It's like she's convened a meeting and told everyone to leave the bar and take their seats. They're lingering at the bar and she's getting impatient."

"Exactly. It's a very clear shot though. That's our girl, no doubt about that. You caught her at the hotel. How about at the airport? Any images there?"

"No," Mike said. "I checked the gate areas for *Delta*, *Southwest* and any other airlines that had direct or connecting flights from LAX, Burbank, Ontario, John Wayne…the complete set. There's always the possibility that she could have driven to Santa Barbara or, well, wherever, but I'd need an army of computer jocks with very long attention spans to cover the multiple possibilities."

"I understand," I said.

"How long was she at the restaurant?"

"Hard to say, but it wasn't a wham/bam/thank you, Mr. Karsh kind of thing. She was standing behind the head chair for two, possibly three minutes."

"So she wasn't worried about being seen or somehow compromised."

"No," Mike said. "Of course this was at the beginning of the dinner service, so the place was starting to perk up with a lot of pedestrian activity."

"Makes sense."

"There was also a little drama going on. If you watch the full movie clip you'll see that she stopped to check her cell phone, slipped it in her purse, paused and looked up, ready for her closeup. Then she checked her phone again and walked away."

"Trying not to draw attention to the fact that she was posing?"

"That would be my read," Mike said.

"One other question before I go. Did you talk to anybody at the bookstore about the availability of their system?"

"No, I just hacked in. It appeared that there was nothing available for the date or dates in question. Probably erased."

"I'll try to charm them," I said. I'm sure they're open now and the restaurant doesn't formally open up until 11:30."

"Happy hunting," Mike said. "I'll keep looking for her in the dark corners of our proud fifty states."

"With my blessings," I said.

I signed off and looked at a local map on my laptop.

'At least I can see why she stayed at this hotel,' I said to myself. 'It's no more than a brisk 15-minute walk to the *Rookwood Pavilion*.'

# THIRTY-FIVE

The manager at *Joseph-Beth* was an old Cincinnatian named Bill Honthorst. He quickly volunteered that his grandfather had once managed Bert Smith's *Acres of Books* before it moved from Cincinnati to Long Beach. "Back in the day it was reputed to have a million books for sale," he added, "including some rare stuff, not the shlock from peoples' attics and yard sales."

"How about yourself?" I asked. "What's your background?"

"I managed a *Borders* before they closed, and a *Brentano's* back in the distant past. The hard copy chains and independents are having a rough time these days, but I was surprised to see that *Barnes & Noble* is somehow expanding. *Joseph-Beth* is doing fine, however. Not because of anything I'm doing that's out of the ordinary. We just don't have a lot of competition and we've got a great location here in the *Pavilion.* 'Adjacent to Norwood' wouldn't have been a big selling point back in the day. This was the part of town with all the manufacturing plants. People came up from Appalachia, worked all week and then returned to their hollers on the weekend. James Lee Burke has a book about it. *To the Bright and Shining Sun*; have you read it?"

"No, I haven't," I answered.

"We have it—over there with his crime fiction."

"Thanks for the tip," I said, anxious to get him back to the identification of our mystery woman. I showed him my Bureau credentials and asked him about their CCTV system. "We're trying to find a woman we'd like to interview. We know that she was in the area about ten days ago and we were wondering if she came into your store."

He looked at the calendar on his *iPhone*. "I'm sure the system was up and running because we've had a lot of recent activity in the store. Emeril was here to sign copies of his new cookbook and one of the retired Bengals was signing a memoir. Can you believe the money those guys make?"

I took heart until he added that their system recycles every week and that it would have been erased for the time in question. Emeril and the offensive-line tackle with the 22" neck had been in 5-6 days ago.

"I'm very sorry," he said.

"So am I, but I appreciate your time," I said.

"There's that Burke book over there that you could check out," he said.

When I smiled he said, "Wait a minute. How about a cup of tea or coffee on the house?"

I thanked him for his hospitality and actually did browse for awhile but at 11:25 I left to visit the *Redlands Grill.*

The manager was a man named Jeffrey Bounds. He was polite to me but his expression said that he would much rather be somewhere else, doing something very different.

"I don't understand," he said. "Somebody was in the restaurant a week and a half ago and you want me to verify that or try to identify her?"

"Not exactly," I said. "We know that she was here because we have a picture of her. What we're wondering is whether or not someone spoke to her or noticed that she did something that might have been considered to be out of the ordinary."

"How did you get the picture? Someone must have been here to take it; they probably know more about her than any of us would."

"We took it as a screen grab from your CCTV system," I said. "That's common practice in an investigation such as this."

"You mean invading our privacy, hacking into a security system owned and operated by a private company."

"Ultimately, it's for your protection, Mr. Bounds. The person could be an upstanding citizen anxious to taste one of your steaks or pastas. On the other hand she could be a criminal who wishes to do you or a member of your staff harm. We simply don't know, but that's the sort of thing that we're trying to determine."

"Excuse me, that sounds like bullshit, but I'll try to help you. Let me see the picture."

I showed it to him and he immediately said, "Natasha."

"Natasha? You know her?"

"No, that's what one of my waiters called her. He said she reminded him of that woman from the Bullwinkle cartoon."

I was somewhat nonplussed. She didn't look like the cartoon character, who was truly cartoonish. A former Miss Transylvania? The companion of a person named Boris Badenov? The antagonists of a flying squirrel and a thickheaded moose? On the other hand, Natasha was a spy. That was more interesting, but most spies weren't initially arrested for throwing rocks at Girl Scouts. The woman who voiced her character was shooting for something like Zsa Zsa Gabor, but Zsa Zsa was Hungarian, not Romanian/Transylvanian. And the character was inspired to some degree by Morticia Addams.

"I know, I know," Jeffrey said, reading my expression. "That doesn't make any sense, but the waiter doesn't usually make a lot of sense. Let me get him for you."

Four members of the wait staff were standing at the end of the pass, adjusting their clothes, making small talk, looking as if they wanted to step outside for a cigarette, though they were probably organizing the prep for the lunchtime service. Jeffrey touched one on the shoulder, took him aside, spoke to him for a minute or two and then brought him over to the table where we had been sitting. The man was short, with slicked-back dark hair and rimless glasses. He was wearing an *Apple* watch and I noticed that he had had a professional manicure.

"This is Louis," Jeffrey said. I wasn't sure whether he was calling him by his given name or surname (Lewis?), but the man stared at me as if he wanted to give me one-word answers and return to whatever he had been doing. Everyone in this restaurant seemed to be impatient.

"Sit down, Louis," Jeffrey said, and Louis/Lewis did, but he sat on the edge of the seat as if this was all being done against his will. I showed him the picture.

"Natasha," he said. "A crown bitch."

"Why do you say that?" I asked.

"Because she was ordering me around. She first spoke with Charles; he was there to assist Mr. Bounds. Charles asked me to help her and she looked at me as if I was some ignorant lowlife."

"What did she want?" I asked.

"She was asking about seating for large groups. She said she had a party of…I don't remember…twelve or maybe fourteen people and she said that they wouldn't want to be squished in among the other tables. She didn't use the word 'squish'; it was something cruder, but that was the point."

"When she stood at the end of the table…"

"Yes?"

"Was there anyone taking her picture?"

"Not that I noticed, but we have people taking pictures in here constantly."

"The table in the picture is at the center of the far end of the room," Jeffrey interjected. "Someone could have been using a long lens."

"Most party-goers would use their phones to take pictures," I said. "We're thinking that this picture might have been more, well, professionally done."

"Possibly," Jeffrey said, but this was at the beginning of the dinner rush. The focus is on the diners. Many are arriving at the same time and they're anxious to be seated. Waiters and bussers are trying to make their way between tables. They're trying not to spill food or drinks and they're sidestepping coats and purses hanging from the backs of chairs. It's loud, distracting. They're not looking for someone with an old-fashioned camera. They're not all that rare anyway. In every large crowd you'll find a person who's an OG photographer, the official picture taker, the guy who goes for a hike with three or four pieces of camera gear hanging from his neck…"

"I understand," I said. "There's no one at the table where she's standing. It's as if she's presiding over something that isn't actually happening."

"They're probably still in the process of setting the table," Jeffrey said. "Maybe she had escaped the seater and was laying claim to it, you know, like holding it before someone else could take it."

"Wouldn't she have been held back, to keep the space open for the people to work?"

"Usually, of course," Jeffrey said, "but like Louis said, this person was pushy, difficult."

I looked at Louis/Lewis and he was growing increasingly impatient. "Do you need me for anything else, Mr. Bounds?" he asked, probably bothered by the fact that Jeffrey had taken over the conversation.

"I do," I said. "I'm wondering why you called her Natasha."

"She reminded me of that cartoon character," he answered. "She wasn't dressed over-the-top or falling out of her dress or weirdly proportioned or anything; it was her voice."

"She sounded…?"

"I don't know, like East European or something?"

"Were you thinking Russian? Natasha is a Russian name."

"No," he said. "I was thinking more like Trump's wife Melania."

"She's Slovenian," I said, "formerly Yugoslavia."

"She just sounded different, not necessarily affected," he said. "Let me put it this way; she didn't sound like someone from Norwood."

"And you didn't see anyone with her?"

"No. Charles just asked me to help her. My station was over there," he said, pointing to a line of two-seat tables along a side wall. "I had to get back to work."

"Was there anything else that she said to you, besides asking about seating for a large party?"

"No," he said. "And I didn't want to stop to chat."

"And she didn't have dinner then?"

"Not that I noticed. She was standing alone. I had the impression that she was thinking about making a reservation for another night and she was just checking us out."

So, I thought to myself. She wanted her picture taken behind an empty table but not in an empty room. She had a vaguely East European or Central European accent. And she was insistent; Louis/Lewis thought she was bitchy, though he may have been overly sensitive. Was this progress?

# THIRTY-SIX

I returned to the *Hilton Garden Inn* and contacted Mike, bringing him up to speed on what I had learned.

"The facial rec software doesn't have a box check for 'bitchy,' but the European accent is potentially very helpful; I'll widen my search. Think about the important thing: a person from a foreign country has come ashore in a remote part of the U.S. of A. The fact that she seems to be in control of her situation suggests that she hasn't been sex-trafficked or otherwise brought in against her will. That doesn't mean that she couldn't be under some form of duress; in fact, that might be why she seemed bitchy. Still, we have no evidence of that."

"Agreed," I said. "And on the plus side, she looks as if she's comfortable in her clothes."

"Too much of a woman's perspective for me to evaluate," he said.

"That's why we're a good team," I said. "Anyway, I'll sit tight and wait to hear from you."

"I already tried to find you something to do this evening," he said. "Unfortunately, the Reds are playing the Pirates in Pittsburgh. That could have been fun; after all, it is the national pastime…wait a sec, there's a touring company of 'The Whiz' at the Aronoff Center. Want me to score you a ticket?"

"I think I'll pass," I said. "I don't have a dog; I left my red shoes at home and I already feel as if I'm surrounded by munchkins. I may just go back to the *Redlands Grill* and road-test some of their offerings."

"You eat; I'll work," Mike said.

"Deal," I answered.

I actually went for a Caesar salad and some prime rib with smashed potatoes. (Smashed? Mashed? Whipped? I know there's a difference but I wondered why the styles kept mutating.) The waitress asked me if I wanted a side of broccoli or mac and cheese and I asked her to bring me some of the St. Francis "Old Vines" Zinfandel.

I skipped the heavy dessert choices and went instead for some English Breakfast tea with a madeleine. When I returned to the hotel and saw that there were no messages from Mike I took a hot shower and turned in for the night. I slept well, all things considered, but before I could make it downstairs for the breakfast buffet I heard the text signal on my phone. Mike directed me to a protected site. "Ready to return home?" he asked.

"Did somebody else break the case?" I asked.

"No such luck," he said, "but your international woman of mystery has just smiled for the camera again."

"Where, Mike?"

"The Senate Office Building."

"Say what?"

"She attended an open meeting of the Agriculture, Nutrition and Forestry Committee. Today."

"Why in the world would she want to do that?"

"Maybe she's concerned about beef prices now that you've doubtless consumed a large portion of the country's supply?"

"Interesting," I said, "but unlikely. Seriously, that sounds like the kind of committee where they'd put freshman Senators. The old white hairs in charge would go for Appropriations, Armed Services, the Budget Committee or the Judiciary…"

"She remains inscrutable."

"I thought you'd need reservations for that kind of thing. Like a month in advance or something."

"Usually you need them for most things around the Capitol, but there are third-party tour operations that will open the gates and pave the way for you. For a fee, of course. The government doesn't charge but they make you wait forever for tickets and then you have to stand in long lines. Hence the middlemen. We remain a capitalist society, after all."

"I assume the picture of our fair lady is en route."

"Yes, indeed," he said. "I'm anxious to hear your take on her outfit."

I heard the image drop and opened the file. "Well, I can say one thing; she's not dressed like a tourist."

"I was thinking more of a formal meeting kind of thing," Mike said. "Not like a cocktail party or fancy dinner but more like a businesswoman rising to a modest occasion."

"Rising to a modest occasion? You sound like you should be a runway reporter in Milan."

"I have my moments," Mike said.

"No pillbox hat," I said, "even though they're back in style, but that might have drawn too much attention. I'd say she looks like a female executive who's anticipating a nice meal at the *Willard* with her political consultant husband."

"*Senior* political consultant," Mike said. "A hamburger with fries and a cup of soup will run you close to sixty bucks there."

"As you learned from bitter experience?"

"All I wanted was a couple beers at their bar. Unfortunately, I got carried away. Or the money in my wallet did."

"I can get to D.C. in early afternoon," I said, "assuming there's space available on the nonstop."

"Peggy's already got you booked. I may have been presumptuous but I thought we knew each other well enough to…"

"Much obliged," I said.

"You know that you'll be flying in one of those tin cans with the low ceiling and an aisle that only accommodates anorexics."

"I'll soldier on," I said. "And thanks again."

The picture of Natasha was standard issue. She was seated comfortably in the gallery, staring into the distance, waiting for the show to start. In this case, however, she had seatmates on either side of her, a middle-aged woman and a teen-aged boy, one presumably a tourist, the other a visitor with a Boys' State group or a high school debating society. They each appeared eager to observe the political posturing, while Natasha looked as if she had been there on countless occasions and was attending dutifully but not entirely happily.

I didn't want to shlep my luggage on the Metro so I taxied to my apartment in Cathedral Heights and changed my clothes. Peggy knew that I was in town and the Director had been briefed on our recent developments. Mike was trying to create a grid that would provide some insight into why an apparent foreign national might turn up in a bookstore in Los Angeles, a hotel and restaurant in Cincinnati and a Senate meeting in the District of Columbia. There was still no identification of the woman now being called Natasha, but I felt as if something in the case was about to break.

That optimism was countered by my concern about Richard, whose location and physical state remained unknown. Nevertheless, Natasha's behaviors were suspicious and I had to believe that her activities and fate somehow intersected with his. Bottom line: it was all that I had and unless and until we knew about her motives and identity I was forced to be patient—not my normal or preferred state.

I didn't learn a great deal after my visit to the Capitol, but I found a Senate page there named Stephen Hunter, a high school junior (as they all are) who directed me to the seat in which Natasha had ensconced herself for the open meeting. I didn't find any hair or fibers or cigarette butts with odd filters, but I found a *Ricola* wrapper wedged on the floor in front of the seat. Unfortunately, she was wearing gloves in the picture, so it was doubtful that the Bureau lab would find any prints or DNA on it. I did, however, learn two things. She had a cough and she was a litterer. The former might have been explained by her movements between the Maine fog, San Gabriel Valley smog and Ohio Valley humidity; the latter suggested that she was arrogant (or, to be fair, under duress and hence distracted). I don't like arrogance or duress, but each of them help motivate me to search for explanations and suitable cures.

# THIRTY-SEVEN

There actually turned out to be a partial print on the wrapper, but it didn't appear in any of the data bases to which we had access. "I would have thought a real American would have used *Hall's* and an affected European would have opted for *Ricola*," Mike said. "Unfortunately, *Ricola* now rules the U.S. in market share."

"I would have thought the same," I said. "Menthol is menthol but I suppose people have to have their share of those Alpine herbs."

"They clean out the throat, sinuses, eyes, ears, brain, shoulders and upper body," Mike said.

When I updated Peggy she asked me if I would be available for dinner with the Director. "Just here in the office," she added. "Nothing formal."

"Name the time," I said.

"8:00," she responded.

"I'll be there," I said.

Peggy had set the coffee table in his office with some silverware and cloth napkins. She added some bottled water from his mini-fridge and old-fashioned glasses. The Director arrived at 8:09 and apologized, explaining that his meeting with the AG had run over.

"What do you feel like, Gwen?"

"Something simple, Sir. Maybe a club sandwich."

He nodded toward Peggy and retrieved a bottle of Buffalo Trace bourbon from his cabinet. "Ice?" he asked. I nodded No, thanks.

He then poured two fingers of golden liquid in each of our glasses and settled back in his armchair.

"I wanted to talk to you about Richard Ingle," he said. "I've tried not to be too hands-on because Richard's a civilian and this is not really our show. It's important to me, however, and I think that my personal connection with the case is trumped by a particular aspect of the case."

That was a surprise; I had no idea that the Director had any personal connection with Richard.

"Let me start with the basic premise," he said. "When someone disappears like this it's either because someone has hidden them or because they've hidden themselves. If the latter is true it means that the individual is, in some way, dirty. He or she has done something or is somehow involved in something that he or she wants to suppress. If they go so far as to abscond, well, it's probably damned serious. In this particular case we simply don't know what has happened, so all that we actually have is our knowledge of the individual and our sense of the likelihood that he could have done something illegal, immoral or very embarrassing. The point I'm getting to is that it is absolutely inconceivable to me that Richard has committed a crime or compromised himself in some serious way."

"Because of your personal connection with him," I said.

"Yes. And I didn't want to involve myself because I wanted to avoid charges of favoritism or even misuse of Bureau resources. I was, however, willing to send one of my top assets to see what, if anything, she could determine. Given my personal knowledge of Richard it now appears clear to me that since he is above reproach he is somehow involved in something indirectly. Our ultimate perp is either using him or silencing him because Richard inadvertently saw or heard something."

"And that person has either eliminated him or, perhaps, is framing him?"

"Quite possibly. This is not a kidnapping; there's been no ransom demand. For that matter there's been no contact with the family whatsoever. Or, as far as we know, with Richard's company."

"He could have simply been killed and buried in the mountains," I said. "As hateful as it would be it's still a strong possibility."

"Yes, unfortunately, but we do have this odd lead with the woman you're calling Natasha. We don't know why she's here and we don't know what she's doing, but the likelihood is that she hasn't done it yet. Hopefully we can track her actions and find that she somehow leads us back to Richard."

"I agree, Sir, and I share your belief that Richard is a person of honor. Above reproach, as you said."

"And you knew him well, if briefly," he added.

"I did," I said. "We were close."

"Let me tell you about my connection with him. Some of it is a matter of public record, but one would have to read between the lines to understand the full story."

I wanted him to keep talking, so I nodded and took a long sip of the bourbon. It was exquisite. Not pricey, but often marked-up because of its rarity. The Director gave himself a fresh pour, offered me one, and continued.

"You probably didn't know this," he said, "but my son Thad and Richard were classmates at USMA. They lived in the same barracks and had the same TAC officer, a man named Greaves. Greaves had made it his personal mission in life to torment my son, quilling him for such things as possessing small appliances in his room that were claimed to be fire hazards. There *are* rules about such things, but they vary in levels of seriousness and punishment (if it is applied at all) is often applied, shall we say, prudentially."

"Why did he single out your son?"

"Probably to prove that he had the authority to do so. It was a way of linking his name with mine, knowing that I would not intercede on my son's behalf. Greaves was to be the one considered bold enough to screw over the General's youngest son."

"Didn't they use to hunt for popcorn poppers in the barracks? That was some kind of academy tradition?"

"Yes," he answered. "That was more of a cat-and-mouse game, because of the smell. If a TAC officer walked into the barracks the smell would be overpowering, like fresh-baked bread. The cadets were essentially saying, 'catch us if you can' and the TAC officers were saying, 'watch us.' Nowadays, of course, everything's electronic and the forbidden objects can be very trivial. The punishment tours, however, are not, particularly when the cadets are forced to walk them on weekends and holidays."

"And that's what Greaves did."

"Yes, and he was noticeably unfair about it. His name was Charles but the cadets' nickname for him was 'Chickenshit'."

"And Richard somehow resisted him?"

"Not so much that; Richard supported Thad. He implicated himself in some of Thad's alleged actions and then walked the punishment tours with him. He also tutored Thad in Math, which remains a key subject at the academy. If the cadets' grades were still physically posted in the Sally ports as they were back in the day, Richard would have been there to support him. Now they're posted electronically and, again, Richard was always there to congratulate Thad or to console him. You know that the academic system there is set up in such a way that the cadets can be evaluated daily, on a single class?"

"Richard mentioned it once; that's a lot of pressure."

"But not like the pressure of being responsible for an Armored Brigade Combat Team of 4,000-6,000 soldiers," the Director said.

"Your son's current role."

"With the 1ˢᵗ Armored Division at Fort Bliss."

"That's a bird-colonel gig," I said.

"He's one of the youngest," the Director said, "and, again, with no intercession from me."

"Whatever happened to Greaves?" I asked.

"He retired as a lieutenant colonel; he was never assigned to command a battalion; the last I heard he was operating a small string of car washes in Midland, Texas."

"Ouch," I said. "So there really is justice and a power above."

"As far as I can see, that would be in the affirmative."

After a toast to justice Peggy entered the room with our club sandwiches, garnished with homemade chips. "Thanks for taking care of us," he said, "as always. Why don't you go home to your lonely husband and let me tell this young woman some more war stories."

"I'll see you in the morning, Sir," she said.

The Director told me some more anecdotes about Richard and Thad. "Thad would have graduated and, I think, prospered," he said, "but with Richard's help he lived up to his full potential. Richard's an only-child; Thad was his surrogate brother."

"I didn't know any of that," I said, "but I can't say that I'm surprised."

"As I said, I wanted to stay on the sidelines, but your investigation turns on the fact of whether or not we can trust Richard without any reservation. From my perspective (which I thought you should be aware of) we can. Now where do we go from here?"

# THIRTY-EIGHT

"Mike is tracking Natasha's movements and trying to find links between them…some commonality…some explanation… some rationale."

"The pattern is weird," the Director said, "but possibly only weird to us. We just haven't found the key that opens that lock. She lands in Maine; she travels to Los Angeles, then to Cincinnati, then to Washington. In California she goes to a bookstore; in Cincinnati she stays near a bookstore but makes her presence known at a restaurant. In our fair city she goes to a meeting room in the Senate Office Building. We have to connect the dots in order to determine her motive or motives."

"It's interesting that she was led to the shore in Milbridge…"

"By the woman in the scarf."

"Yes, Sir, but she now seems to be on her own, at least from what the CCTV cameras are telling us."

"My guess," the Director said, "is that she needed to play follow the leader in Maine because she was being shepherded. She somehow made her way to the island and was taken to the shore by the scarf lady. They were then met by a driver on the edge of the woods that adjoin the mainland shore. Perhaps the other individual did the planning for the operation or was somehow verifying the identity of the mystery woman, protecting against the possibility of any interlopers. The European woman had to get from that remote area of Washington County to an airport down the coast. That presented a logistical challenge and probably some risk. The driver didn't want to pick up the wrong passenger."

"Makes sense," I said. "I wish we knew the identity of the woman in the scarf."

"I understand that all we have is the tip of the thing. Is there any identifiable pattern in it, something unique?"

"The picture is in black and white and the scarf is dark fabric. It has a subtle pattern; we haven't identified a brand name but it doesn't look like the sort of thing you'd buy at *Walmart* or a yard sale. Nice scarf. Not *Gucci* or *Burberry*. Just nice. I wish we had more."

"Lots of shadows from the evergreens, faint reflections from the rocks and then that encroaching fog," the Director said.

"Yes, Sir, they don't help."

"I wonder why Richard's company met at that time of year. It was after ice-out but hardly an optimal time to visit there."

"I think they always meet at the same time," I said. "August is the nicest time to be there but it would also be the most costly. In Maine a lot of people book the same place every year at the same time, because the window is so narrow. It's a good question, however."

"But probably with an obvious answer," he said.

"Mike is on the case," I said. "I have a lot of confidence in him. I just wish I had more patience. Richard is probably in harm's way; I want to be there to help him."

"I know you do," he said. "We'll do all that we can for him. Meanwhile, go home; get some rest."


I slept fitfully, even after some putatively-soothing tea and the comforts of my own bed. I woke up early, checking to see if Mike had turned anything. He hadn't.

I got on my laptop and did some busywork, creating timelines and recording notes that might spark some memories. They didn't.

Eventually I had a light breakfast, went to the Capitol and checked with some pages who were at or near the scene of Natasha's last appearance. No one noticed anything out of the ordinary and I could see them talking among themselves, probably questioning why a crazy fibbie was worried about tourists at a meeting that was likely to have been boring beyond all belief.

That evening I went down into Georgetown and had dinner at *Martin's Tavern*, a kind of poor man's *Musso and Frank*, but with reliable comfort food. I opted for the chili and the meatloaf, topping it off with some Irish coffee. It was comforting enough but I knew that any actual comfort would be on hold until I could find Richard, hopefully in one piece.

I arrived home at 10:00, taking a long walk home via Wisconsin Avenue. I showered and climbed into bed, closed my eyes for ten or fifteen minutes before experiencing a hypnic jerk. It's that weird, sudden feeling of falling. Your brain is playing tricks with you, interpreting your muscle relaxation as a loss of balance.

It had happened before and was caused by overdoing the caffeine, the stress, the anxiety and simple physical fatigue. 'At least you earned it,' I thought to myself. I closed my eyes, pulled my comforter over my exposed shoulder, and five minutes later heard an incoming text. It was from Mike. His message was simple:

**I have a name.**

# THIRTY-NINE

"For Natasha or the woman in the scarf?"

"Natasha. I appreciate your confidence in me with regard to identifying the Scarf Lady, but that's the longest of long shots. Natasha (or Tereza) was much easier."

"I'm all ears," I said.

"Tereza Petrů. Czech. Ballet prodigy. My facial rec picture is dated; she's just a tween-ager, but the numbers and the facial dimensions don't lie. She was expected to end up in the Czech National Ballet Company in Prague."

"A big deal."

"The biggest, for her," Mike said. "Unfortunately, it was not to be."

"How so?"

"She suffered stress fractures in her left foot and had to have an operation so that she could continue to walk. That meant a plate and some high-end (probably titanium) screws that would bankrupt the average citizen. The problem is that when you have that kind of surgery you lose lateral mobility. You can walk but you can't dance in a premier ballet company."

"Isn't she a little tall for a ballerina?" I asked.

"Usually they run around 5'4"-5'7"; the companies like everyone in the troupe to be around the same size. Of course, they'll always make exceptions for exceptional people."

"How long ago was she dancing, Mike?"

"Eleven years and change," he answered.

"What's she been doing since then?"

"When you cut through the euphemisms in the press it looks like she's been clerking in a cosmetics store."

"How the mighty have fallen."

"It explains a lot," Mike said.

"Pretty woman, lots of poise, significantly under-employed."

"And underpaid, I'm sure," Mike said.

"Susceptible to taking on a role where she could use her talents that remain," I suggested.

"How about recent travel?"

"No record of her route to rural Maine. When she flies commercial in the U.S. she uses the name Veronika Bartak."

"That means she's using a phony passport."

"Yes, it does."

"That's a no-no."

"Yes, it is."

"And probably a phony credit card."

"That too," Mike said.

"And where is Ms. Bartak staying at the moment?"

"Would you believe…"

"I probably would."

"She's right down the street from you, at Ye Olde *Four Seasons*."

"Whoa. Palace prices, not *Ken and Mitzi's in the Woods*."

"One of the highest," Mike said.

"Not affordable on a clerk's salary."

"No way," Mike said.

"That means she's working for a high roller," I said.

"Or someone who wants to represent her as a member of the high-rolling set."

"Exactly," I said. "Bonus points to the Chinese member of the Church of Jesus Christ of Latter-day Saints."

"I'll take them," he said. "And I'll even put on my best temple garments."

It only took a few moments for Mike to notify me concerning Tereza's room number as well as the daily rate for that cherished space at the *Four Seasons*: $1950. You could bring that down by booking months in advance but you'd still be well north of a grand a night. I notified Peggy concerning her whereabouts and asked Mike to keep an eye on her movements there. I drove down Wisconsin Avenue and parked as close to the hotel as I could, waiting for Mike's call. The plan was to follow her and see what fresh destinations lay in her future. The unintended result was that I would be waiting most of the day to determine them. I had brought along several changes of clothes to maintain my anonymity and was glad that I had done so, since her actual destination required me to dress for dinner rather than for tracking.

She taxied to the restaurant when she easily could have walked there. *Café Milano* is a Georgetown staple, known for pricey Italian fare and dark corners for clandestine meetings for power brokers and feeders at the public trough. It prides itself on its list of celebrity diners, including past presidents and their first ladies. By the time I was able to park my car and follow her into the restaurant she was already seated with a middle-aged woman who was more or less her same height, thus disqualifying herself for the role of the Scarf Lady.

I positioned myself at a distance, not wishing to draw any attention to myself but close enough to be able to photograph the happy couple. I couldn't identify their food choices but they appeared to be risotto appetizers with fish entrées. I couldn't read the label on their white wine, but the ruffles and flourishes which accompanied its presentation suggested that we were light years away from anything close to $40/bottle.

I eventually took a picture of the two of them and went into the Ladies room to send it to Mike and wait for a possible response. He was able to act on my identification request immediately.

"That was easy," he said. "For starters, Ms. Petrů, aka Ms. Bartak, is doubtless picking up the tab."

"Why do you say that, Mike?"

"Because her dining companion is an academic on a limited budget. Her name is Roberta Winslow, B.A. Smith College, M.A. and Ph.D. Columbia University. Associate Professor of History at Georgetown University. Nine-month salary: $87,500. Probably not a rising departmental star. Age: 46. Specialty: Modern Chinese Diplomatic History. She published her dissertation with the *Cambridge Modern China Series*. Probably her career peak. It deals with Chinese infrastructure-building in certain areas of Africa and Latin America. She's also published a few articles and book reviews."

"Interesting," I said. "What in the wide, wide world of sports does a sometime Czech ballerina have to do with a middle-aged college professor who specializes in China?"

"Above my pay grade," Mike said, "but I figured you'd find it further grist for your mill. And before you say anything more, I'll see what else I can find out."

"With my gratitude," I said.

"Always," he answered.


Terry and Bobby lingered over coffee. Figuring that the ballerina would return to her palatial room I followed the History teacher home. She lived in a modest apartment in Springfield, a nasty commute that involves a crawl across the Shirley Highway (or Dieway as it is sometimes known). If Dr. Winslow was a Chinese agent she was doing so because of some misplaced idealism; she wasn't on any payroll that would contribute materially to her bottom line and quality of life.

# FORTY

The next morning I checked in with Mike. If Tereza had risen for breakfast she had done so via room service. He hadn't turned anything new on the Winslow woman but he had added her to his tracking list.

I prepared myself to spring into action the moment Mike was able to detect any significant movement on Tereza's part. There was none until the following day. While I was grateful for the respite I was becoming more and more concerned about Richard.

When she returned to the Senate Office Building I was following her. Same room. Same committee. Different dress. She positioned herself directly behind the probable location of the witness chair. This time we were live and I could see the full expanse of the room and the female figure who was taking Tereza's picture. It was a young Asian woman who was dressed like a tourist but carrying thousands of dollars worth of *Leica's* best.

I was able to secure a list of the individuals who would be testifying before the Agriculture, Nutrition and Forestry Committee. The subject was the beef and pork industry, with governors from various large state producers. As far as I could tell, the committee's focus would be on costs, since they had scheduled sympathetic economists as well as a representative from the Office of the Secretary of Agriculture.

As soon as I could find a secure area I called Mike. "The Senate committee on Ag, Nutrition and Forestry is meeting again and Tereza has appeared for a preliminary closeup."

"I noticed," he said.

"I need some help," I said.

"I'm at your beck and call," he answered.

"This particular committee met recently…"

"Yes, and the ballerina was there at that time."

"I want you to check and see if there was any overlap between the individuals testifying then and those testifying today. Do you have access to today's list? If you don't, I do. They're on a schedule posted outside the door of the room where the committee is meeting."

"I do. Remember, I'm a historian but also a hopelessly-devoted spy."

"Great. Whatever name or names surface for each event I want you to check against the events on or around the time of our sightings in Pasadena and Cincinnati."

"I can do that. What are you thinking?"

"I'm thinking that someone is taking pictures of the ballerina and then photoshopping her image to make it appear that she was present for those events. That way she could have been there before, during or after the actual occurrences. We didn't notice anything suspicious in her appearances except for their emptiness and banality."

"*Banality*. I like it. And you know what?"

"What's that, Mike?"

"With the current developments in AI the photoshop ploy has been taken to whole new levels."

"I understand. The problem's often in the background. People see the face on the body and the image is convincing, but the background isn't synched. Or the lighting."

"Especially the lighting," Mike said. "It's all in the shadows and how the rays of natural or artificial light fall across such things as the folds of the person's clothing. As you said, we're so taken with the fact that some familiar face is appearing in an unexpected position or location that we forget to check on the fine details. It's no problem for some teenager trying to embarrass a classmate; put a chaste face on a nude body and all of their mutual 'friends' sit up and take notice. The damage is done; the story is out; the tears flow."

"But if we're talking about something far more serious…(and I know that the vicious teenage attacks are serious to the poor kids involved)… but if we're talking about something that's as serious as compromising national security…"

"Or risking the life of a friend and former Bureau agent…"

"Yes. If we're talking about something like that we're talking about serious players and serious players have access to technology beyond the public's current imagining."

"I'll check the names and our other locales," he said.

"Soonest?"

"Always."

I followed Tereza back to her hotel and found a quiet corner where I could sip some ridiculously-overpriced coffee and wait for Mike's call. It took him two hours.

"Harrison Thompson," he said.

"Texas governor."

"The very same."

"He was at both of the committee hearings."

"He was indeed," Mike said. "And he was in Pasadena, flogging his book with the innocuous title."

"Land of Liberty, or something like that," I said.

"*Our Land of Liberty*," Mike said.

"Everybody writes a book before they run for national office," I said.

"Or has someone write it for them," Mike said. "I think he may have actually written this one himself. The advertising material contains some long quotations and they're full of down-home colloquialisms."

"Trying to show that he's not all hat and no cattle."

"Score," Mike said, "but he's also a serious candidate. Some would say the *most* serious candidate."

"So he was in *Vroman's* to do a signing."

"Three days after the ballerina got her picture taken."

"What was the deal in Cincinnati?"

"Fundraiser. Two days after her solo picture was taken. (That might be why she was inquiring about a large table, trying to find out where it would most likely be located.) I was able to check their CCTV system and saw the other people at what turned out to be the center table: a veritable CEO conclave: *P&G, Kroger, Western & Southern Financial Group, GE Aerospace, Fifth Third Bank*…you name it; they were there. Some were hardcore donors; some were probably potential donors, scoping out Harry Thompson's answers to the questions that most affected their organizations."

"I wonder why the people at the restaurant didn't mention it. I can understand *Vroman's*; every major book signer passes through their doors. A senator here, a governor there, a sports hall of famer, a Hollywood star who fell from the skies…but a steak house on the Norwood border?"

"I actually called the manager there," Mike said. "He said, 'you didn't ask'. I think he may have been a little p.o.'d that we hadn't acknowledged his vaunted position on the Queen City gastronomic pantheon. He got a little huffy with me and said, 'we have distinguished guests here every night'."

"I ate there," I said. "*Le Bernardin* it was not."

"I believe he was thinking *The French Laundry* league," Mike said.

"In his dreams. Anyway, good work. The best."

"Care to hazard a guess on what the ballerina was up to?"

"I can guess," I said.

# FORTY-ONE

"**G**o," Mike said.

"Harry Thompson is in his mid-to-late fifties; Tereza is around twenty-two or three. Harry has five kids and a wife with whom he attends weekly mass (daily mass, for him, when his schedule permits). His administration has been free of corruption. He lives modestly, drives a ten year-old car. He's ex-military. Your basic moral paragon…"

"And it would be beaucoup embarrassing to learn that he had been seen in the presence of a foreign ballerina, almost certainly a lover, possibly a spy."

"It would destroy his presidential aspirations and he's not one of fifteen or twenty primary candidates with middling credentials; he's got the pole position."

"And those people with access to the state-of-the-art AI software? They don't much care for him."

"They loathe him," I said. "The Russians, the Chinese, the North Koreans, the Iranians…all of the countries his base and a goodly number of independents fear (and also loathe) would be far happier with a candidate from mush town."

"You need to talk to him," Mike said.

"From your lips to the Director's ears," I said.


"We have to move on this as quickly as possible," the Director said. "I've called Harry; we'll set up a conference room for a late dinner this evening. I'll want you there, of course. Peggy will arrange to bring him to the room without drawing any attention. I don't want someone inferring that he's under investigation or anything like that."

"Understood," I said. "How about his wife? Will she be there?"

"Back in Plano," he said. "He knows the bare outline of our situation and immediately wanted to bring his wife into the discussion but she was already en route to Dulles and any interruption of her plans might have drawn unwanted attention."

"What time do you want me there, Sir?"

"8:15."

"I'll be there."


Peggy brought him into the conference room at 8:20. He looked tired but not disheveled. Wearing a modest suit and tie he could have passed for one of Edgar's best. He wore his hair in the same length as he did when he was an Army one-star but it was now gray around the edges. He and the Director embraced.

"I appreciate this, General," the Governor said. The Director introduced us and the Governor told me that he was aware of my work. "So glad we've got the first team on this," he said to the Director. Then he looked at the punch bowl on the table and said, "You shouldn't have, but I'm certainly glad that you did."

"Artillery punch?" I asked, noticing it for the first time.

"Peggy's handiwork," the Director said. "The most lethal potable known to humankind. Unfortunately, we didn't have time to do the whole sugared lemon peel muddling operation, but we've created a substitute that features all of the essential ingredients: black tea, cognac, rum, bourbon and champagne. There's some lemon peel there for garnish."

"My lord, that's good," the Governor said, drinking half a cup in one swallow.

"You may not be aware of it, Gwen, but Harry was the garrison commander of Fort Sill back in the day. He's a certified cannon-cocker. He subscribes to that old belief that artillery adds dignity to what would otherwise be an ugly brawl."

"Frederick the Great's opinion, right?" I asked.

"I told you this was the first team," the Governor said.

"I appreciate the compliment," I said, "but I'm smart enough to know when I'm in the presence of the actual first team."

They both smiled at that and the Governor tipped his punch cup toward me in thanks.

"In addition to the Governor's role, Harry's still in the National Guard," the Director said. "We don't do business very often but when we do we tend to have a record of success."

The door opened as we were finishing our second cup of punch. The caterer brought in the steaks and baked potatoes along with a green bean casserole dish that contained bacon and crispy fried onions. It reminded me of Thanksgiving at my grandmother's house. The caterer's assistant brought in two bottles of red wine, opened each and invited the Director to taste them. "There are others if these are not suitable," he said.

"They're fine," he responded and the caterers left the room. Neither had made serious eye contact when they were with us. "Souls of discretion," the Director said, "and my apologies…no bourbon and branch tonight."

The Governor smiled. "I think we'll survive," he said.

While we ate, the Director opened a folder, removed the pictures of Tereza and slid them over to the Governor, who looked at each of them. Three times.

As he did so I thought about the fact that if the Governor was elected POTUS he would pick his own AG and, hence, be the Director's ultimate boss, a crass thought, but then I remembered that the chain of command often shifts at the highest levels. Generals call each other by their first names and have a different relationship than other men and women in uniform. Still, Commanders-in-Chief are a different matter entirely.

The Governor looked at one picture in particular, the one from the restaurant in Cincinnati. He finally collected them and stacked them together at the side of his wine glass. "Very pretty young lady but not quite in the league of a Texas head-turner," he said. "I've never seen her before."

"Gwen thinks that they may have been taken to embarrass you; they would be photoshopped with the best AI tweaks and when the finished products were released she would be seen standing or sitting near you on multiple occasions."

"My side squeeze," he said.

"Something like that," I said.

"Damn clever," he said. "A kind of variation on your traditional honeytrap, except that we'd never have to even meet or be in the same room at the same time."

"They would figure that they couldn't succeed in tempting you, so they would have to go for simple guilt by association," I said.

"I appreciate the vote of confidence," the Governor said, smiling.

"Morality is your hallmark," the Director said. "Guilt by association would be more than enough to impugn it."

"The real problem," the Governor said, "would be determining who wants to destroy my reputation. That line is long, Walt."

"The woman was seen having dinner with an academic who specializes in China's more recent geopolitical moves. She was photographed in the Senate committee room by a young Asian woman, whose camera would have put Weegee's old *Speed Graphic* to shame."

He looked at me and said, "Way before your time."

"I know his work," I said. "His specialty was crime scenes, fires, accidents—any and all images from the darkest streets on the darkest side of town."

"If memory serves, he was from the Ukraine," the Governor said. "This woman…remind me…"

"The Czech Republic," I said.

"I thought I was in contemporary America," the Governor said. "Suddenly I feel like I'm the fall guy in a good old black-and-white Orson Welles movie. So what do you want me to do?"

The Director answered.

"Right after the woman entered our country one of our former agents—a man on the scene when she arrived—disappeared. Completely. He simply vanished. No body. No ransom notes. No evidential trail. We want to find him before they're forced to change their plans and they decide that they need to eliminate him (assuming for the moment that he's still alive). The bottom line is that we don't want to precipitate any actions on her part that might spook her handlers. Another less than pleasant point is that it would appear to be the case that someone in your office who would be aware of the details of your schedule has either been sloppy or willing to share them with someone on the opposing team."

His face fell slightly but he acknowledged that that was a possibility. "A lot is in the public record, of course, but I'll give that some thought. No one but my top assistants should know about the finer points of political fundraising, but don't worry. I won't play junior G-man and put the interns, mid-levels and volunteers on guard."

"The best thing that you could do is take a mini-vacation," the Director said. "Go home for awhile, maybe do some dove or quail hunting or something else that would be in character and not raise any eyebrows or set off any jungle tom-toms. Tell the members of your staff that you can be reached by phone but that you want some time to relax and recoup after your book tour, senate testimony, and so on."

"I can do that. On another subject…when do you expect them to attempt to use the pictures against me?"

"Sometime closer to the election," the Director said. "If I'm them and I'm feeling malicious I'd let you raise money, spend it on the primaries and then blow up your chances before you have the time to explain, redeem, or exonerate yourself."

"This is a big deal, isn't it?" he asked.

"Meddling in an American election? Attempting to change the face of global political realities? It's damned big," the Director said.

"I wouldn't bet any serious money on the girl's chances of surviving this," the Governor said. "The moment they've made their point she would become expendable. They wouldn't want her questioned by law enforcement and they wouldn't want her badgered by the press and the chattering class. Your basic dead woman walking. They'd probably get her out of the country first and then arrange the disappearing act. Now you see her, now you don't. Just like your former special agent."

"I can't disagree with that," the Director said. "She's being used. She may not even understand the general direction of their plans and motives. She's been out of the limelight for years and now someone wants her to initiate a modeling career. It's all very sketchy and suspicious but the money is good and she's sleeping at the *Four Seasons*."

"Deep pockets in the shadows," the governor said. "Are you thinking about approaching her? You don't have to answer that if you'd rather not."

"Haven't decided yet," the Director said. "In the current moment we're more interested in protecting our former agent than in protecting her, but if the latter might aid us in the former it would be something we'd have to consider."

"Understood," he said. "Anyway, when all is said and all is done I want you to know how much I appreciate your help in getting us…and me…through this. Ever been dove hunting, Walt?"

"No. I've always specialized in jihadists," the Director answered.

The Governor smiled. We shook hands, said our good-byes and turned the Governor over to Peggy, who made sure that he got out of the building unnoticed.

He turned to me and said, "Sit down, Gwen. Peggy will have made the coffee and we need to talk."

# FORTY-TWO

"What do you think?"

"Solid citizen," I said. "Calm under pressure. He'll partner with us effectively. I could even see myself voting for him."

"Had some combat experience in the past," the Director said. "Good leader. Good instincts. Good values."

"Do you think we should approach the woman, let her know where she stands, the degree to which she's at risk?"

"She surely knows that what she's doing is illegal and dangerous. How do you think she got to the island in Maine? Probably on some boat in international waters, followed by a ride on a nondescript fishing boat. She knew she wasn't on a luxury cruise on *Royal Caribbean* and she wouldn't have been so stupid as to assume that her mission was some innocuous modeling gig. If she was that big of a fool they wouldn't have brought her on for the job. She's also aware that she's traveling under an assumed name. It could well be that she's acting under duress. Perhaps she has family or friends back home who've been threatened."

"Always a possibility," I said.

"If so, we could be of aid."

"True," I said, "assuming she would trust us more than she would fear them."

"Let me mull it over. You think about it as well. Meanwhile, if Harry returns to Plano and tells his people in Austin he's taking a few days' off that will buy us a little time. If, indeed, there's a leaker in his organization the real string-pullers might be suspicious when he or she reports to them but they'll hold off for awhile. Governors *do* take vacations, especially when they can include long weekends."

"Things are pretty quiet in Austin these days," I said. "Everyone knows he's running for the big job and they'll expect him to be spending less and less time in the office."

"What a system," the Director said. "When it comes to politicking and election time (which is now 24/7/365) the regular jobs can somehow be put on hold. What's the implicit assumption? Texas is tiny and there are only 30+ million residents. Small-town mayor's job?"

"Even if you can't delegate responsibility you can delegate authority," I said. "And they do."

"That is a roger," the Director said. "Probably our primary modus operandi these days. And many will also try to delegate the responsibility."


I drove home and texted Mike, asking him to see if he could find a possible leaker in the Austin statehouse, whether or not Tereza had relatives or friends who could be threatened back in the homeland and also to do a deep dive on the Georgetown historian.

He wrote back immediately and asked, "What about the little Asian girl with the big and expensive *Leica*?"

"Her too," I said.

"On it," he answered.


The next morning Mike offered his thoughts on several possible leakers in the Governor's organization. Most of them were eager youngsters whose naivety exceeded their inexperience. "I'll keep working on the specifics, but as long as the Governor keeps his location and plans vague the leaker will be neutralized but not be alerted to the possibility of his or her exposure."

He also had some information on Tereza's family. "Her father died young, in a car accident. Nothing appears to have aroused any suspicions. The wall had fallen; the Czechs were free again. It was simply hard luck. Tereza was raised by her mom whose health is now reported to be 'fragile'.

The family was never wealthy; Tereza's dancing was all state-funded and when that went south she had to work in order for her and her mom to keep body and soul together."

"Luck has never been on her side."

"No, it hasn't," Mike said. "I can easily imagine that she would jump at any opportunity to right the ship, even if it meant bending some rules. Her life has been a succession of small tragedies. Her dancing skills no longer serve her; the only thing remaining is her natural beauty. Her mom is still attractive and her father was good looking as well, at least from what I could see in his obituary and the occasional pictures of the couple in the popular press."

"And there's no one else back in the old country who could be threatened in order to compel Tereza to do her handlers' bidding."

"None that I could see. There were no brothers or sisters and no romantic interest. The principal tabloid in Prague, a paper called *Blesk*, ran a human interest story on her a few years ago. It was a kind of 'where are they now?' piece. The main theme was that her life has been a run of systematically bad events. She's not even the proverbial poor little rich girl."

"Just a poor little poor girl," I said.

"That's about the size of it," he responded. "I've also got some information on that Winslow woman…"

"Let's hear it," I said.

"OK. It's a tale as old as time, at least as old as the days of the Bolshies. And you've heard it all before."

"Student activist? True believer? Useful idiot?"

"All of the above. Smith has something called the Jandon Center for Community Engagement. It looks like young Roberta practically lived there 24/7. If there was a cause she was for it; if there was an enormity she was against it. Not only did she involve herself in every cause de jour, she also involved herself in things that would reasonably be considered beyond her ambit. She isn't black; she isn't a Native American; she isn't gay; she had no coursework in environmental studies; she had no technical knowledge of nutrition or so-called food insecurity. She's not a Latina; she's not a Palestinian…"

"Like Groucho's song, whatever it is she's against it…or, as the case may be, for it."

"Precisely. What she is is a kid from a wealthy family in Armonk. Dad's an investment banker; Mom's a clubwoman extraordinaire. Each probably drives a Tesla (or did, until Elon did something to rub them the wrong way). The interesting thing is that she had her hands (and nose) in so many things that it made the local paper."

"You mean the student newspaper?"

"No, the *Daily Hampshire Gazette*."

"*Pravda*, northeast."

"That's it," Mike said. "They're not generally into humor, but they wrote a piece about her stereotypical activism. Their readership was not amused. They rushed to her defense, using words like 'heroine' and 'dedicated leader' and 'hope for the future'."

"Columbia probably liked that. Actually, they probably also liked the fact that Mom and Dad could pay the full freight for grad school. She would be like one of those highly-coveted, deep-pocketed foreign students."

"Dad's a contributor to Georgetown, even though he has no personal connections there. He went to Yale and Wharton. Roberta's much younger brother is a Williams alum doing a grad degree at Stanford."

"Sounds like Mom and Dad are running interference for their daughter's academic career."

"Nice if you can afford it. Some members of the porcine set always seem to be more equal than others."

"So now she's working for the Chinese government?" I asked.

"As you know, the Chinese have their thumbs in every academic plum pie that could matter to them. A program here…an institute there…a whole pisspot full of paying students everywhere, students whose curriculum includes the requirement that they report back to their Beijing handlers."

"With their eyes on our intellectual property as well as our ideological complicity," I added.

"They have their eyes on *everybody's* intellectual property," Mike said.

"What about the Asian photographer at the back of the Senate meeting room?"

"Chinese. A student at American University."

"I wonder why she's there rather than GU or GW."

"This will not surprise you," Mike said. "AU offers a major in something called 'Computational Media and Applied Perception'."

"Bingo," I said.

"And Ya Qi is one of their students. By the way, Ya Qi means something like 'lucky'."

"Unlike Tereza."

"Exactly," Mike said.

"I'm going to get back in touch with the Director."

"Thought you might," Mike said. "I put the essential information in a folder for you; it includes some pictures of our three fair ladies."

"You're the best," I said.


As soon as I contacted Peggy she put me on hold, returned in a minute and scheduled a meeting for me with the Director. "At his home," she said. "DoorDash at 8:00?"

"Done," I said.

# FORTY-THREE

"Next steps?" he asked, as he mixed some *Bombay Sapphire* Martinis. "I think it's time," I said, "given what we now know about the current principals…"

"You want to rattle some cages?"

"Not so much that. I think we should talk to Tereza and the Winslow woman, let them know that they may be in some danger and suggest that they do their best to stay beneath the radar for awhile. The proximate intention would be to make their handlers queasy."

"Queasy?"

"Yes. Let them know that someone on our side has noticed something. We don't know what. We don't know why. We don't know who. We just know that something's not right."

"You're worried that if we don't do something Richard's condition could go south. And if we do something too…direct…it will definitely go south."

"Right, Sir. I believe that the women, certainly Tereza, *are* at risk. The moment they've served their purpose they'll be considered expendable."

"And liquidated."

"Yes, Sir."

"And probably Richard as well."

"Assuming he's still alive. If the only reason for his disappearance was the possibility that he might have seen Tereza come ashore…well, he could already be lost."

"Perhaps it's the fact that he saw the ballerina's handler."

"Certainly that's possible," I said.

"Or perhaps they have some future role for him to play."

"Fall guy?" I asked.

"That would be my assumption," he said. "The bottom line is that you want to roil their boats with some waves and see how they respond."

"Yes, Sir. Does that make sense to you?"

"It's a risk but that's one of the key reasons why we have such things as patrols—to probe and see if we can prompt a response."

"Recon by fire, Sir?"

"Yes, Gwen, but we start with pistol-caliber carbines and hold off on the naval guns until we know more."

"I think we should keep the Bureau out of the picture, Sir, at least for the moment. Let the ladies think they're dealing with some organization less threatening."

"Just Tereza and Roberta Winslow."

"Yes, Sir. You're not going to turn the Chinese student. She'll obey her handlers, come hell, high water or direct threat."

"So we send in someone from, something like what, the Capitol Police?"

"Forgive me, but I was thinking…"

The Director smiled and took a sip of his Martini. "Maybe one of our people but with one of their badges?"

"Maybe a trainee at Quantico. Someone whose identity can't be easily tracked electronically."

"And when they try to identify the person and fail…that might be another wave against the bow of their boat."

I sipped my Martini and returned his smile.

"You trust our people more than the Capitol Police?'

"I'd keep the circle of trust as small as possible."

"I think that could be arranged," he said.

The Director suggested we send in a woman. "Less threatening," he said, "at least for the ballerina. We can offer the History teacher some sterner stuff."

"Some of us can do threatening," I said, smiling.

"This person's job is to put a gloved hand on the cell and rattle it softly," he said. "I've got you waiting on the sidelines to do the crushing tackles."

I just smiled.

"Besides," he added, "with a woman we'll have longer hair and it will be easier to cover the earpiece."

"In case she needs prompting."

He just nodded.


The trainee selected was named Janice Campagna. Short in stature and a 25 year-old who could pass for 18, Janice was compact and wiry. She had aced every physical test in the training curriculum and was brimming with self-confidence. When asked about her willingness to take on the assignment she had said, "Sounds like fun; when do we start?"

"In an hour," she was told.

Janice wasn't given the full array of information on the larger case but she knew that there was a former special agent who might be in danger. "Let's skip the coffee and start now," she said.

Janice was equipped with a buttoned jacket, one of whose leather-appearing buttons contained a body camera with a pinhole lens. She was also given a nondescript badge with the name 'Mary Louise Gleason' and a long i.d. number. The Director, Mike and I were able to watch the performance and a top Bureau interrogator named Bill Hemmings was able to observe her work and communicate with her if he thought that she needed prompting, correcting or an increase or decrease in intensity. I had seen Bill work in the past; he was the best.

She began the next morning with Tereza, who was having breakfast in the 'Seasons' room of her posh hotel. She was halfway through a plate of waffles with sides of fresh fruit and crisp bacon. Janice approached her and said, "Tereza Petrů. My childhood idol!"

"I am afraid you are mistaken," Tereza replied. "My name is Veronika."

Janice looked at the chair opposite Tereza's table and asked, "May I?" and then sat down before Tereza could reply.

"I have always wanted to dance like you, but I lacked the legs and the feet," she said, smiling and oozing empathy. "How is your foot?"

"I assure you that I am not a dancer," Tereza said.

"And I am not a ballerina," Janice replied, opening her wallet just enough to expose her badge. "I am an officer with the Capitol Police. You were observed in a Senate committee room. Twice. A Chinese student took your picture using very expensive equipment. Before that you were in Cincinnati and, before that, you were seen in a bookstore in a Los Angeles suburb."

Tereza sat silently, putting her fork on the edge of her plate and taking a long sip of her black coffee.

"Facial recognition software is a wonderful thing," Janice said, "and it is…unforgiving. The pictures of your face as a child prodigy contain the same proportions as your current images. There is no question concerning your actual identity. I am here to deliver a message to you."

"And what would that be?" Tereza asked.

"You have not yet been observed committing a crime, but we have no doubt that you are involved with (or are being used by) individuals who would not hesitate to eliminate you once your assignment has been completed. You are, to put it simply, at very great risk."

"Are you truly serious?"

"I believe the proper idiomatic response to that is that we are as serious as a heart attack, though I would expect something more like a car accident or a staged 'suicide'."

Tereza paused before speaking. "And what would you suggest that I do?"

"Nothing," Janice said. "At least nothing that would contribute positively to your handlers' plans."

"Nothing?"

"When I leave there will be a vial of medication left on the table.

The chemicals will incapacitate you for a number of days. There will be symptoms suggesting that you have an upper respiratory infection. Your eyes will redden and water. You will have a cough and a nose that runs constantly. It will not kill you. It will simply be unpleasant. The important thing is that it will keep you from doing any serious 'modeling' work."

"Why are you doing this?" she asked.

"Because we don't want to see you die and we don't want to see your handlers succeed in whatever it is that they're attempting to do."

"And now I suppose that it is my turn to respond by thanking you," she said.

"No need," Janice said. "The vial is unmarked but be certain that you discard it without anyone being able to observe you doing so. I will slide it under the edge of your plate on my right, your left. The CCTV camera to your right (don't look up at it now) will lack the line of sight that could reveal it. When I leave you should shake my hand, force a smile and then add an expression of frustration, as if to say that your time had been wasted. Signal the waitress to refill your coffee and sip it slowly. Check your makeup, put your napkin next to your plate and simultaneously remove the vial, slipping it into your purse. Go to the women's bathroom, enter a stall, ingest the medication and flush the vial down the toilet. Then simply go about your business. If anyone questions you later about my meeting with you tell them that I was a journalist who thought she recognized you but was eventually persuaded that she was mistaken."

"You are frightening me," she said.

"You *should* be frightened," Janice said. "The individuals who are using you would not hesitate to eliminate you once your usefulness is no longer needed."

# FORTY-FOUR

"What a pro," the Director said. "We were lucky Tereza had chosen a dark corner for her breakfast meal. There was no one in the area who could have monitored the meeting."

"And it was perfect that we left out any mention of her time in Maine. The Capitol Police would be worried about a threat to a member of Congress or one of their witnesses. If she takes a risk and talks to the string-pullers they'll know that law enforcement finds her actions very suspicious but has no inkling of her original entrance on the scene and any possible link with Richard's disappearance."

"You guided her, Gwen."

"Yes, Sir. I'm just glad it went so smoothly."

"Next stop: the Department of History?"

"Yes, Sir," I said.


Roberta Winslow's office hours were from 3:00-4:00 that afternoon. When she entered the room she was immediately followed by Janice, who had been standing outside the door, checking her cell phone. This time the meeting was harsher— the kind described by the British as 'without coffee.'

"You're not one of my students," Roberta said.

"Thank God," Janice replied. "I'm a member of the Capitol Police."

"I want to see your badge," Roberta said.

"If you see my badge you'll also see a set of cuffs," Janice said. "You're not under arrest. You're not charged with anything. Yet."

"What do you want?"

"Turn off the campus agitator posturing," Janice said. "You're not in the streets of Northampton talking to a teenager with a handmade protest sign. You're in the District of Columbia and you were observed meeting with a woman from the Czech Republic who's operating in our country under an alias. From every indication that we have been able to establish you are friendly with the government of the People's Republic of China. A student from the PRC was observed taking the picture of the Czech woman immediately after you had met with her. She was in a meeting room of the Senate. The picture was a professional one and there was no one else in the room observing them (they thought). A reasonable person would assume that the picture would be used in a way that would not be in the best interests of our government. Would you like to hear the bottom line?"

"I'd like you to leave and I'd like to report your threatening me. I think you're a pig."

"Technically that would be a sow," Janice said (ad-libbing). "And I'm not hear to threaten; I'm hear to warn. It is our view that you are involved in something that would…shall we say… not redound to your personal benefit. Let me put that more directly. You're not making the world a better place; you're plunging in so far over your head that you risk being crushed like some brown, crawly thing that just emerged from the baseboards of a D.C. tenement. If you think that you are up to dealing in that league, be our guest. In the meantime, you should stick to grading papers and sitting in pointless department meetings. If it were me I might take some long weekends in Armonk, eat out on mommy and daddy's dime and try your best to stay out of the line of fire."

Roberta looked as if she wanted to say something abusive, but instead she simply walked to the door and opened it, indicating to Janice that it was time to depart. As she did, Janice turned her body toward Roberta's and gave us all a closeup of Roberta's right hand that held the edge of the door. It was shaking. Noticeably.

"The 'sow line' alone was worth the price of admission," the Director said. "What do you think is going through her mind?"

"I suspect she's trying to decide on whether or not to travel to New York by plane or by train," I said.

"So now we wait, but not for very long," the Director said. "While Janice was talking to the ballerina we were installing listening devices throughout her hotel room and while she was talking to the History teacher we were filling the activist's modest home with them. They might circumvent our efforts by using burner phones, calling from dark corners at odd hours, but we've circumscribed them a bit. If they think they're safe and alone in their normal domiciles we'll be there, all ears. Listening in on your neighbors in Forest Hills is a little bit trickier, but we're not without options."

He was referring to the Chinese Embassy, approximately two miles from my apartment in Northwest D.C.

"If they make any moves," he added, "we'll follow with our own, but we'll keep it low-key, at least for the moment. Richard's condition is my main concern and I don't want to jeopardize it in any way. Meanwhile, I want you to give this some thought. We'll talk in a day or two."

"Yes, Sir," I said.

# FORTY-FIVE

I had an early dinner, savoring some of *Clyde's* chili, looked over my notes, hoping to find inspiration and insight. Finding neither I drove home and turned in for the night, happy to be in my own bed but unhappy with my personal progress on the case. Mike had been a stalwart and the Director was devoting a great deal of his precious time to Richard's plight (or dilemma, or…whatever it was). I had been too much of an observer and speculative theorist, but no matter how much concern I could muster I always seemed to come up short on actual plans. Perhaps it was the nature of the case.

Normally when I need time to think I drive to Great Falls and let the sound of the waters crashing over the rocks drown out the distractions. The setting is primal; it keeps you focused on the basics—power, beauty, the irrevocable passage of time. This time I decided to change gears and drive to the Blue Ridge. My destination was my favorite Virginia winery, *Naked Mountain*, a 50+ year-old facility that served light meals to thirsty travelers. It's just about a 50 mile/hour's drive from my apartment, enough distance to change both the scenery and my current state of mind. I arrived there a few minutes later than expected, ordered some food and promptly washed down half of a Caprese sandwich with some of their Chardonnay/Riesling blend and stared at the views beyond their deck. There were two families there, each with inquisitive children who were more interested in the local birds than their lunches. A pileated woodpecker and red-tailed hawk were attracting most of their attention, the hawk being a featured part of the winery's original logo.

As I thought about my situation (and, far more important, Richard's) the simple facts suddenly hit me like a 50-ounce baseball bat across the bridge of my nose. The coastline of Maine was dramatic and quaint and lovely in a raw way. It was primal, like Great Falls, but there was little more than a couple hundred miles of it. The continental U.S., on the other hand, had a coastline of nearly 100,000 miles and a collective desert area of some 300,000-400,000 square miles—endless choices for a place to drop off Tereza.

So why do that in Washington County, Maine? One obvious reason would be the fact that the general coastline of some 228 miles was quite different than the bays/coves/inlets tidal shoreline of 3,500 miles—a greater shoreline than that of California. However, as established and ultimately predictable as that shoreline might be it was still subject to fog and nor'easters and other unanticipated actions of Nature. It might offer cover and concealment, but it also presented major logistical problems. I thought about the D-Day Invasion; the German defenses were a formidable obstacle, but the major ringer in the operation was the weather. The drug cartels were well aware of that nexus of possibilities. While they might occasionally use boats they generally relied on porous southern borders and trucks. If you've been to Nogales, Arizona and Nogales, Mexico you realize that the distance between them entails a drive that's probably shorter than the average neighborhood trip to *McDonald's*. You can walk across the border with proper identification and the only significant encounters you're likely to have are with the touts directing you to the local *farmacia* to purchase discount *Viagra*. There are eight lanes for inspecting trucks, but our dependence on Mexican produce eases the path.

In short, there were far easier options for Tereza's entry into the U.S. of A. She entered when Richard's company was holding their administrative retreat. She entered; Richard disappeared. That meant that there was an almost-certain connection between her mission and Richard's company, unless, of course, the conference center/hotel people were dirty, but why would a foreign government or some similar, larger entity deal with them when it had so many other options, particularly options that could involve certifiably-dirty organizations with whom they had long done business. In the northeastern woods you rolled the dice and could be dealing with Larry, Darryl and Darryl. It would be far easier to deal with the experienced, well-equipped and heavily-armed boys from Sinaloa, particularly if you already had a relationship in place through which you supplied them with precursor chemicals for their labs.

The conclusion seemed inescapable. Someone in the *Kommunicom* extended family was directing the operation (or, perhaps, had come up with the idea), someone who was sleazy enough to be trusted by the puppet masters, someone who knew the local territory. Someone greedy and/or a dedicated crusader, i.e., a useful idiot. Someone who (and this was key) would ultimately be expendable. That left one significant problem beyond the identification of that individual (or, conceivably, individuals): the fact that those backstopping him or her could bring significant resources to bear on any threats that they might consider serious.

There was another possibility, one that I had momentarily suppressed. If the larger powers felt threatened they would almost certainly abort their operation and cut their losses. They would eliminate Tereza, the evil-doer or doers from *Kommunicom*, Professor Roberta and, instantly, Richard. If he was to be saved it would have to be done on a small scale, perhaps with some backup but, inevitably, by either a small number of individuals or a single individual, the most likely: yours truly.

# FORTY-SIX

I put down the remainder of my sandwich, took a sip of my wine and called Peggy. She told me that the Director had a dinner meeting with the AG and key leaders within the DOJ—the DEA, ATF, Bureau of Prisons, the Marshals Service…. "The whole alphabet-soup shebang," Peggy said. "It's best that you come in for breakfast. I have no idea how long the AG will want to hold forth after dinner. I also know that the Director's waiting on reports with regard to the principals in your case. He'll almost certainly know more in the morning. It'll have to be quick, however. He has to testify before Congress at 9:00 and he'll want a few minutes to prepare. Come in at 6:15."

"Will do," I said.

Breakfast was a plate of croissants and a carafe of black coffee. "You were right," the Director said. Professor Winslow flew into White Plains last night and is now ensconced in her old bedroom in mommy and daddy's $3.4 mil manse in Armonk. I suspect that she's hiding under the covers and doing her best not to suck her thumb. Tereza is still at the *Four Seasons*, but a maid has reported that she is taking meals in her room and battling the mother of all head colds. She commented in particular about her red eyes."

"They took Janice's advice to heart."

"We're nominating her for an Academy Award," he said. "Oh, and our student—Ya Qi—we're calling her 'Lucky' now… she had dinner last night with a member of the Chinese embassy staff."

"Someone of stature?"

"No, someone toward the bottom of the food chain. Probably for Lucky's own protection. They don't want to signal her presence as a member of their team. She and the woman from International Place dined off campus at a Chinese restaurant on 14th Street: *Great Wall Szechuan House*. I haven't been there. They say that the portions are generous and the prices are low. If you want to open a *Verizon* account you can do so next door."

"Street food; nondescript, anonymous."

"Especially in contrast to the embassy palace. It was designed by I. M. Pei and it's so feng shui-friendly that it's impossible to escape the harmony, peace, prosperity and good health that the French limestone exudes."

"Different menus for the diners at the embassy."

"Yes. Lucky and her friend had spring rolls and Kung Pao Chicken."

"Any reports on the conversation?" I asked.

"I just got the translation from our expert in Mandarin," he said. "It sounds as if they were trying to talk in code. Stuff like…

> 'We are missing your friend.'
> 'She is ill. It is not serious.'
> 'Will she recover soon?'
> 'She is expected to do so.'
> 'We love to see your photographs of her. She is a lovely lady.'
> 'Hopefully she will be able to pose in a few days.'
> 'That would please everyone.'"

"So," I said, "this is very important."

"Right. We now have the connection between the ballerina's activities and the PRC."

"Did they say anything about the Winslow woman?"

"They said that her (i.e. Tereza's) 'manager' was visiting with her family and that she should be returning shortly."

"Did they exhibit any concerns or nervousness about either development?"

"Lucky was playing the loyal servant. What's the expression? A lickspittle? If she was any more obsequious the other diners would have wondered what she was doing at the embassy woman's feet. The embassy woman…well, she was as firm and frigid as Princess Turandot."

"What would Mike Liu say—if you throw a super ball in any bureaucracy you'll hit a dozen people like that?"

"Yes," the Director said. "Their idea of patriotism generally entails the employment perk that the common people will abase themselves at your feet. Anyway, the result of all of this is that we've bought a couple of days. What should we do with them?"

I summarized my thoughts for him.

"So you want to return to western New York and you'd like some backup."

"Yes, Sir. I'd like to have Ben, if he's available."

(Ben, or as he was more often called, *Doc,* had completed every military course in the Army's combat curriculum. Airborne. Ranger. Pathfinder. More recently: Sapper. We had worked together before. As the poet would say, if you looked up the word *lethal* in a dictionary you would find his picture there.)

"He would be my choice," the Director said, "but he is presently in the Ukraine. And he's not on vacation there."

"Is there a second option?" I asked.

"Why don't we do this," he said. "You begin the next stage of your investigation and I'll see if he can be made available."

"Works for me, Sir," I said.

"You've already scoped out the key people at Richard's company," he said. "You're going to want to do some anonymous tracking."

"Yes, Sir. A day's travel, followed by a week or more's investigation…"

"Hopefully I can get Ben rested and ready by then, though he generally doesn't require a great deal of rest."

# FORTY-SEVEN

We decided that a slightly less prominent hotel might help to preserve my anonymity and settled on a *Hilton Garden Inn* in a section of the suburbs called Bushnell's Basin. Peggy made a reservation for me and I went home to pack.

I chose a number of different outfits, packed some miscellaneous implements and cleaned my *Sig*. As I reinstalled the barrel, spring and slide and performed a function check, my phone rang. Since so many of my professional communications were done via laptop or burner phone I was a bit surprised. 'Probably someone trying to sell me long-term car repair insurance,' I thought.

I was wrong. It was Janice Campagna.

"Special Agent Harrison," she said, "I hope it's all right to communicate with you like this."

"Actually it's a pleasant surprise," I said. "And call me Gwen. What can I do for you?"

"I'll get right to it," she said. "I'd like you to help me. I hate the word, but I'd like you to, well, advise me. I can't say *mentor* without gagging. Just…advise."

"I've never been asked to be someone's rabbi," I said. "Maybe it's time that I did. There's a big problem, however. My role in the Bureau is…well, an odd one. The vertical chain of command and bureaucracy is not where I usually live. My cases are sometimes weird and almost always out of the ordinary. I have to respect the ladder but I don't spend much of my time climbing it."

"I don't want to climb the ladder for the sake of rank and titles," she said. "I want to learn how to find the bad guys and take them down."

"Lately I haven't been as successful at that as I would like to be," I said, "but I'd be happy to talk to you about my attempts and misadventures. Unfortunately, I'm heading out on a special assignment in the morning."

"I have an evening's pass from my training," she said. "I'd love to get together tonight."

I looked at my watch; it was 10:50 a.m.

"Where are you now?" I asked.

"Quantico."

"Sit tight for a couple minutes; I'll see if I can get us in anywhere this evening. It will probably have to be very early."

"I can be wherever you want me to be," she said.


I called her back in four minutes. "Success," I said. *L'Auberge Chez François* will take us at 4:30. Have you been there before?"

"No. I'm from Nebraska, Gwen. This will be my first restaurant with a French name."

"It's highly rated and not grotesquely overpriced," I said. "It's out in Great Falls. You'll enjoy the ride in the country. Come to my apartment and I'll drive us."

I gave her the directions to my place. We left for Great Falls at 3:30, just in case we ran into unexpected traffic. We made small talk along the way, mostly concerning the training at Quantico. We arrived at 4:10. Still a family-run restaurant, they allowed us to be seated early and order drinks. She ordered bourbon on the rocks without specifying a brand. I had an Old fashioned with *Maker's Mark*.

We were on our second when we ordered. She followed my lead, with onion soup and Tournedos (passing on the fois gras addition). We disciplined ourselves by restricting our further alcohol intake to a single glass of red wine. Then we got down to business.

"I don't want to waste your time with the obvious," Janice said. "I'm keeping myself in shape, paying attention in class and trying to absorb all of the instruction that comes between the lines. The biggest issue so far is that I've always tried to strike a balance between the needs and demands of a bureaucracy and the simultaneous need to demonstrate initiative and independence. It seems a little harder to do that now. I try to see the Bureau within its larger governmental context. I understand the importance of politics but I don't really care for it. I also have some concerns about the tech demands and the degrees of specialization within the organization."

"My concerns as well," I said. "I know we're not chasing Bonnie and Clyde and Pretty Boy Floyd these days but I don't want to be chained to a computer or tracing genealogical DNA. I understand the importance, even the centrality, of modern technology, but I've always wanted to be a detective, not a technician."

"The Director's Tracker," she said.

"I'm called that, I know," I said, "but it's more than just looking for tracks in the dust or the snow. It's being in the field; it's interacting with…well…soldiers. I have a great computer jock who supports me every step of the way, but I want to kick down doors and look into the eyes of people who thought they were too smart to ever be found."

"Exactly," she said. "And there's room in the Bureau for you to do those kinds of things."

"Yes," I said. "The Director we have now is a straight arrow guy. He's alert to political realities and a great bureaucratic in-fighter, but he knows that our fundamental job is to protect the citizenry. He was Creighton Abrams' aide back in the day. Abe was Patton's primo tanker. Sometimes Georgie followed orders; sometimes he skirted them. The key thing is that he won and the enemy feared him. With good reason. Walt Gradison smiles at that tradition and talks about the 'old ways' but everyone knows, in their heart of hearts, that he is first and foremost a winner and if you try to hurt his people, now *our* people, he'll grind you up in his tank tracks. In old Army doctrine those tracks were considered a weapon. There were cardboard pictures in day rooms of enemy soldiers caught beneath them. He's not afraid to use them."

"The problem is, what if the administration changes and we get saddled with a politician?"

"That's always the risk and always the resulting challenge," I said. "In that case we hunker down and try to insulate ourselves from the politicians and self-promoters. They're always a looming possibility, particularly in this profession, but we still do everything we can to help the Bureau protect the people and take down the most-wanted, not hold political pep rallies and persecute political opponents."

We finished our soup and took a sip of our wine.

"Let me ask you a journalist's question," Janice said.

"OK."

"What's the major lesson you've learned so far in your work?"

"Let me think about that for a second," I said, as the waitress cleared the table and made room for our beef and potatoes and green beans.

"I would say…well, let me put it like this. There's always a lot of talk about instinct and intuition. The inherited wisdom is that you're faced with a situation and your gut tells you to…go. Or to…stop. Whatever. It's part luck and part mystery. It just…happens. I think that's all bullcrap. There are no great secrets. It's all about hard work and learning and experience. When you decide not to walk across the Shirley Highway at rush hour it's not because of any intuition. It's because you've learned the dangers posed by steel vehicles hurtling across the landscape and the degree of protection afforded by a thin layer of gabardine over human flesh.

"I have a mental image of a human being. It's a stick figure with a huge funnel of experience behind him or her. When you act you bring all of that experience to bear. It flows like a wave to a point on a beach, a decision point. It occurs in a singular moment. You're either ready or you're not and if you're ready it's because you've prepared yourself to be ready. First, you have to know what you don't know. You have to be humble. You have to realize that life is very, very complicated and that your knowledge of it is ultimately very, very limited.

"Take a single case, a famous, iconic case—for example, the murder of Elizabeth Short or the old silent movie actor, William Desmond Taylor. These cases have been studied to death (no pun intended) and you can be aware of all of the literature on the cases and still not have an inkling of the identity of the actual perps. You have to keep plugging but sometimes the facts are simply unavailable and the conclusion is going to elude you.

"Then there's the broader learning. This isn't the knowledge of a wise old Greek, aware of the fact that, ultimately, he knows nothing. This is the knowledge of a *Jeopardy* player, not so much with trivia as with broad knowledge of all areas of human experience. I majored in geography, particularly human geography. Why is the west side of town the best side of town? Because the tanneries were on the east side, to spare the wealthy people the smells that came from them. That kind of knowledge doesn't solve a lot of crimes, but it's more helpful than a knowledge of astronomy. Ditto a knowledge of weaponry and psychology and chemistry. Dame Agatha was a nurse and an apothecary's assistant during the first World War. That's why she utilizes poisons in her stories. The Russians like to poison people; Vlad the Impaler was a little more direct in his methods of execution. The mob shoots you twice in the brain with small caliber rounds. The more you know about such things the more cases you can solve…"

"So, study."

"Endlessly," I said. "And practice. Have you seen Ricky Jay and his 52 assistants?"

"I've streamed it. The sleight of hand stuff is remarkable."

"Ask him how you learn to throw a card across the table and land it in some small, circumscribed space. It's not a matter of intuition. It's a matter of endless, tortuous practice. You want to fire a gun, throw a knife, take down a 265-pound man and cuff him? It's not a matter of theory; it's a matter of practice and experience—the old Army 4-P's:

Prior Planning Proper Performance. But also, Prior *Preparation* Proper Performance. By the way, how are the tournedos?"

"I forgot to eat them," Janice said, and quickly cut a slice and tasted it.

"It's why you order a house specialty," I said. "The line cooks have more experience making it. The evening's special? Probably more iffy. Before you order fish in a New York restaurant you read Anthony Bourdain on the local delivery schedules. You want the fresh stuff, the stuff sitting on the clean ice, not the dubious."

We passed on dessert and had some black coffee.

"To be continued?" she asked.

"As soon as I'm back in town," I answered.

# FORTY-EIGHT

As we drove back to Cathedral Heights we reverted to small talk. I could tell that Janice wanted to know more about the case I was working on, but I told her to restrain her curiosity. "I can't talk about it in detail now," I said. "When we wrap I'll tell you what I can."

"Fully understand," she said. "Thanks for dinner and thanks for all of your help."

"Not a problem," I said. "I have no private life and I enjoy talking with friends."

We both smiled at that.

I slept well enough that night but had to rise early to catch the breakfast flight from Dulles to Rochester. I had notified Mike that I was returning to my origin point and needed updated files on my principals—Bethe, Cline, Ruffino, Fuse and Phillips. I wanted information on their residences, spouses and, most important, their recent movements. I figured that if Richard was still alive someone had to at least be feeding him. His living conditions might be spartan but if he was to be of any use to the conspirator(s) he would have to be kept alive. In some ways that was reassuring, because whoever had abducted him would have two basic choices. The first was to simply kill him and eliminate the possibility that he could become an impediment to their operation. The best method would be to create an 'accident' that would establish an actual death and quell any investigations of the larger operation. The second choice would be to keep him alive, but the only purpose of that would be to utilize him in some way to further their operation. If he were to be kept alive he would need to be kept close to home; they wouldn't incarcerate him in some distant site, because that would require them to broaden their field of operations and, of necessity, bring other players into the (I hated the word) undertaking.

Someone outside of *Kommunicom* might be directing the operation in some ultimate way, but the choice had been made by someone deep-within or adjacent to the company to bring Tereza ashore at a place and time contiguous with the work of that company. I was back to my realities-of-the-American-coastline point. The conclusion, however tentative, was that he was being held in some obscure industrial or agricultural site close to town. A perp's basement or attic was another possibility, but more of a long shot because the locals would see his or her comings and goings and/or the spouses and families of the perp(s) would have to be aware of the activity.

This was all hypothetical and provisional but it was also commonsensical. Assuming that Richard was being kept alive he was almost surely being kept nearby. The good thing was that the town was smallish (just over a million people) and not a megalopolis. With all of the numbered highways it was a local truism (reinforced by Tony Giraldi) that you could get to any point in greater Rochester in twenty minutes. The bad thing was that we couldn't flood the area with special agents and signal the perp(s) that we were getting close, close enough for them to feel that it might be time for them to cut their losses.

Ben would be an enormously helpful asset, but he would not be available for several days, days in which the clock measuring the remainder of Richard's life would continue to tick. In the meantime it would all be up to me, with some distant help from Mike.

As I thought about the dimensions of my task I also thought about my personal relationship with Richard and my motivation to save someone I cared about and wished well. He was a sweet and decent man and we had been very close. He didn't deserve whatever was happening to him and neither did his wife, Kathy, or the child who would soon be making an appearance on our troubled scene.

I also thought about Janice, a younger version of myself, and the successful career that lay ahead of her. I liked her eagerness and her attitudes. I thought momentarily about the possibility of her joining me on this investigation, but I realized that she lacked the experience that someone like Ben possessed. That experience would come, perhaps sooner than she expected, but she was not yet ready for the moment of truth, the moment when you take out your cuffs or take out your semiautomatic, the moment when you take a perp into custody or take his or her life. The moment of decision would most likely be instantaneous and it would surely be final.

The flight was a simple one, a little less than an hour and a half, with barely enough time for the most basic of drink services. When I landed I was presented with a Bureau car that looked like a soccer mom's SUV, a two-year old black *Toyota* Highlander. My hotel room wouldn't be ready for several hours so I drove to Richard and Kathy's home in Honeoye Falls.

# FORTY-NINE

Kathy was surprised to see me. I noticed that when she invited me into their home she scanned the street for other unexpected vehicles. That was a good thing.

"I didn't know you would be coming," she said.

"I didn't want to alarm you," I said.

"Has something happened?"

"Yes and no," I said. "We don't have new information on Richard but we have new information on the case. We believe that an individual was brought ashore at the time of the company administrative retreat in Maine. That person's role was to make mischief in next year's presidential election. Richard may have seen that person or he may have somehow been drawn into the situation, against his will."

"That's very serious," Kathy said. "That would involve a large organization or perhaps even a foreign government."

"It might," I said. "That's why I came by. I think you should leave your home for awhile. I don't want you to be at any risk."

"You're thinking that they may be worried that Richard said something to me."

"Yes, exactly. It's purely precautionary but I think it would be prudent."

"Where do you think I should go?"

"Not to any place that would be in the public record like a parent's or a sibling's. And not to any place that would require you to use a credit card."

"A friend's house, maybe?"

"Yes," I said, "but one outside of the immediate area."

"I have a school friend this side of Syracuse."

"Perfect. Don't tell me the name or the address."

"So…you don't want to know so that no one can force you to tell them."

"Standard protocol," I said, stretching the truth. "You still have the phone I gave you…"

"Yes."

"It's untraceable; we can use it if we need to communicate with one another. And it's all perfectly legal, so long as you don't use it for criminal purposes."

"Not part of my plan," she said, smiling faintly.

"I knew that," I said.

"Can you tell me anything else about your investigation?"

"It's pretty unclear at the moment. I'm going to follow up on some of the *Kommunicom* principals."

"You still think that one or more of them is behind this?"

"Someone certainly is and it was that group that was meeting in Maine at the time that the foreign national came ashore."

"And you don't think that they simply…eliminated Richard."

"I don't. If they had there would be no reason to make it look like an abduction or a simple disappearance."

"They could have simply hit him with a car or truck and made it look like an accident."

"Exactly," I said.

"So you think they're going to try to make some use of him."

"That's what I think, but remember that this is all very speculative."

"I understand," she said. "If they're keeping him alive for some purpose he would almost have to be…local."

"I agree."

"They don't want to drive to Toronto each time he needs to be fed. On the other hand, if it's a foreign government involved…"

"They're taking their signals from someone local," I said. "They've committed to an individual they believe they can trust. If the time comes when they begin to have doubts they'll sever their ties immediately."

"Assuming that their plan is to disrupt our country in some way they could have brought the foreign national in in Miami or Galveston or San Diego or Seattle, Biloxi or…wherever. That's why it has to be someone in or near the company."

I thought to myself, 'You're surrounded by intelligent women. She's figured out your case without your having to tell her anything.' I responded to her, "That's right."

"I hate to leave the area if he's somewhere near," she said.

"I understand," I said.

"But you don't want them to be able to somehow control him by getting to me."

"We wouldn't want that," I said.

"I'll start packing and I'll put the timer on the living room light so I won't draw attention to my absence."

"Good idea," I said.


My talk with Kathy had involved an urgency that precluded any time for socializing. When I got back in my car and started driving out of their development I realized that I hadn't yet eaten breakfast. I checked my phone and googled local diners. The closest to my hotel was in Victor, New York, just inside the adjoining county border.

It was the Victor version of *Steve's*, the place I had eaten at in Henrietta. This time I went for one of their so-called love cakes, a pancake the size of a sports arena. I ordered a side of bacon and some black coffee. My waitress's name was Lynda.


"You're not from around here, are you Hon?" she said, taking a small break from her rounds.

Before I could respond she added, "You're not wearing jeans and a Bills cap."

"No, I'm just here for… a reunion," I said.

"My husband won't go to those," Lynda said. "He's afraid everybody there will be millionaires and thin."

"Mine's not a school reunion," I said. "I'm just meeting up with an old friend."

"Not that we're not doing well, ourselves," she said, blowing past my comment. Larry does real estate and these days that's a good business to be in, so long as you get the listings. Then you just sit back and cash the checks."

"Market's still tight," I said, "but hopefully the mortgage rates will continue to go down and people will give up their 3% loans and let go of their properties."

"True that," Lynda said. "It's always about the dollars. Where you're sitting…"

"Yes?"

"You're in Ontario County. A few yards down the hill and you're in Monroe County. Higher taxes. That's why the Mall across the street was located in Victor. Then all the strip malls piggy-backed along the road and the result is that we all have work but we all have to deal with the traffic."

"But it's steady work," I said.

"It is that. Your food should be up soon, Hon."


A few minutes later she brought my breakfast and followed with a coffee urn in each hand. She carried them as if they were western pistols. "It was black, not decaf, right, Hon?"

"Black and bold," I said. "High test."

"You sound like you could be from around here," Lynda said. "Like Larry always says, western New York is sometimes like the Midwest, 'as extended.' He gets that phrase from his work."

"I went to college in the Midwest," I said.

"But you're not from there originally."

"Northern Plains, the Dakotas," I said.

"Big spaces," she said. "We went to Wyoming once for a vacation. Somebody asked us if we had flown to Salt Lake or to Denver. Think about that. Your choices were to fly into other, different *states*."

"They say the miles are shorter out there," I said, "but I had third grade math and I can't quite understand that concept."

"Me neither," Lynda said, "especially with the weather. We were in Laramie in June and damned if it didn't snow. Speaking of our birthplaces, I don't have much of a story to tell. I was born in Greece."

"That's a long way from here," I said.

"Not really. It's a local suburb, maybe 25 miles or so from here. At least it's pronounced the same, unlike the suburb spelled like Chili but pronounced Chie-Lie."

"I think I saw a sign for it on the road by the airport," I said.

"Just a sec," she said, turning and looking over her shoulder as if some sixth sense was telling her that someone needed a coffee refill. "Enjoy your breakfast; I'll check back in a few."

She secured new urns and made a run through the row of booths opposite the pass. Every pour was accompanied by a sentence or two of greetings and questions. I *was* enjoying my breakfast, especially the syrup and butter with which I had slathered my pancake.

My purse was leaning against my left leg and I felt my phone twitch. I always like to keep the purse close when I'm carrying my sidearm. I slipped out the phone, thinking it might have carried a message from Mike, but it was one of those ads in which your grocery store tries to convince you to have your prescriptions delivered to your home. Everybody wants a piece of the Big Pharma action. I trashed it and returned my phone to my purse.

A few minutes later Lynda returned and refilled my cup before I had the chance to ask her to do so. "How was that love cake?" she asked. "I see you managed to eat it all."

"The best," I said, "and I loved the bacon. I like it thick like that but not burned and not greasy."

"Larry always orders a double batch when he comes in. He always asks John, the manager, when he's going to keep the place open past 2:00 o'clock. John always tells him that he's been there since dawn and is ready to go home and rest by then. Then Larry says that we're the best place in town and he wishes he could come in for dinner. John then tells him that it's too hard to find the competent help these days. It's a thing they go through all the time. I think Larry wants John to acknowledge that I'm part of the competent help and that he should appreciate me all the more. He's sweet that way, but so is John. I've been here for years and can't imagine working anywhere else."

"One of the most important things in life," I said, "liking your work."

At that she just nodded and smiled. "You be sure and have a nice day," she said, putting my bill beside my coffee cup. "No rush on that; when you're ready you take it to John, over by the door."

"Thanks for everything," I said.

Again, she just smiled and nodded.

When I got to the parking lot I checked my phone. Still nothing from Mike, so I drove back to my hotel in the Basin, checked in and began to unpack.

# FIFTY

When I got to the hotel I had the sense that it had been retrofitted to accommodate the *Hilton Garden Inn* brand. The configuration of the floors didn't feel quite right. Peggy had secured me a room with a king-size bed and I was grateful that I had enough room to spread out and, if I had the time, kick back.

When I had my clothes arranged in the drawers and cupboard and was ready to begin my actual day's work my secure phone rang with the comfortable ring sound I had recently selected. It was Mike.

"Before I bury you in information I thought I'd check in with you and see what you needed. My thought was that I'd set up files for you and as soon as they're completed you could use them any way that you saw fit. If it's OK I'll do at least one every day, depending on the availability of information. I'll try to stay a day ahead of you in case you hit a snag or want to change direction, but there will be a lot of information."

"You can't have too much," I said.

"Right. And if you need more I'll get you more. Anyway, I'll direct you to a site in a moment or two. I've got the file on the security guy ready to go and I'll have the information on the production guy soon after that.

"Tom Fuse first," I said.

"Right," Mike said. "So you'll have his name and address, car, license plate, any second family car information, his wife's vitals and his kids'. I've also thrown in some pictures in case he tries to throw a curve ball and change his hair or glasses or whatever..."

"Sounds great, Mike," I responded.

"I've also put in some maps with expected migration routes and whatever deep background material I could scavenge: education, majors, athletics, military service, etc. along with the usual height, weight, hair and eye color, etc. If you have any questions concerning identity I've always got my facial rec software up and running and I can do quick checks if you need them. Medical records are a little more iffy, but a lot of the locals there use docs from the U of R and the U of R system uses software from *Epic*, so if the files are in order and the creeks don't rise I can see the messaging between the individual's family doc and the various specialists the person has seen."

"You're going to turn them every which way but loose."

"That's my intention," Mike said. "The ringer is always their phone traffic and if they're using burners that will complicate both of our lives. Of course, if there's any indication that they're using burners that fact will draw our mutual attention. Are they talking to a drug dealer, a secret girlfriend or…someone at the Chinese Embassy?"

"I get it," I said. "And if they'll betray their spouse in one form they may well be prepared to betray their country in another."

"Given the fact that they're working in a defense industry they're supposed to be pure and upright. Everyone has secrets, of course, but we want those secrets to involve a special Valentine's Day gift for the spouse or a birthday present for one of their kids, not treason."

"Exactly," I said. "I can start with any of the gang of five, so we'll begin with Tom and see what we can turn."

"I'll send you the site information for his file," Mike said.


Tom Fuse lived in Perinton, an adjoining town with a village called Fairport. A few yards west of my hotel was a street called Kreag Road. Turning north on Kreag took you into Tom's particular neck of the woods, but I had followed him from *Kommunicom's* headquarters, checking to see if he might lead me to Richard before he returned home. I have to admit that I had doubts concerning Tom's possible guilt since he had been a member of the NYPD and had moved upstate to support his widowed mother, but I couldn't allow myself to go soft and give him a pass because of his prior activities. Bureau protocols (and common sense) told me that I was not awash in possible suspects and the need for thoroughness trumped any personal inclinations.

He left work promptly at 5:00, which might have been considered suspicious, but then he drove directly home. Another point in his favor was the fact that he drove a forest green Sienna—a car for large families. It might have accommodated a kidnapped body but it was far more likely to contain an array of children's car seats and space in the rear for a Golden Retriever. When I had arrived at the company headquarters in mid-afternoon I had actually inspected Tom Fuse's car. There were no children's seats but there was some sports equipment and bedding that might have lodged a terrier or two.

When Tom got home he was greeted by an impatient wife who was checking her watch as he passed through the door. Twelve minutes later they both reappeared, accompanied by two teenage boys, each of whom was fidgety but dressed for dinner. Using my best *Nikon* binoculars I could see Tom set the house alarm in his well-lit hallway. I noticed a kind of hurried affection between him and his wife. Both were in their late 40's. She had been worried about their timing, not about her husband.

They drove into the Basin, turned right and drove along the Canal into Pittsford Village, driving through meandering streets past a bank, the local library and a pizza joint called *Pontillo's*. Now on Monroe Street they drove into the town's commercial zone which featured a large, upscale strip mall called *Pittsford Plaza* on the south and a host of independent stores and mini-strip malls on the north. They drove into Brighton and I noticed a number of Hasidim walking together along the street. Their conversations seemed earnest and intended to persuade and convince. Tom then turned into a small strip mall on the north side of Monroe and parked diagonally in front of an athletic clothing store.

Finally I saw their destination: a store front restaurant called *Max*

*Chophouse. Max's* on their green awning, but *Max* on their website. The frontage was clean and presentable but the establishment could just as easily have been a mom 'n pop that specialized in grilled cheese sandwiches and tomato soup, served on *Formica*-top tables with paper napkins and worn cutlery. Instead, it was the leading steakhouse in the city; it offered the possibility of tasting some actual *Pappy's* from their amply-stocked bar and the certitude of finding a perfectly-cooked medium rare Prime Cowboy Ribeye for a modest king's ransom.

It was somebody's birthday, perhaps Tom's, though there were offerings on the menu which would have appealed to the female of the species. I myself was dining in my car on a club sandwich I had picked up earlier from the *Cheesecake Factory*. I couldn't wash it down with anything interesting because I was on the clock and needed to be able to follow the Fuse family without being detected.

Their dinner (doubtless including dessert) was of 2 hours+ duration. Tom was walking upright, with an impressive degree of sobriety. Taking on a designated-driver role after a celebratory occasion earned him more points on my mental checklist. Security was, after all, his stock-in-trade.

After they returned to Perinton I observed them from a distance, predicting their movements as lights went on and off from the hallway to the home's second floor. I waited another half hour after the lights were fully extinguished, just in case Tom had scheduled some illicit midnight run.

He hadn't. The next morning I arrived early in bright sunlight, grateful that I had my best binoculars and that Tom lived in what the Brits call a leafy neighborhood. The last thing I wanted to do was raise suspicions among his neighbors or, flatly, blow my cover.

He emerged at 6:45, coming through the garage, which also revealed a second, newer-model Sienna, this one in Ruby Flare Pearl, or, as some would say, red. His first destination was *Starbucks* and the size of his purchase was what they term a 'Venti', or what the rest of us call a large, 20-ounce. I doubted that it had any foam or floating cinnamon gracing its tideline.

His next stop was *Kommunicom*; again, I gave him extra points for being up-and-doing, reporting earlier than expected (perhaps to compensate for his early departure the former afternoon) and retaining the purest image of sobriety. The small ocean of coffee was a requirement that I had acknowledged, in part because it was one that I shared. I had actually taken two cups from my hotel buffet.

If Richard was still alive and if Richard was still in the Rochester area and if he was still under the direct care of someone at *Kommunicom* it wasn't likely to be Tom Fuse and if he was being guarded and fed by some small group of criminals it was difficult for me to conceive of them being directed by a man in a green Sienna. At the same time, it was difficult for me to imagine that man, a former NYPD officer, being directed by criminals or, for that matter, individuals from a foreign government.

That evening Tom worked until 6:15 and stopped on the south side of my ingress/egress route to pick up subs from a place called *Salvatore's*, a local chain with a new incarnation in the Basin. No Cowboy Ribeyes tonight, but the family would not lack for calories or the joys of a large dining room- or kitchen table surrounded by full mouths and smiling faces.

I let Mike know that I had completed a fourth of my task, a fifth if I decided to follow Rudolf. The good news was that a nice man had likely been fully exonerated; the bad news was that I was running in place, no closer to the goal of finding Richard.

"We're not without other possibilities," Mike said. "Your next file is ready."

# FIFTY-ONE

CC T he production director?" I asked.

"Signor Ruffino," Mike answered.

"Gabe," I said.

"Actually Gabriele," Mike said. "5'9", 195 pounds, brown eyes, black hair (unlike the more usual brown). Fifty-two years of age; wife Clara; two daughters, Isabelle a junior at Colgate and Julia, married to a dentist named James Carovillano, living in Boston. More precisely, in Andover. Nice. Gabe and Clara have duelling *Lexi*; he drives a red RX 350 and she has a white NX 350h."

Gabe and Clara lived in a pretty development on the west side of Mendon Center Road, a few miles from the Basin and a few miles from *Kommunicom*. I knew that I would be spending more time with the Ruffinos (or the Ruffino) because it was now Friday and Gabe had the whole weekend in which to either make mischief or prove himself to be an upstanding citizen.

He left work in Henrietta at 6:45 and drove straight home, parking in his garage and (I had to assume) passing into his home via a connecting door. There was little evidence of activity inside except for a few overhead lights and a glow from a distant wall that must have been issuing from a television screen. An hour later a small van pulled into their driveway, bearing the *Salvatore's* livery (increasingly the brand of choice for the locals). The driver carried a square box and a large bag. Someone was going for the pizza, someone else for the chicken parm. Or the pasta with meat sauce. Or, in this part of the world, the wings with multiple dipping sauces.

It could have been movie night or just fall-in-front-of-the-TV-on-the-leather-sofa night, but either way the work week was over and they were in for the night. I checked Mike's file and saw that Clara was an interior designer, working for a drape and blinds shop in East Rochester. She advised and measured while their trim carpenter installed. While Gabe supervised employees all day in a noisy space she schmoozed and drove all over the metropolitan area, doing measurements, offering choices and taking orders. Both were probably ready for some beer, wine, pepperoni, green peppers, Italian sausage and something fried.

The next morning Gabe was up early, making a run to the *Sunoco* station in the Basin where he loaded up on high-octane gas and *Dunkin' Donuts*. The rectangular box was large; he may have been expecting company or shopping for the whole weekend. He returned home with a handful of sugar, grease and carbs and (again, I had to assume) he and Clara went for the couch and coffee table.

In the early afternoon they drove to the Eastview Mall in Victor and attempted to walk off part of their breakfast. They began by window shopping at *Williams Sonoma*. From what I could determine from my odd angle and limited view they were looking at the $1,000.00+ coffee makers and $20.00+ bottled sauces. From there they proceeded to a mini- *Barnes & Noble*, again shopping but not buying. The *Apple* store nearby occasioned a comment and some gestures (probably concerning the hordes waiting for service), but they stayed in their line of pedestrian traffic and walked through a third or so of the mall, passing an array of booths of middle-eastern individuals reading their phone and tablet screens but available to change your cell phone battery or sell you any number of gawdy protective phone covers.

After a steady heel-and-toe for twenty minutes they returned to the *Williams Sonoma* corner with an adjoining *Starbucks*. The line was twenty-deep but they soldiered on and made their selections. Gabe went for the Venti black, while Clara did something with foam, to which she added what was possibly chocolate powder but more likely cinnamon. They then turned left and found a pair of pleather chairs in which to relax and enjoy their coffee.

Fifteen minutes later they made their way to a department store called *Von Mauer*. It was strictly 'traditional' with upscale clothing, crystal geegaws, *Coach* purses and an endless selection of perfumes and colognes, brand-name shoes and what may have been the nicest restrooms in a modern mall store.

Then they were back to the serious walking, stopping by the food court carousel to watch excited children with their eager grandparents and then moving on to *Penney's* to actually buy some fitted sheets with matching pillow cases. They then returned to the *Williams Sonoma* wing, walked outside and enjoyed a late lunch/early dinner at *P. F. Chang's*. My view of them was obstructed but I imagined Gabe was replenishing his fluids with a large Asian beer and Clara was sipping something with punctured fruit beneath a paper umbrella. They then shared a huge tureen of soup and a single entrée with a side order of white rice. I envied them, since I was subsisting on packets of peanut butter crackers and dark chocolate candy bars.

The one thing that was certain was that Richard played no part in Gabe's plans for his Saturday. Someone else may have been feeding him but Gabe was not. When he and Clara finished their meal they drove directly home, perhaps planning on a later snack of day-old pizza and what was left of the morning's donuts. I watched their garage door for an hour and a half but it remained closed. After a hot meal at a pub in the Basin (a former bank with a humongous safe sitting opposite the *Guinness* tap) I returned to the Ruffino household and waited to see if Gabe would be slipping away on a criminal errand. He wasn't.

The next morning began late, perhaps with something more healthy for breakfast, but while Clara made a run to the *Wegmans* in Henrietta Gabe stayed home. All in all, a lost weekend, but not one that would call

Gabe's character into question or offer some indication that he might have been involved in Richard's abduction. When I returned to my hotel on Sunday evening I contacted Mike.

# FIFTY-TWO

"I take it that nothing of note happened," Mike said.

"Nothing," I said.

"At least it's nice to know that people you thought were legit actually turned out to be legit," he said.

"There is that," I said, "but I prefer to hunt bad guys rather than snipe."

"Understood. So who do you want to do next? I've got both the H.R. person's and the R&D person's files ready to go."

"They both seemed nice when I first met with them…let's do H.R."

"Marianne Phillips," Mike said. "Got your map screen up?"

"Yes."

"OK. I'll give you the macro and you can put in the micro when you need the street-by-street directions. You're going to be driving into the village and turning right, crossing over the Canal. Your former hotel—the *Del Monte*—will then be on your left. You'll drive straight ahead and eventually turn left onto East Avenue. It's a major migration route that bends around and then ends up downtown. You'll pass some golf courses, colleges and churches en route. Nice neighborhood.

"The H.R. woman lives in a Tudor mansion that was recently converted into three condos. Hers sold for a tidy $975K, five years ago. She's unmarried, has no children and drives a silver/blue *Lexus* ES 350h sedan. Early 40's, 5'7", 135, blonde/blue. Good looking woman."

"I remember her," I said. "She was helpful or at least tried to be. Decent human being, not a bureaucrat who buried you in forms and tried to spend her works and days attempting to make you feel subservient to her."

"*Rara avis*," Mike said.

"Yes, I thought so," I said. "Tell me about her background."

"Tippie College of Business."

"Tippy? As in Tommee Tippee?"

"No, as in the B-School at the University of Iowa."

"OK."

"Old and established," Mike said. She grew up in Des Moines. She was married for about a decade but her husband died of pancreatic cancer. Good guy; former Navy lieutenant."

"Tough," I said.

"Right. She worked awhile for *Westinghouse* and then got her MBA from Wharton."

"Impressive," I said.

"Richard's company appreciates her. She draws a salary that is steadily moving from six figures to the sunny territory of seven."

"Sweet," I said, "but she's unassuming and cooperative. No question that she's highly competent, but she doesn't lord it over the mere mortals she regulates."

"Maybe that's why she makes the big bucks."

"*Rara avis*."

"As we said," Mike added. "Sounds like a long shot for criminal activity."

"She doesn't need the money," I said.

"Let me know if she proves us wrong."

"Will do," I said.


I followed her from her driveway at 7:05. When she got to the *Kommunicom* parking lot there was only one other car and a truck parked there. The first was British and expensive; the second was aged and streaked with rust. Rudolf's and the cleaning crew's. I was impressed by the fact that she didn't stop for coffee on the way in; she was probably setting up the machine for everyone else in her building.

There was steady pedestrian traffic to and from her building throughout the day, with most individuals carrying file folders or an occasional briefcase. She didn't go out for lunch, probably munching on a vending-machine salad at her desk. Between 5:00 and 6:00 the parking lot began to clear. At 7:00 she was still there, but she left at 7:10, drove directly home, changed into clothing which was slightly more night-on-the-town than business/casual, got in her luxury ES Hybrid (what Mike called silver/blue, or as *Lexus* calls it, Iridium), turned right onto East Avenue and headed for downtown Rochester.

We passed the Eastman House on the right; Marianne drove just under a mile and turned left into the parking lot of the Genesee Valley Club. When I later checked on their estimated dues I wondered if she was piggy-backing onto a company membership or using a personal one. She drove to the rear of the lot—a kind of spillover area—and parked her car. I had parked as far from her as I could, turned out my lights and taken out my binoculars.

She had slid open her interior rearview mirror, illuminated the front seat, touched up her makeup, run a comb through her hair and then returned to near darkness. There was enough ambient light from the Club building to allow me to see her answer her phone and then click off. A minute later she emerged from her car and walked over to the side entrance to the Club. A dark, shiny and very expensive *Lincoln* Navigator drove up to her and a man emerged. At that distance it was hard to see specific aspects of his dress, but his demeanor said 'money,' as did the tailored lines of his clothing. He was also unmistakably Asian.

# FIFTY-THREE

"Damn," I said aloud. By the time I was able to exchange my binoculars for my long-lens camera they had already entered the building.

I sat in the darkness for the next two hours and forty-five minutes, waiting for them to emerge and hoping that I would be able to take a picture of him that Mike could check out with his facial rec software. When they did I dropped my coffee cup in the Highlander's holder, grabbed my camera and aimed and shot as if I had been armed with a small machine gun. Then I got lucky. The Navigator reappeared and Marianne and her dining companion stood under the light, saying their good-byes. I got at least three good shots of the Asian man before I sent them to Mike and followed Marianne out of the lot and onto East Avenue.

The Navigator had turned left and while I expected Marianne to drive straight to her condo she threw me a slight curve ball and turned into the *Wegmans* lot on the left side of her return route. She was there for no more than fifteen minutes and emerged with a small plastic bag with the *Wegmans* image on each side. A milk run? Bread?

Whatever it was it was for her and not Richard because she stayed in for the night and drove directly to work the following morning.

With the time difference between western New York and Salt Lake City Mike was up early. As I followed Marianne to Henrietta he filled me in on the results of his midnight research.

"You were wondering if the man of mystery was the puppet master or his/her direct representative."

"It had crossed my mind," I said, "though I hoped it hadn't been true."

"Rest at ease," he said. "In the first place, the man is Korean, not Chinese."

"Don't take this personally, but how exactly can you tell?" I asked.

"Call it my personal intuition or my extensive experience," Mike said. "The Chinese are usually more tan than the pale Koreans. There are also some differences with regard to the flatness of the nose, the fullness of the lips and the roundness of the cheeks and jaws. In the light available to you at the time it would be a tad more difficult to make an exact identification. However, the whole process becomes much easier if you go broad-brush and happen to land on fifteen or twenty pictures of the individual's well-known face, smack dab in the middle of what we call your basic public domain."

"And…?"

"His name is Ye-jun Choi. His mom and dad emigrated from Seoul back in the day and dad taught math at the University of Illinois-Chicago (or as we used to say, Chicago Circle). Their daughter Soo-min is a reconstructive plastic surgeon in Dallas. Her brother—your guy—Ye-jun, studied engineering at the University of Illinois, Champaign-Urbana."

"John Bardeen country," I said.

"Good memory," Mike said. "Two Nobels. Anyway, Ye-jun went on to Caltech for his Ph.D."

"A lot more Nobels," I said.

"Mmm-hmm. From there he went to Georgia Tech and to MIT. Eventually he landed at Carnegie Mellon where he currently serves as the Dean of the College of Engineering. He also carries a named-professor title as well as a named-dean title which accompanies the gig."

"He's interviewing for a job at *Kommunicom*. A big one."

"My guess would be that he's interviewing them."

"In what sense?"

"Gotta back up for a second and tell you that your friend Rudolf ambled across my screen just before the pictures of the Korean Dean. He just bought a home in Austin."

"He's got a new gig there."

"No announcement yet, but there are enough high-tech firms there to choke a herd of wild horses. It's also the kind of place where you wouldn't generally buy a vacation home, particularly not one in his price range."

"So the Korean is probably his replacement."

"My guess?"

"Sure."

"As soon as Rudolf signed on the line that is dotted he let his overseers at *Kommunicom* know. They called a consulting firm; the consulting firm made some discreet calls and Dean Choi quickly rose to the top of their list. With a private company you don't need search committees and faculty consultations. It's outside the normal boundaries—sort of like hiring an Athletic Director or Head Football Coach at a college. A dean at a top engin school will make a sweet base salary along with his consultancies and board seats at local companies, so the *Kommunicom* job will have to pay big bucks, because the dean already makes big bucks and Pennsylvania taxes are more attractive than New York's, so they will have to pull out the usual stops and actually woo him. Hence my guess: the H.R. director is widely trusted and she knows where the heavy hitters are ensconced and the bodies are buried. The folk at *Kommunicom* in Stockholm like her and trust her so she was selected to give the dean the skinny on what life is *really* like at their company."

"She also has no vested interest the way a division head would; her priority would be the general health of the company."

"Right. There's something else I haven't mentioned…"

"Yes?"

"Ye-jun was in ROTC at the U of I. Signal Corps. (Actually a *combat-support* branch, but you probably knew that.) Logged some time in the Sandbox under serious conditions. Bronze star with a **V**-device as well as other forms of recognition. The **V**-device looks legit."

"An actual hero who also knows radios," I said. "Big time."

"That's why they probably went for the big steaks, the top wines and the aged cognac at the GVC."

"You're starting to sound like a local, Mike."

"My form of cover and concealment," he said. "I love to maintain my anonymity."

"Bottom line: a match made in heaven and probably a significant step up from Rudolf."

"Yes, and a gazillion-to-one chance that he would have any relationship to Richard's disappearance."

"Warms my heart but doesn't help me find Richard," I said.

"At least you're narrowing the list."

"There's not much list left," I said.

"Patricia's file is ready for you. You'll like her house. And by the way, her husband Jon was just appointed associate dean of the School of Arts and Sciences at the U of R."

"I think he does Philosophy," I said.

"Hume and the Scottish Enlightenment," Mike said.

"One of my favorite forms of it," I said.


The Clines lived in Pittsford, outside of the village but not in one of the recent developments like Gabe and Clara's. They were in a low-slung ranch home that sprawled across an acre of land in the Stone Road/ Tobey Road area. I wouldn't have wanted to pay their landscaper bills, but aside from the daunting real estate taxes and maintenance costs the neighborhood was lovely. Patricia would drive into Henrietta on Jefferson Road, a major East/West artery that fed into the village on the east and through miles of restaurants, big box stores, an occasional boutique and string of hotels on the west. When I waited to accompany her to *Kommunicom* the next morning she surprised me.

At first light both she and her husband pulled out of their garage together, she following him in her new RAV4, he in the family Land Cruiser. They drove across Jefferson and eventually turned south on

West Henrietta Road, then turned sharply right into the local *Toyota* dealership. Jon was bringing in the car for service. After he handed off his keys and signed his paperwork she drove him to the U of R and his work.

She then drove directly to work, no stop for coffee, no passing of GO, no paying of $200. She had lunch with Gabe and Tom (a tiny break in their usual patterns) but made no other trips or stops during the day. In the late afternoon she drove back to the *Toyota* dealership, where she rallied with her husband. I figured he had hitched a ride there with a university colleague. The dealership had washed the Land Cruiser as well as serviced it and the two of them stopped at *DiBella's* for subs on their way home. A work day, not a date night.

The next morning she stopped at a *Tim Hortons* for coffee and donuts. The box was huge; she was the office public benefactor, feeding the troops and filling the room with smiles and sugar highs. That night she stopped on her way home but her destination was *Wegmans* on Calkins Road, not some holding cell where Richard might be languishing. Her three bags of groceries probably set her back at least $150.

By now I was becoming more than frustrated. I was worried about Richard and even beginning to wonder if he would ever be seen again. Mike hadn't turned anything new, aside from the fact that Rudolf's appointment in Austin had been formally announced and *Kommunicom* had issued a congratulatory statement, thanking him for the many ways in which he had advanced the company's interests.

Then the unexpected happened.

# FIFTY-FOUR

At 9:15 the next morning one of my burners rang; it was Patricia Cline calling. Had she seen me? Had my cover been blown?

"Agent Harrison?" she said.

"Yes. Is this Patricia?"

"Yes. How are you?"

"I'm fine," I said. "How about you?"

"Well, I'm about to get a new boss, assuming that our top candidate takes the job."

"Mr. Bethe is leaving?"

"Yes, he's going to Texas. More or less a parallel move, I hear, but he's always wanted to work in his new company's area of operations and he expects to have better weather there."

"I take it he's never experienced a tornado."

"He's mostly contemplating the use of a year-round pool. He doesn't know what kinds of things can blow into one."

"What's the feeling among the people at your level?" I asked.

"The person that we're courting is fabulous. Rudolf was more than a figurehead but his most attractive features were his presence, his appearance, his personality and his steady hand. The new person has a research background as well as a managerial one and he has actual field experience with our products. Combat experience."

"Sounds like a great fit," I said, wondering momentarily why she hadn't mentioned the fact that the possible new boss was the dean at her own alma mater.

"We're all pretty excited," she said.

"Unfortunately, I don't have any significant updates for you on our search for Richard Ingle. I'm glad to hear your good news; I just wish I had some from my end."

"We figured that if you had you would have notified us," she said. "That's why I'm calling. My husband has some thoughts and we'd like to talk to you about them. When will you be back in our area?"

"I could be there this evening," I said, avoiding any talk of my actual location.

"In time for dinner? I could cook and we could talk more privately than at a restaurant."

"Give me ten minutes to check flight schedules and I'll get back to you. What time would you want me there?"

"Seven?"

"And you'll text me your address?"

"Sure."

"I'll get right back to you."


I called her in twelve minutes. "7:00 is no problem," I said. "It took a moment or so with the car rental."

"Jon could have picked you up."

"I appreciate that," I said, "but if your ideas are helpful I'll want to stay in the area longer."

"*Ideas* is the right word," she said. "We don't have specific facts or new information, but Jon's always got useful thoughts. He's a philosophy professor."

"You told me that, I think," I responded.

"The level-headed kind."

"That's the best," I said.


When I got to their home I could smell the roast in the oven. It smelled peppery.

"She greeted me with a hug, which surprised me. So did her husband, a barrel-chested man who looked more like a heavy equipment operator than an academic specialist in British empiricism.

"I want this to rest for awhile," she said, removing a beautiful standing rib roast from her oven. It was dotted with black peppercorns and the scent of the juices was exquisite.

"My mother's recipe," Patricia said. "She would have wanted to keep it in the marinade longer, but I think you'll enjoy it. While it rests Jon can get us some drinks."

"Scotch OK?" he asked from the adjoining room.

"Fine for me," I said.

"Ice? Water?"

"A little of each," I said. He was pouring 12 year-old *Macallan*, the kind aged in sherry oak. Not a life changer but a solid $100 bottle of whiskey when you could find it. Patricia liked hers with multiple cubes of ice and an equal amount of water; Jon drank his neat.

"Jon actually studied at Edinburgh," Patricia said.

"There's something special about working in David Hume Tower," Jon said. "They later changed the name because of some of his comments on race. He hated slavery but he was a man of the eighteenth century, not the twenty-first. Still, his detractors held him accountable and did what they could to cancel him. We call that 'presentism.' He was also the greatest philosopher between the Greeks and Kant, but let's not let that distract us from enjoying our Scotch. The Tower wasn't a very handsome building anyway."

The Scotch was excellent. While Jon and I made small talk Patricia prepared some potatoes and asparagus. When we settled in around their dining room table Jon opened a bottle of red Bordeaux.

"I'm anxious to hear your thoughts on our search for Richard Ingle," I said, looking at each of them in turn.

"Nothing terribly profound," Jon said, "but it may be something you could use."

I cut a piece of my beef and waited for him to continue.

"I was just made an associate dean," he said. "Nothing permanent.

It's more of a glorified internship. They rotate department chairs in and out of the dean's office. The notion is that you'll develop a greater appreciation of the way the place actually works and share your knowledge with other members of the faculty. The faculty used to run everything, of course, but with the bureaucratization of things a distance has crept in; this is a way of closing the gap. That's the theory, at least."

"Sounds like a good idea," I said.

"Especially with the capital-D deans spending so much time on fundraising and public relations," he answered. "And in litigation."

"Plenty of that everywhere," I said.

"Yes, well, once you're in the dean's office you hear interesting things. For one thing there's the table of organization and equipment. You have the dean, the more-or-less visiting associate deans like me, the baby deans who carry the titles but basically hold hands and pass out Kleenex…and then there's the R.D."

"The R.D.?"

"The real dean," he said. "Usually a middle-aged woman who's been in the office since the dawn of time. She knows all the rules and regs; she knows all of the campus players; she's an expert in what we now call 'system navigation' and, most important, she's the person the so-called Dean turns to when the journalists are calling, the students are protesting and the bureaucrats are swarming."

"Like a *consigliere*," I said, "or should I say *consigliera*?"

Jon smiled. "The term apparently goes back to a CGS meeting several generations ago."

"CGS?"

"The Council of Graduate Schools; it's the large-umbrella group; the AGS (Association of Graduate Schools) is the arm of the AAU schools, the so-called elites."

"OK…"

"Anyway, the CGS was meeting in D.C. and a group of the deans went out to dinner one night at Duke Zeibert's…"

"A local mainstay. At L Street and Connecticut," I said. "It later moved."

"Yes," Jon said. "The power broker's home away from home. TV personalities…Redskins' owners…the place to see and be seen. The food wasn't necessarily great, but Duke was a charismatic guy and the business flourished. Anyway, one night the deans were there and, horror of horrors, a brown-banded cockroach strolled across their table. Imagine a round table with a clock face at 6:00. The bug was taking a slow constitutional from bottom to top. One of the deans, a woman from what was then called SUNY-Buffalo, reached across, crushed him with an open palm and then proceeded to remove what was left with her thumb and index finger. 'How would you like to have to go to her for a special exception to the grad school rules?' one dean asked. 'She's what we call the Real Dean,' another responded."

"Great story," I said. "I wonder if she promptly washed her hands."

"Apparently not," Jon said. "That was the coda of the story."

"So what you're saying is that if I want to find Richard I should be looking for the Real Dean?"

He looked back at me knowingly and took a long sip of his wine.

# FIFTY-FIVE

"Who would that be at *Kommunicom*?" I asked.

"Karla," Pat said. (The more she shared the more her name transmuted in my mind from *Patricia* to *Pat*.)

"I talked to her briefly," I said. "She was Rudolf's assistant."

"More like executive assistant," Pat said.

"And *consigliera*?"

"He leaned on her a lot," Pat said.

"But when I got there I was introduced to him by a young man."

"Teddy Wilson," Pat said.

"OK," I said. "I remember thinking that he was like Gertie and Karla was more like his Della Street. Gertie did the scut work but Della got to sit in on the important meetings."

"As in Perry Mason," Jon said.

"Right," I said.

"Except we never saw Gertie," Pat said. "At *Kommunicom* you never see Della."

"Tell me more," I said.

"In the first place, she's been there forever. She worked for his predecessor, Matt Andersson. Matt as in Matteus, not Matthew."

"Corporate memory is a heavy source of power within organizations," Jon offered.

"She has *that*," Pat said, "but not much else."

"In what sense?" I asked.

"She's not married. To my knowledge she has no children.

And not to be unkind, but…well, she has no personality and she's physically unattractive."

"Tell us what you really think, Pat," Jon said.

"Just trying to be honest," Pat said.

"I don't remember hearing her last name," I said.

"Hosek," Pat said.

"That would be, what, Czech?" I asked.

"Usually," Jon said, "but in the old country it would have a diacritical mark over the *s*. Pronounced *Ho-shek*. It's also Jewish."

"What does it mean, Jon?"

"Something like *to do good* or *please* in Czech, but in Hebrew it means *darkness*."

"Her view vs. everyone else's?" I asked.

"Possibly," Pat said, "but I suspect that most people try not to think of her at all. Most of the people in the company give her a wide berth."

"So maybe more of a Rasputin than a Della Street?" I asked.

"I don't know about that, maybe more like the distant relative you'd rather not see around the Thanksgiving table," Pat said.

"Interesting," I said. "I suppose that could cover a multitude of sins."

"She's not the funny uncle type or the person with crazy political views," Pat said. "She…well…let's just say she keeps her own counsel. She…stews. She sits silently and you wonder what she's thinking, or if you're somehow being judged. Her expressions never seem to change."

"Secretive."

"Yes," Pat said, "maybe *inscrutable*. On a good day, *reclusive*; on a bad day *dark*."

"Why would Rudolf tolerate that when he's the schmoozing type? Good cop, bad cop?"

"Yes, in part," Pat said. "He has a pleasant personality but not a strong one. He doesn't like confrontation. I suspect he'd be happy to see someone like her take on the more difficult tasks."

"So she might be available for things like unpleasant negotiations; she'd miss out on the great perks but earn a larger share of the resulting pie. While the director was toasting the clients at the pricey steakhouse she'd be sitting in the shadows, poring over the fine print."

"Yes, I could see her doing that," Pat said. "As I said earlier, she's been there forever. People may not like to deal with her but after years of experience they've learned how to do it. The company division chiefs and the heavyweight purchasers have all had to conjure with her personality and methods. My guess is that she's at least become predictable in the sense that you know what you're getting into with her."

"Familiarity breeds contempt, but it's also reassuring in that what you see becomes what you get."

"You could say that," Pat responded.

"The smart ones might eventually learn how to use her as a workaround," I suggested. "Feed her ego and you feed yourself."

"Possibly," Pat said.


I made a point of drinking another cup of coffee so that I could make a plausible trip to the bathroom and contact Mike. "Code 1," I said. I could hear him put down his own cup in the background.

"You want me to stop watching my ballgame and check out someone at Richard's company."

"One Karla Hosek," I said. "The CEO's executive assistant."

"The real power behind the throne?"

"Quite possibly."

"You got it."


"So you see why we wanted to talk to you," Pat said.

"Yes, but just to be clear…you don't have anything in particular that could link her with Richard's disappearance."

"Nothing," Pat said, "but she's the one principal in the company you haven't spoken with and there are aspects of her personality that could give you pause."

"Understood," I said. "And much appreciated. Do you happen to know where she lives?"

"Yes," Pat said. "In the Park Avenue neighborhood. It's a strange place for *her*."

"How so?" I asked.

"I should have been more precise," Pat said. "It's a nice old neighborhood, not far from the Eastman Museum. What's strange is that the houses are huge. Five, six bedrooms sometimes, but a hundred+ years old. What would she do with all that space? And why would she want to maintain it? I'd figure her for a nice condo like Marianne Phillips'; I'm sure she could afford it."

"Maybe she settled in there back in the day and chose not to move," Jon said. "There are restaurants in the area; you're close to downtown and there are boutique stores…card shops, candy places, shady streets and old sidewalks for dog walking. The Museum also does some nice lunches."

"That's true," Pat said. "With me, well, where you live is in some ways who you are. If I was single I'd live closer to work, probably by one of the country clubs in Pittsford or by the Henrietta border. You could eat there, maybe meet someone there, have some kind of social life, even if it means going to Bridge night or Wine-tasting night, or whatever…"

I was going to speak but I let Jon speak for me. "Maybe she wants to be alone," he said, "or to hide."


I thanked them profusely for their help, asked if I could call on them again if I had any questions and walked slowly to my car, not wanting to appear overly anxious. Once inside and a block away from their driveway I was on my phone on a secure line, talking to Mike.

"Too early for any results," he said, "but I did have something else to share."

"What's that?"

"The Chinese girl who was taking pictures of the ballerina at the Senate Office Building…"

"You've got a full name."

"I always had a full name. I just didn't think it was important. Her name is Ya Qi *Chen*."

"She's a student at AU."

"Yes, but with a mom at the Embassy: one Ting *Chen*."

"And?"

"Ting Chen is a putative cultural attaché. She's actually a member of the Ministry of State Security."

"Their counterpart to the CIA."

"Unh-huh."

"Not uncommon to have Company types presenting themselves as cultural attachés at our own embassies."

"No, but how many of them have a direct link to the ballerina's operation (which appears to have a link of some sort to Richard's disappearance)?"

"None. Anything else on her background?"

"What we call your basic leather ass," Mike said.

"A desk rider and pusher of paper."

"Yes. Technically an analyst, never involved in field work to the Bureau's knowledge."

"And nothing in her background to suggest that she was ever involved in wet work."

"Other than to analyze it," Mike said.

"The daughter's connection is interesting," I said. "It keeps mom at a distance from the action but risks implicating the daughter in it."

"Heartless, I'd say."

"A lone wolf operation? Something beyond the Embassy's walls?"

"Possibly," Mike said, "but the smart money will be on some degree of Embassy involvement. Somebody had to pay to get the ballerina from Prague to the open water to Mary's Island and, eventually, to the Milbridge shore and parts west. And perhaps even more difficult: someone had to foot the bill for her travel and that gargantuan tariff at the *Four Seasons*."

"The Chinese are involved but also maintaining some distance."

"My guess," Mike said.

"Ya Qi had dinner with someone from the embassy; they ate at a crappy Chinese restaurant."

"That was Xinyi Li, an assistant to the Foreign Ministry Spokesperson. Ya Qi was probably trying to get some photography gigs. Her mother works in a different division."

"That's very helpful," I said. "Thanks."

"There's one other thing for now," Mike said.

"Yes?"

"I talked to Peggy. She asked me to tell you that a person called the Doc is being freed up to work with you but that it may take him slightly longer to join you than you might have wished."

"Estimated ETA?"

"Probably more like days than hours," he said.

"Thank her. I'll talk to you in the morning."

# FIFTY-SIX

With Mike two hours behind me on Mountain Time I wanted to give him as much opportunity as possible to gather information on the Hosek woman. I *was* able to secure her address from several directory sites and was considering paying her home a visit while she was at work. Any evidentiary material would be inadmissible but at this point I was more interested in saving Richard than in prosecuting Karla.

Before entering into a longer interchange Mike sent me a preliminary note: "Ting coming your way on a late-afternoon flight." That was very interesting news but not good news. Our adversaries might have gotten wind of our operation (or simply become sufficiently nervous over Tereza's health and Roberta's road trip to mommy and daddy's house to think about cutting losses, covering tracks and destroying evidence). I never like the sound of a ticking clock, particularly when I don't have a plan or a lead-pipe cinch evidentiary chain for its proper silencing.

While Ting Chen was packing for her trip north I was following Karla Hosek from her home on Canterbury Road to *Kommunicom*. She came in early but didn't stop along the way. She was driving a late model *Audi* Q5. Pricey but not top of the line. She parked at the CEO's building. I waited a few minutes but when she failed to reappear I returned to her home and prepared for an off-the-books entry.

I always carry a magnetic side plate with a vague logo signifying some form of civic officialdom to mask my actual intentions. I parked several blocks from her home, placing it in the center of the driver's side door. My accompanying tool is a basic clipboard with small-print illegible text in parallel with a set of boxes begging to be ticked.

The Hosek house occupied nearly 80% of its lot and shared a driveway with its neighbor. For me that could have been a deal-breaker, but the driveway had been properly maintained, particularly in an area that undergoes the frequent scraping of snow blades. The three-story structure was constructed of actual stone and wood clapboard. It had been painted a faded mustard color with dark wood trim around its large and numerous windows.

I scanned the house and its neighbor for cameras and was surprised to find none there, not even the Nest doorbell that you often receive as part of the purchase of a security system. For that matter there were also no security system signs on the external corners or in the windows of the Hosek house. I have a number of ways of detecting the presence of such a system, but the windows were positioned in such a way that I had a good view of the building's interior and could note the lack of motion and window sensors as well as the absence of a control panel in the hallway entrance. I did a Wi-Fi/Bluetooth scan just for personal reassurance, walked around the side yard, ticking boxes on my clipboard sheet and (after being pleased by the line of shrubs and fencing providing me cover and concealment), picked the lock on the rear door. It took me less than a minute. The lock was an ancient but still functioning *Sager*, standard builder's quality. Purchased later by *Yale and Towne*, it passed out of existence in the 1950's. If Karla was a leftist spy she still held traditional values (or was fond of pinching pennies with an intensity that would make Abe cry out in pain).

The downstairs included a rear solarium with single glazing and an assortment of stacked lawn chairs, boots and tennis shoes. The dining area was twice the size of the attached galley kitchen. Everything was orderly and neat, including the living room, which featured a large bay window and a functioning wood burning fireplace surrounded by antique tiles. Near the front door was a very small powder room installed beneath the steps to the upstairs bedrooms, of which there were six.

The room formerly known as the 'master' bedroom was smallish. A queen-sized bed provided just enough space for parallel nightstands, a small corner chair and an oak chest of drawers. There was no *en suite*, but there was a 'family bathroom' across the hall with black and white tile and a nice clawfoot tub. The two adjoining rooms on that floor were probably once a nursery and a sewing room. The third floor would have been for the children. A new bathroom was installed there, with the pink and blue godawful tile of the 1950's. The rooms were now largely used for storage (one was simply vacant).

Before I did a closer search I quickly checked the gothic basement. It had whitewashed stone walls, a dusty floor, *Whirlpool* washer and dryer on wooden stands near a floor drain and a certifiable relic—a *Timken* boiler. Karla wasn't a hoarder but she wasn't one to seek contemporary products if hers still functioned. I wondered to myself which would be easier to find—the Lost Colony of Roanoke, or replacement parts for the *Timken*.

The macro-search complete, I homed in on the micro-. I knew what I was looking for but I didn't expect to find it. Any skilled criminal would have discarded it, but Karla's taste for the tried-and-true extended to her personal items. The chest of drawers in her bedroom was filled with sheets, pillowcases and blankets. Her bathroom contained a side table with an antique comb and brush set. I checked her medicine chest to satisfy my curiosity. There were some statins for reducing cholesterol (and reducing blood pressure?), *Advil* and *Tylenol*, melatonin to help her sleep and antacids to quiet her stomach. Medication minimalism.

The sewing room no longer contained a vintage *Singer* or *Bernina*, but it did feature an inexpensively-fabricated closet with drawers and racks of various sizes, but no safe or more secure container for jewelry, cash or important documents. Working drawer by drawer it took me ten minutes to find the ultimate object of my search. Bob Sharp's picture of my Czech ballerina and her guide was in black and white, but if you looked closely at the guide's scarf you could see that it was dark in color and had a pattern that was technically double herringbone with art deco accents. It was more stylish and subdued than one might have found in high-end Parisian flooring. It turned out to be maroon. I liked it. Even more, I liked the fact that I had found it, sitting quietly and unobtrusively at the bottom of a stack of four others. Karla couldn't part with it, but she should have.

# FIFTY-SEVEN

As soon as I got back to the car, drove a few blocks, parked, and removed the ersatz logo from the driver's door, I called Mike.

"Were you reading my mind?" he asked.

"I don't think so," I said.

"I was just about to contact you. I have some interesting information on Madame Hosek."

"So do I," I said. "So do I."

"Flip to see who goes first?"

"You go ahead."

"OK. First off, she's from Cali. Dad taught Urban Affairs at San Jose State. His first and last job. Never rose above the rank of associate professor."

"Ouch," I said.

"And never, so far as I could see, was able to afford a house."

"A lifetime renter, telling everyone else how to structure their cities and their ways of life."

"He was into things like sustainability, environmental impact, regulatory strategies, climate change mitigation and everything that could be shoehorned into the box labeled *social justice*."

"Not to be judgmental, but I'm hearing a voice in my head that suggests he may have been a tad bit preachy?"

"Probably a lot. He turns up more often in the local newspapers than in the scholarly journal literature."

"How about Mom?"

"His good and faithful servant, usually standing by his side, wearing a bandanna and holding a hand-painted, political sign."

"Immigrants?"

"Ultimately, of course, but not recently."

"Siblings for Karla?"

"Nope. Only child."

"Studied at…?"

"Berkeley."

"Studied what…?"

"Kind of an amalgam. A major in computer science, with what their propaganda calls 'robust GIS training' via an interdisciplinary minor in Geospatial Information Science and Technology—all run through the Geography, Environmental Science and City Planning Departments."

"Sounds like she was trying to outdo her father by working on the same kinds of things that he did, but with larger data sets, electronic maps, mega-mainframes and much better jargon."

"My thought as well."

"You know I did Geography in school."

"Yes, but more like Geography cum History, Sociology, et al."

"Right. More contextualized, with a lot of attention to economics, culture, etcetera."

"So you're soul sisters?"

"I wouldn't go that far," I said. "I just went through her house and the only computer there was several generations older than anything stored in *your* basement or attic. It was in a nook in her kitchen and looked like the kind of thing that an aged grandparent would use to send emails to her children's children."

"So she didn't keep up."

"Either that or she has her real equipment in her office," I said. "Or in some secret hidey-hole."

"S.P.E.C.T.R.E. HQ," Mike said.

"Possibly. Her home was full of other relics, so it may just be that she was too cheap to discard her old *Dell*."

"You haven't asked me about my best find," Mike said.

"I can't wait to hear it."

"When Karla was at Berkeley she had a roommate."

"Let me guess…hmm…Ting Chen."

"How did you know?"

"Educated guess. Ting's en route to the Roc for old home week. How did you find out about their time together in Berkeley?"

"Easy, when you ask the right question. I hacked into their old school files and saw that they shared a street address as well as an apartment number."

"They've been in contact ever since," I said. "Count on it."

"Nothing in the public record," Mike said. "Chen was a Chinese student doing Mechanical Engineering."

"That could contribute positively to a range of illicit activities," I said.

"Right. She returned to China after graduating from Berkeley and then surfaced years later."

"In Bureau files?"

"Company files, initially," Mike said, "but nothing with regard to specific clandestine operations. She just shows up now on routine watch lists."

"OK. Want to hear my information?"

"I can hardly wait," he said.

"When I checked out Karla's house and went through her drawers I found a scarf."

"*The* scarf? The *Milbridge* scarf?"

"The very same."

"The dotted lines are connecting," he said.

"Their scheduled reunion time is tonight," I said.

# FIFTY-EIGHT

They rallied at a hotel on East Avenue. Technically a *Hilton Double Tree*, it was called the *Strathallan Rochester,* a largeish facility with an active singles' bar and restaurant on the ground level. The central area included a succession of side booths but it was very noisy, with a lot of standing-room-only patrons swilling pricey wine and trying to be heard above the din.

I would have loved to be able to plant a listening device below their table but I wasn't prepared to put Richard's life at risk in the process. I did, however, have Karla's license plate number and was able to locate her *Audi* in the ample unpaved lot behind the facility. I installed a bug behind the door handle of my adjoining Highlander in the hope that she and Ting Chen might say something of interest to one another after they had completed their meal.

That meal chiefly consisted of scallops, shrimp, oysters and crab cakes, accompanied by one of the house white wines and followed by some tea which, I'm sure, failed to live up to Ting's expectations. I was able to film some of their conversation with my phone but I was operating at a considerable distance and there was an unending parade of individuals obstructing my view in an attempt to jockey for the best positions at or near the bar.

When dinner was finished I had hoped that they would travel together to the site where Richard was being held (or had been disposed of), but that was not the case. Ting did follow Karla into the parking lot but she then returned to the hotel where, Mike later confirmed, she was actually staying. I allowed Karla to drive out of the lot, retrieved my bug and followed her across East Avenue, back to her home on Canterbury Road. The bug turned out to be largely useless. The only conversation it recorded consisted of formulaic chit-chat and a promise to join one another the following day.

I sent the footage I had taken within the restaurant to Mike, who promptly enlisted the services of a lip reader who was able to reconstruct a few fragments:

> "We must complete this…"
> "Tereza is acting strangely. I wonder if she…"
> "We may already have enough…"
> "We should be able to…"
> "I will help in any way that I…"

Certain things were clear. The two were participating in a joint operation of some sort. The operation involved the Czech ballerina. The operation was coming to a close. Whether it was coming to a close because it had been successful (or not) remained unclear. It was clear to me that both Karla and Ting were hearing the same ticking clock in the back of their heads that was occupying my days and disrupting my sleep.

The next morning I checked in with Mike. He had been able to secure Ting's rental car license number. I swung by her hotel and noted that her car was still there. The one advantage that I had was that Karla lived less than five minutes from the *Strathallan* and I was able to both check on Ting and have time left to follow Karla out of her driveway.

Sensing that we were reaching some point of finality I had double-checked my *Sig*, strapped a small, light *Smith & Wesson Bodyguard 2.0* to my ankle and added some other devices to my purse and person. I wondered what I would need and how soon I would need them.

Karla surprised me. She didn't drive to work and she didn't drive to the *Wegmans* near her on East Avenue or the one on Calkins Road by *Kommunicom*, the end points for seemingly half the city's daily traffic. Instead she drove toward their flagship store on Monroe Street, but then drove right past it, continued through the village and drove to the highly unlikely *Target* store in Victor, where she purchased a large bag of dog kibble.

At first I wondered why she was going so far out of her way to buy it. Was she aware that I was following her? My tracking skills were strong but none are perfect. The second thing that concerned me was the fact that there was no evidence of any canine presence in her home on Canterbury Road and she most definitely did not appear to be the sort of person who would ever run errands for a friend.

My next thought was that she might be taking her 'cautious' route, the one that always preceded some action or other with which she did not want to be associated. The following guess was that her destination may have been guarded by a hungry Rottweiler, Doberman or Mastiff. Only one of those thoughts proved to be correct.

When she pulled out of the *Target* lot she turned left, leaving behind her a string of big box stores located beneath the Eastview Mall. She then drove to the Basin on the Pittsford/Victor road, past an array of banks, office buildings, test labs, jewelry and sporting goods stores. Passing my hotel she continued through the Basin, turning left onto Thornell Road, a long artery that linked a succession of neighborhoods of different ages and architectural styles.

Again, I was struck by the presence of cornfields and other remnants of an agricultural past that had been sustained by local environmental regulations. Hitting the T-intersection at West Bloomfield Road she turned right, passed a Catholic church on her right and then turned left, driving past a large Middle School on Barker Road. At the next T-intersection she turned left onto Mendon Center Road, approaching the subdivision where Gabe and Clara Ruffino lived.

She was full of surprises this morning. I had no reason to expect that she was involved with Gabe in any way and I felt a certain degree of relief when she drove past the entry street for his neighborhood, reinforcing my faith in his and his wife's innocence and instead driving toward the New York Thruway, which was actually visible on the higher ground in the distance.

Then, suddenly and unexpectedly, she turned right into what appeared to be an abandoned farm property with a dilapidated barn at the end of a weed-covered gravel driveway. I drove past without slowing or stopping and eventually positioned myself in such a way that I could observe the corner of her *Audi* without her seeing me.

She returned to her car in fifteen minutes. I could see the small puff of smoke from her right exhaust tip and I expected her to come out of the driveway and turn left, returning to town. I did not want her to see me parked on the opposite side of the road, and when she did turn left I felt comfortable that she hadn't, unless she had followed her intuition and looked for me in her rear-vision mirror. She was driving faster when she departed than when she arrived. Perhaps she had one or more additional stops to make and her task on the derelict farm had taken longer than she expected.

When she was finally out of sight I pulled into the driveway and parked on the far side of the barn. I had already made a cursory inspection for security cameras and had seen none on the barn nor on a nearby garden shed. The farmhouse proper sat at least 150 yards beyond the barn and the angles for potential televised surveillance from the house would have been too indirect and too distant to be of much use to any observer. The space by the barn was unfortunately barren, with the exception of a fallen oak tree that was now a broken and shriveled home for thousands of insects. There was a power line running from the public road to the barn but it looked as if it had been installed just after the harnessing of electricity.

While the siding of the structure was in varying stages of rot, with light shining through at multiple points, there was a sturdy door on the building's north side with a fresh *Yale* lock made of solid brass. It took me several moments to open it. I entered the barn and saw an array of rusted equipment and a vehicle covered by a dusty canvas tarpaulin. I lifted the corner, saw the New York license plate and the three interlocking horizontal and vertical ellipses of the *Toyota* logo. My heart fell and then recovered. I had recorded the plate number. It was Richard's car.

# FIFTY-NINE

The loft above ground level was accessed by a cobwebbed ladder that hadn't been used in years and the raw plank flooring of which it had been constructed was spaced sufficiently to reveal its emptiness. I looked for a space below ground level and eventually located a trapdoor. It was also secured by a *Yale* lock, this one again made of solid brass but with a shackle made of hardened steel. I bypassed the lock itself and found a rusty implement that I was able to use to loosen and then pry off the strike plate. I opened the trapdoor and saw the ladder below. It was steep but it was equipped with a handrail on each side and the space below was lit by a flickering light. I could hear a sound in the distance that was vaguely human.

The dirt floor was marked with Karla's fresh prints. The space was segmented by stacked, heavily-weathered lumber and small hay bales riddled with the presence, remains and droppings of insects and other vermin. Eventually I found Richard.

His legs were shackled and the chains bolted to the remains of a steel I-beam, but for some as-yet unknown reason, the shackles were cushioned by soft linings. The shackles' pins were secured by heavy-duty locks and tip welds that expanded their diameters. Richard would have been able to maneuver slightly, but in his current condition it was doubtful that he had much desire to do so. His pupils were pinpricks, his breathing shallow, his faint attempt at speech slurred and his arms and legs marked with needle tracks.

There were three buckets by his body, one containing water, one containing dog kibble and the third in use as a hit-or-miss toilet. The dominant odor was one of vomit combined with the smells of body waste. He was clothed in underwear but he had been given a comforter and pillow, each of which was heavily stained. The roadside-throwaway mattress on which he lay sat above the dirt floor on a set of splintered, pine skids.

When I first looked at him there was a slight glimmer of recognition in his eyes, but he was nodding off and had difficulty focusing. I estimated his weight loss at 30-40 pounds. He hadn't shaved in weeks and looked like a mad or dying hermit.

My mind and body were swirling with emotion. I wanted to free him but didn't have the tools at hand to enable me to do so. I was doing my best to keep from screaming in anger. If Karla was standing before me I would have emptied each of the magazines for my *Sig* into her face and heart and then clawed at her eyes until my fingernails were broken and bloodied. While I was relieved to find him alive I was enraged by his condition and the unspeakable treatment to which he had been subjected.

I spoke his name but he was suddenly unresponsive. Karla had come to replace what passed for his food supply, inject him and further degrade him. I had heard (and used) the expression of 'profound disgust' many times in my life but what I was feeling now was more like a sea of rage coursing through my veins and demanding an act of violent retribution.

The urgency of my need for some form of revenge was warring with the necessity to do something to save the nearly lifeless form that lay at my feet, a twisted figure that had suddenly replaced all of my memories of a dear person, one whose humanity had now been systematically ravaged by the powers of evil and darkness.

The first thing that I did may have been pointless, considering his condition, but I removed a clean handkerchief from my pocket, dipped it in the bucket of water that sat near his head and began to clean his face and mouth as best I could under the circumstances. While Richard was unable to respond I continued to dip, wash and wipe, but suddenly

I heard another voice, one that seemed to emerge from a hell forged of nightmares.

"Who in the hell are you and what are you doing here?" the voice said.

I turned, settled myself, and said, "I'm a special agent for the Federal Bureau of Investigation. Before you begin to wallow in self-satisfaction you should know that the satellite office in Rochester, the field office in Buffalo and our central headquarters in Washington are all aware of my presence here. They are also aware of your plotting with Ting Chen and your utilization of the Czech ballerina, currently operating under the alias of Veronika Bartak. Your prisoner here is a former member of the Bureau and we defend our own. To the death. Before you add any additional crimes to your rap sheet I would advise you to leave while you still have the opportunity to do so."

"Very bravely said," she responded. "Unfortunately, you have no evidence of any of that and you are now no more than a simple prisoner. I will deal with you directly and I can assure you that it will not be in a way that you are likely to enjoy." (Her tone was odd; it was as if she was attempting to intimidate me by reciting lines from a high school play.) She pointed her gun at my eyes and shook it to the right, directing me to step away from Richard. She then placed her thumb and left index finger over Richard's nose, still pointing her weapon at the center of my forehead. "Remove your weapon," she said, as his body spasmed in panic and desperation. "Do it with your left hand."

I pulled back my jacket and removed my *Sig* from its holster on my left hip.

"Slide it toward me and pull up your slacks."

I did so and revealed the S&W strapped to my ankle.

"Slide that toward me as well and crawl over here."

When I did she ran her left hand along my thighs and inside my belt.

"I trust you enjoyed that," I said.

She sneered and told me to scoot back and sit against a filthy bale of moldy hay.

"Tell me something," I said. "Why the padded shackles? Are you trying to dress the body for later investigators?"

"Someone has to be held responsible for the operation," she said. "It fell to his lot to play that role. His body needed to be more or less intact and any chafed or bloodied skin would have defeated our purposes. When his body is found the authorities will conclude that he needed money to fund his habit and eventually betrayed his company and colluded with some foreign government to secure the means to do so. The only things he had to sell were *Kommunicom's* secrets. When he was finally overcome with guilt he overdosed."

"Given his background as a Bureau agent and a decorated combat infantryman I would seriously doubt that anyone could find something that preposterous to be even marginally plausible. I hope for your sake that you have an alternative explanation." I was stretching out my sentences, looking for the time and opportunity to make my move.

"What you believe or doubt is unlikely to be of any consequence," she said.

"And how long have you been colluding with your former roommate?" I asked.

"You know about that? I'm impressed. Actually, for quite a long while," she answered. "Our work together is really nothing out of the ordinary, more like a simple instance of standard principles and protocols."

"In what sense?" I asked.

"When the Chinese permit you to enter into a commercial relationship they routinely expect to enjoy access to what you would call your *intellectual property*. *Kommunicom* was, shall we say, recalcitrant. More to the point they were operating in western New York, not mainland China. With my pivotal presence within the organization I was able to sustain their standard practice and send along information that they would find of use."

"That's treason, of course," I said.

"I wouldn't characterize it in that way," she answered, "but, as I said before, your opinion is really of no consequence."

"And this farm…it was one purchased by the Chinese, back in the day, before we became aware of the extent of their holdings and intentions."

"The title is now buried in an unsearchable list of holding companies."

"One other thing…"

"You know," she said, "you are beginning to bore me and I have to move on. I'm losing interest in this conversation."

"You don't yet know how much I know," I said. "This conversation could affect your survival as well as the satisfaction of my curiosity." After I said that I scooted around, displaying discomfort at my positioning.

She stared at me passively, waiting for me to continue with my questions.

"Why in the world would you do this?" I asked. "You don't need the money. You live in a relatively spartan fashion. Your Berkeley days of useful idiocy are in the distant past…"

"You have no idea of who I am, what I might desire or what interests or concerns might motivate me."

"I was hoping you would tell me," I said. "I don't really see any personality or, for that matter, humanity, in what you are or what you may have done. That's interesting, in and of itself."

I scooted some more in an attempt to communicate my growing physical discomfort.

"Did I detect some evidence of a personal relationship between you and Ingle?" she asked. "I have to say, the Florence Nightingale routine was deeply affecting." As she said it she smiled. "Well…?" she asked.

"Unfortunately I don't have any time for personal relationships. I usually find myself running down people who are simply incapable of them."

That received a cold stare. I decided to continue.

"You realize, of course, that the Chen woman is operating under orders from her superiors. If you believe that she has confided in you in good faith you are an even greater fool than I think you are. The moment that the operation is threatened your usefulness will have passed. She will probably be the one who kills you, helps cut their losses and then buries your body near Richard's. Ultimately you mean nothing to her."

"You think we're doing this with the full knowledge of her government?"

"I don't really care," I said, "but I'm certain that her government will use her in the same manner that she will use you. By the way, who made the first overture? I suspect it was awkward, probably even pathetic."

She paused for nearly a minute before responding. "There was no *overture*," she said. "It was a natural outgrowth of our longstanding friendship."

"Not a word that plays much of a role in their lexicon, I'm afraid. You're dealing with greedy ideologues who are both corrupt and power mad. Your heart and body are likely to have the same fate as Richard's. You'll be the thing that's fed to the dogs."

"You have no idea," she said.

"But I actually do," I said. "One last question…"

"Finally," she said.

"Do you think you're James Bond?"

"What the hell do you mean by that?"

"You're carrying a *Beretta*," I said. "Bond later realized that the *Walther* was a far better weapon."

"My weapon will kill you without any difficulty," she said.

"Perhaps," I said, "but it's a *Beretta Pico*. One of its significant problems is the fact that it tops the list of the most difficult weapons to rack. Have you ever even tried to do so? Have you ever used it in an actual field operation?"

"Of course," she lied.

"I actually doubt that," I said. "You're a glorified secretary, not a soldier. You speak like a person in a bad play. Go ahead. Try to attempt to rack the slide."

Her eyes were now flaring and as I expected she made the mistake of the most inexperienced amateur. Rather than use the standard push/pull technique to balance her effort she simply tried to pull, thus turning the weapon away from its intended target. By then I had retrieved the knife that was concealed in what we, in more polite society, would call my gluteal cleft. This was made slightly more difficult by the necessity of sheathing it in material that would prevent its razor-sharp edges from cutting into my flesh. As I retrieved it and positioned my index figure along the top, thus maintaining its no-spin status, she caught a glimpse of my movement in her peripheral vision. By then it was already in the air, finding its way to the general area of her larynx and esophagus.

The next sound she was able to make was a mix of gurgling and heaving, as the blood spurted from her mouth and became a set of rivulets darkening the top of her open blouse.

# SIXTY

"If I were you," I said, "I would be very careful now. You know, of course, that you have carotid arteries on either side of your throat and if you attempt to remove the knife you could nick one of them and hasten your death."

By then she had dropped the *Beretta* and was grasping at the knife, the blood flowing through her clutched fingers. She tried to issue a call for my help, but the /h/ sound is unvoiced; the vocal cords do not vibrate and the result is more like a gentle sigh. This one, however, was accompanied by burbling, a water sound but one suffused with breath and blood and heaving.

"The knife is an *AceJet* 'Stinger'," I said. "Top quality. It will run you around $90. Its successful use requires a great deal of practice and experience…"

She was now staggering, clutching and gurgling.

"I counted on your lack of experience with actual wet work," I said. "Not all have the stomach for it. You had the stomach for cruelty and the most sordid form of violence in addicting Richard, but it's one thing to desecrate the body of someone who's incapacitated and quite another to defend yourself against someone who's undergone professional training and has real-world experience."

She fell backwards at my feet, her chest heaving, her torso soaked with frothing blood. By then I was standing above her, looking at her overdressed body as it churned next to Richard's.

"Here," I said, "let me help you with that," and drove the heel of my right foot into the back of the knife, plunging it into her spinal column. After a few seconds of seizing, the electricity exploded in her brain and she came to rest, her right leg (which she had used to brace herself in an attempt to rise) slowly sliding into parallel with her left.

I looked at Richard and he seemed to have awakened momentarily, his eyes looking first at mine and then beyond. Before I could respond to him a voice came from the shadows beyond the ceiling light.

"Thank you very much," the voice said. "I am in your debt. You have done my work for me."

"Welcome, Ms. Chen," I said. "I was wondering when you were going to arrive."

"I wouldn't be that happy to see me if I were you," she responded. "You'll be joining Karla in a moment or two, as well as your addicted friend."

"You intend to murder me."

"Of course."

"But then you'll be forced to abort your operation to destroy Governor Thompson's political career."

"Why should we have to do that?"

"Well, in the first place, my associates are on their way here and you have neither the time nor the strength to extricate Mr. Ingle from his shackles and dispose of three bodies. Not to be too catty about it, but Ms. Hosek is particularly weighty. You have no digging equipment here and those steps are narrow and steep."

"I have no intention of removing them," she said. "All I need to do is pose them."

"Much easier said than done," I responded. "Lines of fire and other features involving positioning are now analyzed with 3D laser scanning. We are not naïve fools, Ms. Chen. There is also the not inconsiderable fact that the room and the bodies will be covered with your DNA. New York may not have the death penalty, but the Feds do. The best thing that you could do now would be to escape (assuming that you would have the skills to do so)."

"I will have diplomatic immunity," she said.

I laughed and said, "I wish I had 100 Yuan for every time I've heard that."

She looked into my eyes and racked the slide on her *Glock 17*.

"One last question," I said. "Was this operation Hosek's idea or yours?"

"Harrison's political success is a simple fact. It is also obvious that my country would prefer other candidacies to his. Hosek knew of this crippled ballerina and suggested we use her to destroy Harrison's chances."

"And did she agree to do this for money or was pressure applied to her?"

"You said 'one last question,' I believe."

"Humor me."

"The woman's mother is still alive in Prague. We could, shall we say, make life even more difficult for her than it already is."

"Thank you for clarifying that," I said.

"In death the satisfaction of curiosity is of little consequence."

"Yes, in death," I said. "I, however, plan on remaining in western New York."

As I said that she offered me a smile that was filled with hate and self-satisfaction. "I think not," she said, and raised her handgun from its position opposite my heart to one opposite my eyes. At that moment her head exploded silently as if it were a pumpkin on a wall surrounded by a thousand teenage boys armed with BB guns and pellet rifles. Some of the blood and brain splatter made its way to my face and shoulders.

"Messy," I said, as Ben walked into the full light above us. He was carrying a *Heckler & Koch MP7A2* submachine gun with a suppressor and 40-round magazine.

"Sorry I was a little late on my house call," he said.

"I never doubted you'd come," I said, "but I did take some personal precautions."

He laughed as I removed my *Smith & Wesson* from my left pocket and my *Sig* from my right. "While the Chinese woman's comadre was stumbling and gurgling I took the opportunity to retrieve my handguns. I wasn't sure if she would appear or not, but I wanted to be prepared."

"Good scout," he said.

"Thanks. The problem was that I wasn't sure if she would have a helmet or body armor or whatever. I'm probably 70-80% effective with my left hand, so I figured I'd use that for the center mass rounds and my right for the head shots."

"Good thinking," he said, looking more closely at Hosek's throat. "*AceJet Stinger*," he said. "Very nice toss."

"Try not to be distracted," I said. "As I was saying…when I had a knight in camo armor appear with a handy-dandy HK my precautions proved to be unnecessary. How are you doing, big guy?"

We embraced and he kissed me on the forehead.

"Good to see you again," he said.

I smiled and kissed him on the cheek.

"What do you say we free this young man and dispose of these two bodies?"

"Works for me," I said. "Unfortunately, I don't have anything at hand to remove those shackles."

Ben bent over and looked at them. "Just give me a sec," he said, and climbed the stairs to the ground level. He returned in five minutes with a small handsaw equipped with a tungsten carbide-tipped blade.

"This blade significantly reduces sparking and other effects that Richard's legs do not want or need." He quickly cut through the shackles and removed them. "Kind of them to use the padding."

"They wanted him to play the fall guy, with the addiction interpreted as self-inflicted. Drooling and seizing would be OK, but they didn't want to leave any marks that would indicate that he was being held against his will. No indication where they would have eventually left the body. I suspect that if you check Hosek's car you'll find syringes, probably one to serve as the hot shot that he would have putatively used to kill himself. What do you want to do with the bodies?"

"We can give that some thought," he said. "It would be nice if we could protect Richard's company from the bad publicity of having a Chinese agent in their front office. With the Chinese woman? My vote would be to drop her off at their embassy. Eventually they would be able to identify her but they would never claim her. It would be a nice way of reminding them that we have an eye on their activities. For now I'll just put them both in my trunk, and, as we say in the Army, take down my little cloth house and steal away into the night."

"The most important person now is Richard," he added.

"Of course," I said. "I'm sure there are plenty of private facilities for long-term care. Let's just take him to a hospital, have him evaluated, cleaned up and made as comfortable as possible."

While Ben carried the bodies to his trunk I called Kathy.

"First and foremost, he's alive," I said.

"Thank God!" she said. I could hear her hyperventilating.

"He's been held captive and subjected to opioid addiction. It appears that they wanted to use him to take the fall for a political operation. Their story would be that he got involved because he needed the money to feed his addiction. I know that sounds ridiculous, but our first operating principle is that you simply cannot fix stupid. Anyway, I can't really go into the details now. We'll have ample time to talk. At the moment he's suffering from days of physical neglect. We'll get him to a place where he can be stabilized and put on a path to full recovery."

"Where and when can I see him?"

"Soon," I said, "but we should have someone check his vitals first. He'll be going through withdrawal soon. Fortunately that's not as horrendous as it once was. Do you have a favorite hospital?"

"My OB-GYN is at *Highland*. Where are you now?"

"On the edge of Pittsford."

"You're closer to *Strong* but they may be overwhelmed in their ER."

"We'll go to *Highland*; you'll be more comfortable there."

"The parking is awful, but the ER is easily accessed."

"We'll find it," I said. "I'll make some calls while we're on our way. We'll get most-favored-nation status for Richard. You should relax, catch your breath, wait a few minutes and drive in carefully. I know you're excited, happy, relieved and still worried. We want you to arrive safely. I'll leave a message at the front desk for you; we'll make sure that his privacy is insured and that he's getting the best care available."

"I don't know what to say…how to thank you," she said.

"Don't worry about it. We'll talk later."

When I ended the call I looked down at Richard. His eyes were open. His nose was running uncontrollably but he forced what appeared to be a smile.

# SIXTY-ONE

We used my car to transport Richard. Ben strapped him into the back seat, promised to follow me and backed out of the way so that I could pass him and turn onto Mendon Center Road. He had also secured the fobs from Chen's and Hosek's bodies and moved their vehicles to the side of the gravel road that led to the old farm house. They were now out of sight from the road beyond, reduced to minor problems that could be dealt with later.

*Highland Hospital* was located in a residential neighborhood lined with row upon row of parked cars. Every available foot of public parking space was taken. As I pulled into the facility I saw the ER intake point in the corner of the building. When I stopped the car a set of individuals approached. They were led by a tall African-American man who looked as if he could have had a Sunday job as an NFL defensive end.

"Special Agent Harrison," I said.

"James Washington," he said. "We've been expecting you. We'll take your passenger. You can park in the facility at the top of the circle," he said, pointing to a multi-level structure with an enclosed entry/exit booth. Take a ticket; they'll validate in the hospital. Your passenger will be in this room." He handed me a plain card with a room and floor designation.

I dropped off Richard and drove to the parking structure which was connected to an adjoining office building that housed several floors of doctors and clinics. 'One-stop shopping' I thought to myself.

Kathy was right about the parking. I had to park on the roof level, but I was closer to the elevator for the hospital than to the ramp that serviced the doctors' building. By the time I got to Richard's room I realized that the corridor was particularly quiet. He had been sequestered, as we requested. I entered the room and saw that Richard was being held upright in a chair in the shower, with two individuals scrubbing him down. The steam was thick and the scent of the soap strong. I wasn't sure that he was aware of the intensity of their efforts, but *I* certainly appreciated them. His hair needed a good cutting, but at least it was now much cleaner and those attending him were rinsing and repeating and constantly combing. Except for the scraggly beard he was looking far more human.

They dried him off, dressed him in a hospital gown and took him to a bed that had more high-tech attachments than the cockpit of a B-2 bomber. An orderly entered the room and used a scissors and standard safety razor to clear his cheeks of the hermit's beard. "Almost there," he said. "This is a change for me. I usually shave the tops of heads or…lower abdomens… for surgery."

"I appreciate your efforts," I said.

"All in a day's work," he responded.

When he was finished, a nurse appeared at the door. She was carrying a syringe in a tray, but before injecting him she pulled up the crisp sheet from the base of the bed, placed it on Richard's body and then removed a blanket from the adjoining chest of draws, removed its plastic protective bag and covered Richard's legs and torso. She then swabbed his left shoulder with an alcohol prep pad and injected him.

She didn't volunteer any information concerning the medication and I didn't ask. A few minutes later a young doctor entered the room. He looked impatient.

"I'm Dr. Shepherd," he said. "Paul."

"Special Agent Harrison," I said. "Gwen." There were no handshakes or hugs.

"We've injected the patient with buprenorphine," he said. "It interrupts the ways in which the nerves signal pain between the brain and the body. Reduces the effects of withdrawal."

"I'm sure he'll appreciate that," I said.

"We call this the *Ritz-Carlton* room," he said. "The hospital director received a call from Washington. We were asked to make the patient a top priority and provide him with the best possible care. We were also asked to protect his identity and keep the press at bay."

"His situation was a matter of some speculation in the local press," I said. "The case has implications that extend beyond this area."

"We'll do our best," he said. "We've assigned him the name 'Lawrence Dennison'; I don't know who picked it. He doesn't look like a Lawrence Dennison to me."

"Nor to me," I said, smiling, "but we'll take him off your hands as soon as possible. At this point we wanted him cleaned up and checked for any problems beyond the addiction, which, as you probably have concluded, was inflicted upon him."

"I'm seeing him for the first time," he said. "I didn't draw any conclusions. Usually the addicts go directly to expensive private clinics, the street people to morgues. When you receive calls from federal agencies…which very seldom happens…you assume that the case is… well, exceptional."

"His wife should be here momentarily. I'd appreciate it if she could have a minute or two with him before you begin to run your tests."

"Certainly," he said.


Kathy arrived five minutes later. Her eyes were red and her breathing was elevated, but she was also overcome with feelings of relief. When she saw him she hurried to his side and took his hand in hers. He remained still for a moment but finally opened his eyes and recognized her. He then turned his head and saw me on the other side of his bed. Clutching Kathy's hand as tightly as he could he also reached toward mine. It was as if he had been faintly aware of all that had happened.

# SIXTY-TWO

"They're protecting his identity," I told her. "His hospital name is Lawrence Dennison."

"Not what I would have chosen," she said, smiling.

After a few seconds of lucidity Richard had returned to sleep.

"They've given him some medication which controls the pain signals between the nerves and the brain," I said. "It makes the withdrawal process easier and less painful."

"That's a blessing," Kathy said. "I take it you've met with the doctor."

"Paul Shepherd," I said, googling the hospital site. "Bachelor's from Dartmouth, M.D. from Washington University in St. Louis. Board certified in internal medicine. Fifteen years' experience."

"Sounds like the first team," she said. "What did you think of him?"

"No nonsense-type. Straight to the point."

"My preference," she said. "I'll do the hand holding; I want someone highly capable to do the healing."

"He'll check back with us after they've done some tests. My guess is that that will take several hours. How about some coffee?"

"I'd love some."

I made a deal with the person behind the big desk at the nurses' station. She would text me when the doctor was ready to meet with us. As I had expected, that turned out to be a matter of hours. The three of us assembled in an empty waiting room in the corner of the hallway containing Richard's room. The doctor sat on the edge of his chair.

"The news is good," he said. "The thing that we worry about most is the state of the lungs, because the opioids can have a serious impact upon a patient's breathing. Bottom line: there's no tuberculosis and no pneumonia. We're not so much concerned about the psychological profile because the patient was injected against his will, so we're not worried about antisocial personality disorder, depression, and that kind of thing. Ditto with things like sexual dysfunction. I'm also happy to say that whoever was injecting him may have been evil but he or she wasn't incompetent. There are no scarred or collapsed veins and no bacterial infections of the blood vessels or heart valves. There are also no abscesses or soft-tissue infections.

"We assumed there was no needle sharing, but we checked and found no evidence of Hepatitis B or C and no HIV. He was injected; he didn't snort, so there were no nasal issues. The runny nose is characteristic, regardless of how the drug is ingested. Almost anything that you shouldn't put in your body can cause it, particularly if you're in a period of withdrawal.

"If I had to give you a straightforward summation I would say that there were two things working in his favor. The first was the fact that he was not addicted over a long period of time, so that the interference with the opioid receptors in the brain did not result in the brain's *rewiring*. I don't want to give you a three-hour lecture on neuroscience but if you google the interactions between the brain and drugs there is copious information on the internet that will help answer your questions. Right now I would say that the recovery process should go very well and that what the patient needs is your presence, your comfort, your love and your support."

"You said there was another thing working in his favor," Kathy said.

"Yes. His general health. He took care of himself. His body was resilient. It was assaulted but ultimately the assault failed."

"And it was heroin, right?" I asked.

"Yes, without any fentanyl. That's a good thing. Unfortunately, it's become a relatively uncommon thing, but this wasn't the usual bargain-basement garbage. You should be grateful for that."

"We are," Kathy said. "How about the next stage of care?"

"We've got to change his diet," the doctor said. "They were feeding him dog food. I don't quite understand that, but he survived it. His captors had strange ideas about economics. Anyway, he's here now; he's free now. We'll ease him into a wholesome diet. He'll be having breakfast, lunch and dinner from a tube first, but then you'll want him to gain his weight back and improve his muscle tone. With his low A1C he could probably tolerate a diet of ice cream, pizza and cheeseburgers. They might also lift his spirits, though I assume that your presence and support would serve him equally well in that regard."

After he left and we returned to Richard's room, an orderly brought in a rollaway bed for Kathy. "We'll bring you some towels and a travel packet with shampoo, soap, toothbrush, paste and deodorant," he said. "You can order your meals through the hospital. We'll try to find you something besides the rust-colored Jell-O and the lukewarm consommé."

We both smiled. "I appreciate all you've done and all that you're doing," Kathy said.

"The gossip on the floor is that someone called from Washington and told us to spare no expenses. We know how to do that."


When he left, Kathy and I embraced and I returned to the lobby. Ben was sitting in a corner, reading a novel by Jeffery Deaver, probably giving no thought to the fact that the trunk of his car contained two bodies drenched in blood.

"I think we've earned some dinner," I said.

# SIXTY-THREE

"**Y**our choice," Ben said.

"I know a place," I said. "Richard's wife recommended it."

"I'll have to ride with you," he said. "While you were waiting for Richard's tests to be completed I checked in with the Buffalo field office. They've sent three individuals to tidy up. The most important will be the Cleaner for my Bureau car. The two cars back on the farm will also be picked up and taken to Buffalo. They'll look for anything interesting that might be found there and they'll check for prints, collect DNA and whatever else might strike them as noteworthy, mostly just for the record."

"What will happen to those cars?"

"I think they'll probably return the Hosek woman's car to her garage."

"Fine irony," I said. "The judgment could be that she simply disappeared, like Richard."

"Depending on what they decide to do with the body. That neck wound will raise a lot of questions and questions are something that we don't need."

"If the clouds of guilt are hovering over her head instead of Richard's that might quell the curiosity of the local press."

"Yep," Ben said. "Some story would be cooked up concerning his disappearance and the press corps would automatically be refocused on her. It would rivet the public's attention for a day or so and then slowly be replaced by something more compelling, like the price of groceries and mortgage interest rates. As to the Chen woman…well, that's a more interesting situation."

"The Bureau could bury her in the Adirondacks or drop her off at the front door of the Chinese embassy. The spies and bureaucrats there will have already deduced that their operation had gone awry."

"Assuming they're aware of the operation," Ben said. "There's always the possibility that the two women really were lone-wolfing it and then hoping for medals and future pats on the head when the Texas governor's presidental run was in the crapper."

"Long shot," I said. "The Chinese don't like lone wolves."

"I agree, but they may have wanted to keep the plotters at arm's length so that they could have deniability and wring their hands in unison with ours when the bodies turned up."

"They remain inscrutable," I said, smiling.

"Let's go eat," Ben said.


The restaurant was called *Black and Blue*, a kind of play on surf/turf or steak/fish. Located in the *Pittsford Plaza* upscale strip mall, it was a favorite spot for celebratory dinners and, as a result, a place with a high noise level and the generous spread of cash.

"Richard's wife said that we should ask to be seated in the back room if we want to be able to speak and hear."

"I can do that," Ben said.


We had some Maryland-style she-crab soup, medium-rare ribeyes with brandy peppercorn sauce and shared some French fries. This was all incidental to the two courses of dry Martinis with which we began and the *Duckhorn* Merlot with which we continued.

Half way through the second round of Martinis Ben received a text.

"The Chinese woman's car was a rental," Ben said. "Very traceable and very amateurish, unless she was trying to 'hide in plain sight' or something equally foolish."

"We could check it out and then check it back in with the rental car agency and no one would be the wiser," I said.

"Right, perhaps even drop it off in some distant location. Pittsburgh instead of Pittsford. Send a message to the Beijing brotherhood."

"And mystify the press. Win/win."

"I'll be more interested in what happens to the bodies," Ben said. "For now they're in a deep freezer somewhere, surrounded by ground chuck and bags of frozen green beans. They won't be in any conventional morgue."

I smiled approvingly before pausing and talking logistics.

"You'll need a ride to the airport," I said. "Not sure when you'll be able to get out. There are hotels nearby. What can I do?"

"Not to worry. I'm flying private."

"The Director let you use his *Gulfstream*?"

"Special treats for special people. He thought you needed me ASAP and as we all know he has a soft spot for you."

"I think he felt that the mission was important enough to justify it. He's very protective of all of his people, including those who are no longer working for the Bureau."

"I'd bet hard currency that he wished he could have come along with me. He loves to keep his 'hand in' as he says."

"Well, there *was* that incident on the streets of D.C.," I said. "He and the guy formerly known as the SecDef were accosted by a demonstrator who waved his placard in the SecDef's face, nicking his nose."

"I remember that," Ben said. "The General responded with a heel-of-the-hand blow that crushed the demonstrator's nose against his cheeks. He bled like an inattentive sparring partner working with Mike Tyson."

"The press were persuaded to see it as an instance of self-defense," I said. "The Director called it an 'on-the-spot-correction'."

"We don't deserve him," Ben said.

"But Richard does," I added.

"I'll drink to that," Ben responded, raising his wine glass and savoring a long sip.

"So you'll go back to…?"

"Some sunny village in the Ukraine," he answered. "Not sure which one yet."

"I always do enjoy our collaborations," I said.

We passed on desserts but downed multiple cups of black coffee. Every now and then our dining experience was punctuated with loud voices and impromptu songs issuing from the main dining room. They prompted us to take additional sips.

"How about you?" he later said. "Where do you go from here?"

"Probably back on my lecture tour," I said. "I've been working several of the field offices, giving pep talks, opining on special cases, trying to stimulate thinking with interesting anecdotes."

"I can imagine you doing that," he said. "What about Richard?"

"I suspect the hospital will keep him there for a day or two, make sure he's fully stabilized and then happily turn him over to the Bureau. If I had to guess I'd say that they'll send him to San Antonio. The med center there handles addiction cases. I'd guess…maybe…what…six weeks or so there and then he'll be ready to return to work."

"From what you said earlier he'll be working for a new boss. One thing's for damned sure; that boss will have the welcome opportunity to pick a new executive assistant."

"True that," I said.


When we finished I drove Ben to the airport and watched the Director's G550 take off. "He may have other, more presssing uses in mind for it," Ben had said. "We don't want his thirty or forty million dollar carriage to turn into a pumpkin."

"Like the Chinese woman's head," I said.

"Just so," he answered.

# SIXTY-FOUR

I checked in with Kathy the next morning. She sounded happy and refreshed.

"How's Richard doing?" I asked.

"Smiling a lot and speaking in short sentences," she said. "He's heavily medicated but a few minutes ago he said something about loving me and wanting something good to eat."

"I'll stay in touch," I said. "Just remember the important things…"

"Take care of Richard and avoid the press."

"Bingo," I said.

Tony Giraldi met me at the airport later that morning, took the car and wished me well. "Next time you're here…you call me. We can do a tour of the Italian restaurants."

"I'd love that," I said.

That night I slept in my own bed. The sleep was restful and uninterrupted. I called Peggy first thing the next morning and she told me that the Director was ordering me to take the day off. "Dinner at his home tomorrow night," she said. "8:00."

"I'll be there," I said.

"He also said that he wants you to continue your talks, but that you'll have the full weekend and the better part of next week to prepare. The schedule has changed. You'll be going to Tampa, Nashville and New Orleans."

"Sounds more like R&R," I said, "but I'm not complaining."

"Something like that may have crossed his mind," she said.

I spent most of the day at the facing malls at Tysons Corner. I did a lot of window shopping but didn't purchase anything of note. Mostly I walked and looked and worked the bloodiest recent memories out of my system. There's nothing like a solid rush of capitalist indulgence to clear the head and improve the muscle memory. I also relished the anonymity and the ability to go for hours without saying any words or playing any roles. That evening I arrived at the Director's home in McLean at 7:55. He had been there awhile. The coat and tie were gone. He was wearing cotton slacks and a cashmere cardigan sweater that he had probably owned for two or three decades. He greeted me with a hug. Everyone was hugging me these days. I liked it.

"Happy to see you safe and sound," he said. "How is Richard?"

"I talked to his wife this afternoon, Sir. He's doing well. He's got some skin issues from the crappy bed and the confinement but the dermatologist said they're nothing to worry about. I think that he's doing well with the detox/withdrawal process because he never wanted to be drugged in the first place. It's one thing to have chosen a path and another to be dragged down one. There was anger there, anger that was motivating."

"Good point," he said. "Plus they have drugs of various kinds now to ease you through the process. My prediction?"

"He'll be climbing the walls in the detox facility after a week or two and they'll have to tie him down to force him to complete the program."

"Exactly. I didn't know him beyond a handshake at our son's graduation and commissioning ceremony but when I looked at his file I knew that he was a fighter."

"The best," I said.

"Hungry?"

"Yes, Sir."

"I should say before we start that this goes against everything I stand for…"

I just cocked my head like a Scottish terrier, waiting for him to clarify. He smiled, walked into the kitchen and returned with a champagne bucket. The top of the bottle was sloshing slightly in the ice and water surrounding it.

"Somehow I just thought it was time for something more festive," he said. "Richard's back; you're safe; Ben's back on his day job; the bad guys have been neutralized. As much as I enjoy other things I decided we should have one of Monsieur Moët's finer products."

For all of his talk about bourbon, scotch and red wine he handled the champagne perfectly, holding the cork firmly and twisting the bottle while pulling gently, a reverse of the process of racking the slide on my *Sig*.

"Hope you're up for some peasant food," he said. "It was one of my wife's favorites. We always seemed to attract other kids from the posts and this was something she could whip up easily. You take some pork chops and sauté them in butter until they have a nice golden crust. You then put them in a roaster pan. You put six cups of rice or so on top of the chops, and set it all aside. Then you slice six onions, sauté them in butter until they're translucent and add six cups of beef broth. You bring that all to a boil and pour the oniony liquid over the rice, cover the roasting pan, pop it into the oven and an hour later Robert's your uncle."

"It smells wonderful," I said.

"I put it in around fifteen minutes before you arrived," he said. "Give us time for a chat and a debrief."

We settled into comfortable chairs in his living room and sipped our champagne. "I'd like to start," I said. "I want to thank you for making your plane available to Ben."

"Time was of the essence," he said, "though I gather you had things in hand when he arrived. Both hands, Ben said."

"Contingency plan," I said.

"One of your specialties," he responded. "Let me run down a few things for you. We've been thinking through the matter of Richard's disappearance and have come up with a backstory. We'll say that he was doing some very high-level consulting work with regard to the military's needs and his company's most advanced products. This had to be kept secret; his wife was informed and so was his boss. They were all sworn to secrecy and did a commendable job of sustaining the story and giving him time to do his work."

"Sounds plausible," I said. "He *was* gone for quite sometime, but no one would doubt the power of the bureaucracy to increase that time exponentially."

"Exactly," the Director said.

"I'm worried about the ballerina," I said. "I'd hate to see her as collateral damage, particularly when she was being coerced."

"We've relocated her and are bringing her mother over from Prague. Their biggest problem now will be to get used to life in the Dakotas. With the energy boom in that area there will be plenty of available work opportunities, perhaps even some romantic opportunities."

"For each of them, perhaps," I said.

"That would be sweet," he responded. "We've also spoken with Ms. Chen…"

"The daughter. Ya Qi."

"Yes. We made her an offer that she found attractive. She turned over all of the remaining negatives and photos of the Governor and his putative girlfriend. In return we agreed to let her keep her student visa and continue studying at AU, rather than returning to China to work in the rice paddies. She and her mom proved to be embarrassments for the PRC because of their unapproved operation, so the fate that we offered was far more attractive than anything her government might have provided."

"How about Ting's body?"

"It was returned to the embassy and, as they say on 'Mission Impossible,' the government disavowed any knowledge of her actions."

"That's laughable," I said.

"Our guess is that they approved it but told them to play at their own risk. When they saw the results of Ben's HK they distanced themselves even more."

"And the Winslow woman? Still camped out under her bed at her parents' place?"

"The useful idiot."

"Yes."

"We're letting her sort out her situation without our help. When you consciously decide to lie down with the canines you're responsible for eradicating the fleas."

"How about the Hosek woman?" I asked.

"We were lucky there. She has no living relatives or, for that matter, friends. The official story is that she has retired and moved to some island in the Caribbean."

"To rest among the sharks?" I asked.

"More among the dirt, rocks and trees of western New York," he said.

"In some ways it was a sad case. She really did deserve the word *pathetic*. She thought Ting was her friend; this operation was her way of reaching out for, what…companionship? Validation? Attention? Affection?"

"I agree," he said, "but when those actions are directed against our friends and our country…"

"We don't hesitate to intervene."

"Never," he said. "By the way, that *Stinger* maneuver was a world-class throw. The proximity to the arteries…"

"I was happy to help," I said.

"How many times had you practiced it?"

"A few thousand," I said. "I didn't keep count."

"Ben was very impressed. We won't talk about the manner of its concealment."

"Best not," I said. "It had the special virtue of deterring searches."

He laughed heartily and refilled our glasses.

Dinner was simple and wonderful. "My compliments, Sir," I said, "to you and to your wife."

He smiled and went into the lower compartment of the breakfront in his dining room, retrieving his best cognac.

"So you're going back on the road now," he said.

"Looking forward to it," I said.

"I'll want you to check in with Richard when he's completed his program."

"Already on my calendar, Sir, pending your approval."

"So what will you tell the people in the field offices, Gwen? What's the golden nugget? I'd love to hear it."

"Hopefully several," I said. "I do have a favorite."

He topped off my snifter and scooted comfortably in his leather chair.

"Monsieur Moët started his business in the 18th century," I said. "That's where I start, with Sir Joshua Reynolds…"

"The portrait painter."

"Yes."

"Abe said to me once that it would have been marvelous if he had had the opportunity to paint Georgie. Many tried, but never quite captured the soul within. I think one of Reynolds' best portraits is of a naval man…"

"Commodore Keppel," I said. "They actually knew one another. Keppel joined the navy at the age of 10. National hero. The picture depicts him in full command of himself and his men after his ship had been wrecked."

"So what do you tell field agents about an 18th century painter?"

"It's more about what he said in one of his discourses," I responded. "He's talking about the notion of what we would call *intuition*. We sometimes think it's something spontaneous and spur-of-the-moment, something irrational, a reaction from the gut. He doesn't agree with that and he's not pleased with the usual notion of the imagination as something that's fanciful or other-worldly. He says that the imagination is actually like a storehouse. It's filled with all of the ideas and perceptions and experiences which have formed our lives. When we act in what appears to be a small and spontaneous way we are actually tapping into what he calls 'a great system of things.' We are not so much following 'reason' as we are drawing upon what he calls a 'mass of collective observation.' He says we should think of it as 'habitual reason'."

"So, we're confronted with a situation and all of the occurrences and thoughts in our lives come to bear on that decision point. We have to be decisive but we also have to be wise and experienced."

"And we can trust that experience, particularly if we've prepared for it."

"A singular moment," the Director said, "but backed by a lifetime of knowledge and experience. Like…throwing a knife into the center of a throat…"

"Or wanting to take Third Army into the Falaise gap," I said.

"Georgie was right; Bradley was wrong."

"Violated the commonsense principle: when you've got a big gun (like Patton) you should never hesitate to shoot it."

"Nice," the Director said. "Very nice."

"Hopefully it helps them to think and to focus," I said.

# SIXTY-FIVE

As my lecture tour came to a close I flew to Rochester to visit with Richard and Kathy. Tony Giraldi met me at the airport and refused to take no (or 'maybe later') for an answer when he proposed that we go out for dinner. The place was unprepossessing. Situated in a crowded strip mall on East Avenue, it was called *Lucano*. Inside, however, it was a warren of dining rooms with interesting murals and highly-professional waiters with black bow ties and persuasive recommendations.

"It may look like a neighborhood pizza place outside," Tony said, "but the inside is a different matter entirely. Family-run. Very authentic. Rock-solid food."

We ate Italian wedding soup, lasagna with meat sauce and profiterols for dessert. Following Gino's recommendation we enjoyed a multi-varietal Italian wine made by *Ruffino*. "In Gabe's honor," I said.

Tony was appropriately circumspect with regard to our operation. "I understand that everything was resolved," was his only comment.

I thanked him for his hospitality and he told me that the satellite office was always ready to do its part for the greater good. There were no attempts to wheedle information from me, just the offer to help Richard in any way that they could, should the need arise. All in all the dinner was a lovely gesture and the food was exceptional.

The next morning I was scheduled to meet with Richard and Kathy. I asked if I could bring anything. "Bagels? Donuts?"

"I've been fattening him up," Kathy said. "He's excelling at the process. Just bring yourself."

Both of them greeted me at the door. Kathy was wearing pink sweatpants and a matching, loose sweatshirt. Richard was wearing plaid cotton pants and a heavy, solid-color cotton shirt, more a set of pajamas than something approaching street clothes. Each of them hugged me at the door.

"Forgive the outfit," Richard said. "I can't break the habit. Part of my experience with withdrawal involved chills. It was hot in San Antonio but these kinds of clothes were commonplace. After awhile I got used to them."

"It's a big step up," Kathy said. "At the clinic he wore the jammies, a robe, wool socks and a scarf."

"You've gained weight," I said to him. "That's good."

"Muscle mass also. When I wasn't being medicated I was being forced to exercise."

"Military operation," I said, "not a country club or spa."

"But I wanted the spa," he said, smiling. "After weeks of abandonment I wanted to be surrounded by people giving me and my little body some serious attention."

"All in good time," Kathy said, patting him on the back of his head.

It was all very domestic and comforting, precisely what we all needed. We sat down for breakfast. Kathy had made waffles and bacon and served them with 'Adirondack maple' syrup, fresh-squeezed orange juice and steaming black coffee. We ate quietly and when we finished she asked if we could talk.

"Of course," I said.

We went into the living room with fresh cups of coffee and she told me that she wanted to hear the whole story. "All the details," she said. "All of them."

"Well, you know the outline," I said. "The Hosek woman and a woman at the Chinese embassy had gone to college together at Berkeley. They got back together recently and developed the bright idea of interfering in the presidential election by linking the PRC's least-favored candidate with a young and attractive Czech woman. He's a family man, a pious, authentic traditionalist whose candidacy would be destroyed by any evidence of an extramarital affair. Richard was drugged and held in reserve. He would be seen as the director of the operation, his crimes resulting from his need for money to finance his habit."

"One thing I don't understand," Kathy said. "His shackles were cushioned but he was fed dog food."

'I know," I said. "It was weird. They didn't want anyone to know that he had been held against his will. At the same time (and this is just a guess) they wanted his body to appear to have been ravaged by the addiction. The kibble may have also underlined his desperate need for cash and the fact that the habit was all-consuming."

"That was stupid," Kathy said. "Didn't they know that I would have taken care of him?"

"We don't know where his body would have eventually been found or what kind of backstory they would have fabricated."

Still stupid, I think."

"Wisdom is not usually a criminal's long suit," I said.

Richard sat quietly, sipping his coffee, as Kathy continued.

"And you were able to identify Hosek as the primary person responsible and followed her to the farm where you found Richard."

"Right."

"But she returned and found you there."

"Yes. We're not sure why. She may have been concerned that she had overdosed him or she may have been preparing…"

"To actually kill him," Kathy said.

"Yes."

"They were going to kill him eventually and they may have felt the walls closing in on them. They were forced to abort, or, perhaps, ready to complete their 'operation'."

"We really don't know. They had fabricated the pictures of the woman with the presidential candidate and they could have released them then…"

"But they didn't."

"No."

"And they won't."

"Not now," I said.

"And you had a partner who killed the Chinese woman after you had killed Hosek."

"Yes."

"Did he shoot her?"

"Yes, he did."

"Where?"

I could feel Richard's movement, even from five feet away. He was becoming nervous about the direction of the discussion. When he started to say something Kathy put her hand over his and squeezed gently.

"It may sound grisly but it's a matter of protocol," I said. "You don't know whether or not an armed person who's threatening you is wearing body armor…"

"So he shot her in the head."

"Multiple times. It's not one of those moments in which you can afford to indulge any doubts or hesitations."

"And you killed the Hosek woman with a knife?"

"Yes, I did."

"She had seen that you had two handguns, but she wasn't aware of the knife."

"Right."

"That must have been difficult."

"She lacked experience; I had practiced."

"You threw the knife into her throat."

"I did."

"That must have taken a great deal of skill."

"More than she anticipated," I said.

"I wish I had been there," Kathy said.

Richard tried to change the subject. "I was there," he said, "but largely indisposed. When we returned from Maine she called and asked if we could meet at what she described as 'her' farm. When we did she jabbed a needle into the side of my neck. That was pretty much all I remembered clearly until Gwen took me to *Highland Hospital.* I mean, I knew that I was unable to escape and I knew that I was dependent on the drug, but everything was a kind of numb blur, with intervening pain and a lot of difficulty breathing."

Kathy smiled at him and continued to hold his hand. Then she turned to me and returned to her earlier point.

"She must have been staggering and panicking. She must have been having a difficult time speaking and she felt the blood flow through her hands and over her chest. She was gurgling and losing consciousness. She wanted to remove the knife but knew that she could cut an artery in the process and bleed out immediately."

"Yes," I said, without elaborating.

"Do you think that there was any remorse at that moment? Did she realize how evil her actions were? Did all the events of her life race through her mind as she stared into the darkness?"

"She *was* the darkness," I said.

"And then you rammed the knife point into her spinal column."

"How did you know that?" I asked.

"Because that's exactly what I would have done. And because Richard is your friend."

"You're scaring me, sweetheart," Richard said.

"You've forgotten why we do our best to keep women out of war, darling."

"Because we don't want it to become that violent," I interjected.

"The worst thing a hunter can see," Kathy said—"a mama bear with long claws and wet teeth, racing down the road to greet him."

Just then I heard a cry from the hallway beyond the kitchen. It startled me. It also reminded me how distant my life was from Kathy's. I hadn't noticed the reduction in her belly because of the baggy sweatshirt, but I also had been so focused on saving Richard that I had somehow suppressed the awareness that he was about to become a father.

Kathy stood up; I noticed a slight twinge in the movement of her hips. She went down the hallway and then reappeared in about five minutes. The baby was blanketed and her lips were moving, ready for breakfast. There was a tiny bit of waxy substance beneath her eyes and a tiny bow in her ample blonde hair.

"Here," Kathy said, placing her in my arms. "I'll get her bottle." Before she left the room she pointed at her eyes. "Be good for your aunt," she said.

When Kathy returned she was testing the milk's temperature by drizzling several drops across her wrist. That awakened memories. "Do you want to do the honors?" she asked.

I told her I'd love to and propped the baby's head against a throw pillow on the couch as I scooted her into position. The drowsiness had left her eyes and as she started working the silicone nipple seriously she stared at me intently.

"She's really focused," I said. "Not that I'm an expert…far from it…but I'm thinking, serious gene pool here. We're talking gifted-and-talented from the nursery school to college."

Both of her parents smiled politely.

"To answer your unasked question, she was born two weeks ago," Kathy said. "Richard was in the clinic and I was in the maternity ward. Duelling patients."

"And Richard was ripped from the comforts of his spa and handed his Daddy certificate," I said.

"He's doing a great job," Kathy said.

"This may not be the best time to bring this up…" I said.

"What's that?" Richard said.

"Speaking of jobs…a message from the Director. He said that if you wanted to consider it you could be reinstated in your Bureau position. Your choice of role; your choice of field office."

"That's very kind," he said. "Very, very kind."

"Indeed," Kathy said. "You should give it some thought."

"I will. It's very comforting. I'll thank him for thinking of me. I'm still in touch with his son; we were classmates together."

"My partner in the takedown…"

"Yes?" Kathy asked.

"He was flown here on the Director's plane."

Kathy was taken aback. "Oh my God," she said, "just the thought of the possible political fallout…the opposition in Washington could demand that he resign."

"They could," I said, "but he wouldn't worry himself over it. He always does what he considers the right thing. As he says, it makes everything easier and clearer."

"First principles," Kathy said. "Rare these days. I'd love to meet him."

"I'm sure I could arrange that," I said. "Maybe even a nice dinner. We'd have to add another place setting, but all the little one would need was some milk and some loving arms. She wouldn't yet be ready for a steak with some bourbon and branch on the side and a cognac back."

"We haven't told you her name," Kathy said.

"No, you haven't. What is it?"

"Gwendolyn."

Now it was my turn to be taken aback. "That's Welsh, you know," I said. "And far easier to pronounce than what my Native name would have been."

"She who hurls knives and draws much blood?" Kathy asked.

I broke into a smile and said, "Seriously, I'm truly honored."

I looked down at Baby Gwen. The bottle was nearly empty and her eyes were still locked on my face. I wondered what thoughts were coursing through her head. Probably things that were very basic, but basic is good; basic is essential. When I smiled at Richard and Kathy I could see the moistness beneath their eyes. The drapes behind the couch where I was holding Baby Gwen were suffused with sunlight and her lips looked as if they were forming the slightest of smiles.

9 798989 899271 97